Praise for

I0658954

St. Hawk's Medical

I really enjoyed reading about Brandon, Evan and Griff. They all seemed to have the perfect chemistry when they got together. Such a sweet passionate story of two men in a solid relationship finding their third that completes them. Lots of flirting and scheming for this to happen. Wonderfully written with great details and hot, steamy sex between the three. Fantastic read. Highly recommended. ~ *MM Good Book Reviews*

ST. HAWK'S MEDICAL
Volume One

Take Heart

Give Chase

WILLA OKATI

St. Hawk's Medical Volume One
ISBN # 978-1-78430-478-2
©Copyright Willa Okati 2015
Cover Art by Posh Gosh ©Copyright 2015
Interior text design by Claire Siemaszkiewicz
Totally Bound Publishing

TAKE HEART

Dedication

For J.L., Kimberly, and Jambrea.

Prologue

During the daylight hours the view from the broad, shallow steps of St. Hawk's Medical couldn't be beat—unless one walked half a mile to the next overlook. In Brendan's opinion, it wasn't too shabby at night, either. Lights sparkled in the valley below like fireflies darting from leaf to branch, and below him, Blue Creek's main street crackled with life, noise and celebration.

He unfolded the glossy flyer, its crisp edges tamed from reading and re-reading since he'd come to this small town and smaller hospital, and fanned the pages open. Though he couldn't read its printed text in the dark, he'd unintentionally memorized the whole thing.

Held once a year, the Festival of St. Hawk's isn't just any holiday... Since the town's founding in 1902 by James Ryan and his dearest friend Cedric Montgomery, who had originally come West for the prairie cure and didn't stop wandering until they found the former settlement waiting to be restored...

*Policies of healthy body, healthy mind, and not taking no
for an answer...*
The midnight fireworks display is not to be missed.

Brendan pressed a button on his sports watch to
check the time. Eleven fifty. He'd be needed back in
the hospital before long, but he could wait for
midnight. He'd like to see something described as 'not
to be missed'.

Maybe he could make a wish. Fireworks weren't
shooting stars, but they might do the job in a pinch.

"What the hell do you want a job at the hippie
hospital for?" his old mentor had asked, frown lines
etched deep on his forehead, when Brendan had told
him what he had planned.

Good question.

Blue Creek sat nestled midway up the Cascades.
They got their fair share of rain, but also sunlight as
thick and sweet as honey, as gentle as a mother's hand
on his forehead, and it was only an hour's drive to the
beach. The view from every room framed up
mountains and sky that seemed to go on forever. They
didn't have more than fifty inpatient beds, but what
the hospital couldn't manage, they referred. That
wasn't a hell of a lot. Somehow, as far as Brendan had
seen, St. Hawk's brand of care seemed to work in
ways medicine just *didn't* elsewhere.

He didn't know a lot yet. Not much at all. But he
hoped he could learn, and in learning then
somehow—some way—he could change his ways.
Refresh his spirit before he had to go back to the real
world.

The guys on the street below sure as heck seemed to
have figured out the secret to happiness. Brendan
chuckled quietly to himself as he watched them. The

nearer it got to midnight, and the more beer he suspected had been consumed, the freer everyone became with their affections. And why not? As long as they didn't wind up in the emergency room, more joy to them. Even if he wasn't used to that, from where he sat he liked this view best of all.

Case in point—some rowdy types with cowboy hats and biker boots were passing out sparklers on the sidewalk. Brendan laughed behind his hand, charmed by the sight. *Big, burly bad boys with balls of fire.* You couldn't beat that with a stick. As if sensing his attention, and pleased by it, one of the men—their ringleader, Brendan thought—turned to tip his hat at him. He had short dark hair beneath, sweat and energetic excess sending it up in spikes, and the kind of grin that mommas warned their daughters about.

Talk about healthy body, healthy mind.

As Brendan watched, they corralled a lean, comfortable-looking type in yoga pants and a singlet who'd been otherwise occupied ambling down the sidewalk at his own pace, to the beat of his own drum. Their ringleader pressed a double handful of unlit sparklers on him, as well as the Stetson he'd been wearing. The man they'd accosted waved the sticks as if he meant to batter them about the head and shoulders, but he was laughing. They all were.

Ringleader pointed up the steps, at Brendan, and gave Yoga Pants a friendly push. At first Brendan thought—surely not—but then Yoga had started to climb the wide, shallow steps two at a time, sparklers out in offering.

"Since you don't have one yet," he explained as soon as he got close enough for Brendan to pick out individual words. He dropped the hat casually on

Brendan's head. "You're supposed to light them when the fireworks go off."

Brendan laughed. "*Should* I make a wish?"

"If you want. Why not?" the man asked. He had a sprig of something green tucked in his bronze curls, rakish as a feather, and an air of gentle serenity that made Brendan think of hugs and quiet nights in with a cup of hot chocolate. He wore his far-too-light clothing with casual grace—as if he wore nothing at all—and that made Brendan think of other things entirely. Things that made his mouth go dry.

You're beautiful. The thought echoed in Brendan's head.

It was true. Twin copper hoops in his earlobes caught the light when the man tossed his head and smiled—not grinned, there was a difference—down at Brendan. "You're new here, aren't you? Or at least I haven't seen you before. Don't worry." He gestured deftly at the street. "This might all seem like a bit much, but we generally mean well. Most of us."

Brendan opened his mouth to answer, but as the man stretched to push a fistful of sparklers at him, he saw it. An old scar down the middle of his chest—not too old, maybe five years or so. Long and thin. Surgical.

Scars like that usually meant—

"Heart transplant," the man said simply when he caught Brendan looking. He waved off any apology before it could begin, soft brown eyes not puppyish or sad, but safe and happy as he produced a box of matches and touched off the sparkler he'd given Brendan. "Everyone deserves a second chance, and it gives me all the more reason to celebrate. Welcome to St. Hawk's!"

He loped down the stairs and away before Brendan could think of a reply, joining then disappearing into the crowd on the sidewalk. Brendan bit the inside of his cheek. *Damn.* Not even a chance to get his name, and —

Overhead, the first of the fireworks ignited — a Roman candle of blazing purple, red and blue. Brendan tipped back the cowboy hat, a size too big for him, and parted his lips in awe at the brilliant sky.

This is beautiful, too. He opened his hand to let go of the regret that he hadn't made more of the meeting. If he'd had a permanent job then maybe, but as it was... Well.

Every story had to start somewhere, didn't it?

Chapter One

Wednesdays were underrated. Anything could happen on a Wednesday.

Evan dropped the magazine he'd tried — and mostly failed — to keep himself occupied with, waiting. Dr. Kelly could get behind on his schedule before the day even started, and he'd learned a long time ago to come to his check-up appointments prepared for a good old-fashioned campout.

Momentarily distracted, he ticked the list off on his fingers. Sudoku, if he could find a book with puzzles left undone *and* a pencil. Snacks if he could get away with them, fresh sweet almonds or a granola bar with a touch of fresh-ground peanut butter on the top. A travel mug of herbal tea at the very least, hot and fragrant and sweet with a spoonful of raw clover honey mixed in.

He'd forgotten to make enough tea to take with him when he'd rolled out of bed that morning. *Shame.* Some days started flurried and didn't let up, but that was all right. Good things happened to balance them out.

He lifted his head at the cheerful rapping on the door that heralded the arrival of one of his favorite nurses. Darry, as big and broad as the side of a barn, topped off with a full blond beard, poked his head in and grinned at Evan. "Don't worry, we didn't forget you. Dr. Kelly called in sick."

Evan cocked his head to one side, curious. "Doctors can do that?"

"Can and do," Darry said. "Would you mind if we brought a sub in for the last fifty yards?"

Once a football player, always a football player. Evan grinned to himself before answering, "Sure, why not?" He only needed a quick once-over, after all. Regular check-ups weren't too much to pay for the gift of a new heart.

"Good man. Hang tight, and we'll get you sorted out soon." Darry cocked his head. "By the way, did you know you have fennel in your hair?"

"I do?"

"Not on purpose, I take it," Darry said with a rumbling chuckle.

Evan plucked the bit of greenery free, looked at it, shrugged, then tucked it behind his ear. "I'm starting a new trend."

"Why not? Stranger things have happened." Darry gave him an air-five as he saw himself out.

Evan chuckled quietly once the door had closed. Who needed sudoku? Darry's antics kept St. Hawk's Medical plenty lively. He didn't mind seeing a replacement doctor, either. It'd given him something to think about, after all, and interesting beat *waiting* any time, any place.

He slipped his phone out of his pocket and fired off a quick text message.

Feel like doing me a favor?

* * * *

"You're still here? Excellent. Wait. What are you still doing here?"

Brendan splashed a double handful of cool water, soft and smelling faintly of minerals, on his face before he checked up in the mirror above the sink. He'd felt a shadow fall across him when he'd had his head down, and only one guy he'd met so far at St. Hawk's had quite the same sort of presence. "I could ask you the same thing," he said, tired enough for a hint of the Hebridean accent he'd had as a boy to slip through and soften his vowels. "Any towels left on the rack?"

Darry had a grin as wide as a slice of sweet orange, and muscles the size of bowling balls. Wherever he came from, they must grow their native sons with extra fertilizer and double-strength sunshine. He tossed Brendan a clean washcloth still in its sterile laundry wrapping. "I thought you worked second shift yesterday."

"Ahh, you know how it is. One thing leads to another and in the end it was easier to crash here for an hour or two." Brendan gestured in the general direction of the lounge and its couches, deeper and softer than most of their ilk. Hospitals didn't often cater for comfort, but St. Hawk's Medical Center prided itself on marching to the beat of a different drummer.

"God knows I've been there and done that," Darry said with a yawn and a brisk, efficient stretch. "As long as you're not planning to jet in the next half hour, feel like doing me a solid? I'll pay you in back rubs. I give a mean massage."

Brendan couldn't help shaking his head, amused. "We'll see about that. What have you got?"

"Double bookings. I'm wanted down in the pediatric emergency department, but I've been covering Dr. Kelly's calendar too. Would you mind?"

Brendan didn't, but… "It's been a long time since I did my cardiology rotation," he warned.

"It's just follow-up appointments, I checked. Taking vitals and making referrals if need be, and —"

"Enough, already. You don't have to sell me on the deal," Brendan chided, taking the patient file from Darry and dealing him a light swat on the shoulder. "I — *huh*."

"Problem?"

"No, no," Brendan said. He turned pages with his fingertips. All their charts included a photo for visual patient ID. "I think I know this one. I've seen him around town."

"Not a problem, then?" Darry asked. He was already raring to go. Brendan knew the signs.

He waved Darry off, losing himself in the chart again. "I'm fine." More than, actually. He might finally get the chance to say more than hello to the quiet beauty from the night of the festival. That'd go quite a bit further than a splash of water for waking him up.

Familiar faces lifted their chins in greeting as Brendan passed them by on his way to the exam room. Nurses, doctors, physician's assistants, midwives, lab technicians, all of them sporting crisp coats and badges and a sense of purpose. Most of them happy to be there, even.

Unusual? God, yes, endlessly so.

And fascinating.

Maybe he could—maybe he should—try to learn from that. Figure out how to change his ways before it was too late. Maybe this would be where he could start.

Exam Room Seven, here we are. Brendan tucked the patient chart under his arm, rapped his knuckles quickly on the door and let himself in, eager in his curiosity—

And, for once, rewarded.

Waiting for him on the exam table, leaned back as casually and comfortably as if in his own home, was the answer to his wish. Eyes alight as he, too, recognized Brendan. "I know you, don't I? The doctor from the steps."

"Evan Alders," Brendan said, pleased. "Nice to have a name for you too, to match to the face." And a pretty face it was. Sweet and finely-featured, framed in bronze curls. He wore small copper rings in both ears, and he'd stuck a sprig of fennel behind his ear the way an absentminded writer would stow a pen. "How have you been?"

"I've been well." Evan looked honestly pleased to see Brendan. Relaxed and happy, too. It'd been a long, long time since that'd happened for Brendan. "Are you covering for Dr. Kelly? A resident came back a few minutes ago and I think she's already taken care of almost everything."

Damn. Had they? A quick flip through the chart showed the proof of Evan's claim. Under other circumstances, Brendan would have been grateful. "I'll just take a quick look. No troubles to report? Immunosuppressants doing their job?"

Evan patted lightly over the finely healed scar Brendan had caught a glimpse of before. "No problems. Good as new."

"Glad to hear it." Brendan hooked the rolling stool with one foot and pulled it into place behind him, then unwound the stethoscope from around his neck. "Incoming, and fair warning—it's cold. Guard yourself."

Evan chuckled quietly. "Not my first rodeo. I'll live."

Brendan liked the look of Evan up close even better than he had from afar. Bits and pieces of him invited deeper consideration, which Brendan far preferred to blatant beauty. Those smile lines at the sides of his eyes, for one. He'd spent more time pleased than angry, and that was a kind gift for life to have given him. He smelled like honey and herbs, and was gentle when he nudged Brendan's knee with the tip of his sandal.

"See? Ticking away like a gold watch."

"Your surgeon did good work. If I didn't have your patient chart in hand, I doubt I'd be able to guess just from looking at you that you'd had a transplant. I wish all patients recovered so well." He sat back to check Evan's ankles for any signs of swelling. "How long has it been since your surgery?"

"Almost five years. Dr. Kelly says I'll be good for fifteen to twenty more, for a start."

Brendan would believe it. Evan's smooth skin glowed with good health as much as his open, friendly face did with excellent humor. "Amazing," he murmured under his breath. He'd seen far too many patients in worse condition for infinitely less worthy reasons. "Honestly, I think there must be something in the water around here. You should bottle it. You'd make a fortune."

Evan laughed. "Nah. I don't need a fortune. I've got just about everything I could want. It's a good town for that. Lots of live and let live, a really good farmer's market, and then there's all the walking trails I could ever want."

The firm springiness of his calf muscles told its own tale. Brendan would bet he walked five miles or more on a regular basis. A wisp of daydream floated across his mind—an image of Evan fresh from a ramble, skin honey-warm from the sun, hair clinging to the back of his neck with clean sweat, and smiling. He'd rarely met anyone who seemed so contented with their life. Brendan let go of his leg and turned to make a note in the chart. "And here my first guess would have been yoga."

"I just like the pants." Evan flexed his ankle. "I never sit still if I don't have to. Life is too short to waste by lazing around, don't you think?"

"I do," Brendan said, hands falling still as he looked up at the man. He had a fine, full fan of lashes as dark as soot that turned his plain hazel eyes into something amazing when he looked at a man that way. "Very much, I do."

Evan beamed at him, warm as the dawn, and— *Well. Why not?*

"Come for a walk with me?" Brendan asked, the words slipping in a rush over his tongue and past his lips. "Will you?"

Uh-oh, Evan thought.

"That didn't come out quite right." Brendan made a rueful face, nose crinkled, smile unpracticed but genuine. His hands were warm, and gentle, and his manner suddenly hesitant. Less professional, more personal, not crossing any lines, but rich with hope— and he hadn't seen it coming. "I'm overdue for a break, and I'd like to get to know you better. May I?"

When Griff heard about this, he'd tease for *weeks*. "Brendan, I need to tell you—"

A brief staccato rap sounded on the door half a second before the knob turned.

"Tea boy," Griff announced himself as he jostled the door open with one hip and stepped inside, juggling two tall paper cups that gave off the rich scent of jasmine and pekoe. "Hotter than hell and twice as sweet as the sins that'd send you there." He tossed his head to settle his long, dark-russet braid neatly down the middle of his back, away from the spiky tribal tattoos that curled around the nape of his neck, and flashed Evan one of the devil-may-care winks that'd made him fall in love with the man, way back when.

The kind of smile Evan couldn't help returning, and meaning with all his patchwork heart.

Even when Griff had a shit-eating grin the size of Texas dawning on his lips. Let no man call him slow on the draw. He saw the situation and comprehended it fully in point-five seconds as he passed the tea off to Evan. "Oh, babe. Caught another one, did you?"

"Not on purpose!" Evan said.

"Uh-huh. Accident, then. You need a keeper, darlin'." Griff didn't so much offer his hand as take Brendan's without asking. Callused and dry and strong, he had the sort of greeting shake that Evan saw made Brendan's fingers automatically close around his without second-guessing. He saw, too, how the cheeky twinkle ever present in Griff's eye, like the points of light in a glass of good brandy, invited the world at large and Brendan as well to come and play. "My name should be on his paperwork as next of kin, but everyone who knows me calls me Griff. You are?"

"Brendan," Evan said with an internal hands-up of surrender because that was mostly the only way to roll during times of trial. "This is Jack Griffiths. My partner."

"That I am, by the grace of God," Griff said, settling himself into a comfortable lean on the exam table. He cocked his head to get a better gander at the new doc. "I've seen you around, haven't I?"

"I..." The doctor—Brendan, was it?—gave his head a good sharp shake and blinked twice, like a man coming awake without much warning. Griff guessed he must have thrown the guy for a good and proper loop-de-loop. He saw it now, that indefinable something that'd made Evan peg him right away as lonely. Lonely and proud and stubborn. *Huh.* Damn shame.

On the other hand, the man did have a good face. A kind mouth.

"On Main Street. You were leading that gang with the fireworks," Brendan said, lifting his chin in a way that underlined Griff's first impression of *stubborn*. He had the faintest hint of an accent that only came out now, with a roll of 'R' across his tongue. "I ended up with your hat. I'd have brought it back if I hadn't been on duty."

"Is that what happened to it? Damn," Griff said with a pang of regret. Took months to get a Stetson worn in *just* right.

A grin cracked the grim stoicism of Brendan's face, and did all kinds of wonders for the looks of him. Made him seem younger, more approachable, downright human, and like a human Griff thought he might like to get to know.

"Don't worry. I saved the hat. As far as I know it's on a shelf in the back of the lost and found closet. I'll bring it down for you later, if you'd like." He cleared his throat. Faint hints of red crossed his cheeks. "Look, before this gets awkward I'll go ahead and say I'm sorry. If I'd known you were together, I wouldn't have trespassed."

Evan tucked the corners of his mouth in something between sympathy and a frown. He had a heart as big as the great outdoors. Almost as much heart as Griff had mouth. "No, don't do that. How were you to know?"

"Hell, it's not a problem," Griff said. He rested one hand at the small of Evan's back and grinned at the good doctor. He couldn't go for long without teasing Evan, or anyone else for that matter. God must have been in a puckish mood the day he'd set his mind to creating him. "It's happened before. He's bad at figuring out when people are interested. I damn near had to tackle him and sit on his face before he put the pieces together."

"True," Evan said, patting the back of Griff's head in his affectionate way. "But I'm only bad at telling when people are interested in me, while you're an all-around hell-raiser with no manners, so that makes us just about even."

"Blackjack, no take back," Griff fired off with a crinkle of his nose. He returned his full interest to Brendan, studying him from stem to stern before making up his mind in the confidence that Evan would back his play. "Now, he's going to tell me to apologize for yanking your chain, so I'll go ahead and get that out of the way. Forgive and forget?"

He could tell Brendan's nature made him want to resist, but that he had enough gumption to push past that first instinct. Griff liked that. Liked it just fine.

"Don't mention it," the doc said, polite as could be. Drawing back, putting a safe distance between them. It didn't suit him. "It's in the past, now."

Evan nudged his shoulder against Griff's. Pleased with him, Griff thought, which spurred him on. "I'll tell you what, though. You're new around here, yeah? Not had a chance to get out and find your feet yet? Trust me, after a few years with this one and all his time in and out of St. Hawk's Medical, I know doctors. Too busy to tie your shoes most days, and hell, it's not easy for anyone, starting off alone."

Brendan frowned again, a hair deeper this time, but he didn't interrupt. *Good.*

Griff spread his hands open—*there you go.* "Friday night," he said. "Mark it on your day planner, Doc. Seven p.m."

Evan picked right up on Griff's train of thought. *Good man.* "Barbecue?" he asked Griff.

"Too cold out. Better to range out," Griff replied. "Chicken or steak?"

"Both," Evan said. "Or neither. I'm thinking Cajun. Palomino?"

Griff brought his hands together in a sharp clap. "That'll do."

Meanwhile, Brendan's eyebrows had shot toward his hairline. "What—? Come again?"

Griff manfully bit down on the joke that wanted to pop out. If Brendan could behave, so could he. "Friday night. There's a good place up on the hilltop, and we like company. You're either coming with us, or meeting us there." Bless his heart, he looked so flummoxed by the mere notion it only made Griff want to do this all the more. "Peace offering, and I won't hear 'no' as an answer."

Beside him, one of Evan's sweet smiles curved his lips. "Please."

Griff's own grin went wide. When Evan pulled out that particular big gun, it'd take a harder man than either of them to say no. Call it a done deal already.

And so it was.

* * * *

Evan waited until the pair of them were on the sidewalk outside St. Hawk's Medical, comfortably walking side by side, to reintroduce his elbow to Griff's ribs. Gently, though, so Griff knew not to take it deeper than the surface. "Someday I swear I'll teach you to be nice to strangers."

"What? I was plenty nice. Gentlemanly, I'd say."

Evan wound an arm around Griff's waist. "Keep on dreaming, *darlin'*."

Griff chuckled as he tossed his truck keys in the air and caught them, jingling. "He dished back as good as I served up. He's got some sweet and some spice going on there."

"Mmm," Evan vocalized, enjoying himself tremendously.

Just as he'd thought. The effort it'd taken not to laugh out loud when the flirting started, Lord. While he might not be the best in the world at being the center of attention, he could see plenty from the sidelines... And to be honest, he'd liked the view from where he stood. It wouldn't be the first time, after all. What he and Griff had might not be strictly by-the-book, but it worked for them, and Griff always did look lovely seen from that angle, sharing what he had to give, and what Evan was willing to lend.

Not that—as far as he could tell—either Griff or Brendan had a clue as of yet. Which was a shame, but easily corrected, and a chance to watch Griff wait for the penny to drop for a change wasn't anything to sneeze at.

"Oh?" he asked, mostly to see what Griff would say. "How's that?"

"I don't know yet," Griff said, thoughtful. "But I won't lie. I'm looking forward to finding out."

See? Evan remarked to himself with satisfaction. No need for embarrassment. Everything happened for a reason, and most things usually worked out in the end.

This was going to be fun.

* * * *

"Enjoy your time with the Odd Couple?" Darry knocked on the doorframe to announce his presence. His version of a *rat-a-tat-tat* sounded more like a jackhammer solo, but with as much hearty good cheer as a bowl of robust chicken soup. Usually. This time, he stopped mid-pattern and let loose with a guffaw. "Good God, man. What happened here? You look like you just tangled with a freight train and lost."

"I think I might have," Brendan said, rubbing his fingertips over his mouth.

"Yeah?" Darry thumped him companionably on the back. "Okay, now I'm really interested. What did happen?"

"Honestly?" Brendan asked. A breathless laugh slipped free. "I have no fucking idea."

Because surely he'd imagined that flare of interest in Griff's eyes. *Surely.*

But if he hadn't? Would there have been a matching gleam in Evan's, if he had looked? What then?

Chapter Two

A shadow fell over the hammock and blocked the honeyed sunlight from Evan's face. He blinked his eyes open to see Griff holding an arm above him. He looked like five-thirty on a Friday afternoon, roughly stubbled and worn out, but grinning in fiercely pleased pride, with a gleam of anticipation in his eyes.

Evan reached to take his hand and hummed when the sun fell on him again uninterrupted. He swung Griff's hand lazily, touched the back of it to his mouth, and laughed at the wry twist of Griff's lips. "Not a word. You like it."

"Uh-huh," Griff said, but didn't take his hand away. He cocked his head to one side. "Peace, love and hippies. You're in a mood. Good day?"

"Not as good as yours, from the looks of it."

"Kicked the ass off that '65 Mustang I told you about," Griff said with a growl of satisfaction. "You ought to hear it run now. Purrs sweet as a jaguar neck deep in a kill, fine as wine." He dropped to a loose crouch by the side of the hammock, low enough to the ground—they needed to brace the posts again—that he could get comfortable and still keep an eye on Evan. "We still on for tonight with Dr. What's His Name?"

Evan uncurled his arms from behind his head and stretched, curling his toes. "As far as I know. I haven't heard anything to the contrary."

"You think he'll show?"

"Definitely." The look of loneliness and stubborn pride he wore told him Brendan would fight the temptation he didn't yet understand, but the kind of mind that made a doctor would make him give in to curiosity. "He'll be there. Trust me. Have I led you wrong yet?"

Griff snorted, but he took Evan's hand and landed a scrape of stubble on the soft underside the way he knew Evan liked best. "You know something I don't," he said. "I'm almost sure of it. Any chance you'd let me in on the secret?"

Evan chuckled and closed his eyes. "That'd take all the fun out of it. You'll just have to wait and see for yourself. And you will."

Healing came in all shapes and sizes. He'd see. They all would.

* * * *

"I'd say it was just what the doctor ordered, if I didn't know better. With my compliments, Dr. West."

A drink appeared in front of Brendan. He blinked at it — something with way too much fruit and enough rum to make his nose tickle — and blinked again at the man who'd brought it to his table by the edge of Palomino's outdoor seating. Which was, more or less, the last bit of solid ground before the plateau dropped off a hundred and fifty feet to the valley floor below.

Not at all the sort of bar and grill he'd expected from Griff's suggestion—he'd thought maybe somewhere with peanut shells on the floor and neon on the walls, not a scenic overlook.

Still, a good place to people-watch from.

Of course, that would have worked better if he'd been paying attention.

He shook his head to clear it. "Sorry, come again?"

"Now there's a straight line." The man—a physician's assistant he remembered seeing at St. Hawk's Medical—grinned at him. A long, tall drink of water, he wasn't exactly handsome but had a rakish, devil-may-care charm that Brendan suspected he knew worked very well for him. "But then again, I'm getting the feeling 'straight' isn't a problem. I'm Magnus, and if you're not waiting for anyone I'd love to keep you company tonight."

Good Christ, there *had* to be something in the water around St. Hawk's. Brendan could and had gone months in Los Angeles without a single hit on his radar. Getting lucky was part of the motivation for any vacation, but still!

"Brendan West, and I'm..." He hesitated, words caught stumbling on his tongue. "I'm here waiting for some friends," he said at last. It wasn't quite accurate but it'd do. "Sorry."

"Why are you sorry? It's good to have friends. Sexy accent, by the way." Magnus didn't push his luck so far as dropping into one of the empty seats opposite Brendan, but he leaned on the chair back with a sort of cosmopolitan casualness worthy of admiration. He propped his chin on his hand as he asked, "And who are your friends, Dr. West? Ah. I'll bet I know—the rebel cowboy and the hippie. Am I right?"

Brendan fumbled with his hands. "How did you know?"

Magnus raised one shoulder. "They're the town welcoming committee. They like taking newcomers and baby birds under their wings."

"I see." Brendan's ears warmed. So that was it—kindness to a stranger. Nothing to do with *him* at all.

Damn.

Although... Wasn't it just as well, since he wasn't there for keeps?

"Don't take it personally," Magnus said in what might have been mild reprisal or sly teasing. Brendan couldn't tell for sure. "It's happened before, and it will again. I'm sure they would have told you themselves. They're a great couple. Very solid. Very odd, but very much in love—well, as far as I can tell. Never been in love myself."

Brendan cleared his throat. He wondered if his face had gone as red as it felt, and looked down at the table to avoid Magnus's intense study of him. "Me neither. Who has the time?"

"I thought you were on vacation," Magnus said.

"A working vacation, and not for much longer."

"All the more reason to enjoy yourself while you're in town." Magnus nudged the untouched drink he'd brought closer to Brendan. "But as they say, sensibly. Keep that in mind. And—here. It'd be a shame to waste it. And if your friends don't show..."

Cheeky son of a gun, isn't he? Brendan had to laugh, quietly, but meaning it. "I'll keep that in mind."

"You do that." Magnus touched his shoulder, light but lingering, as he stood to walk away.

Great. Brendan lifted his head, almost tempted to call out after him, and—

"There you are," a warm, soft voice said behind him, startling him away from the view of Magnus wandering off to try his luck at the other tables.

"Good lord," Brendan said over the rush of blood in his ears. He glanced over his shoulder to find Evan, looking patiently amused, and Griff, looking just plain entertained. They'd cleaned up nicely, both of them. More than. A touch of dryness made Brendan's lips feel clumsy when he asked, "Do you make noise when you walk?"

"Plenty of it. You were distracted." Evan waited for Griff to pull his chair out. Griff pretended to tip an invisible hat, and winked at Brendan. "I'm glad you're here."

He meant it, too. Brendan wasn't sure he'd stop being amazed by that. Was it just Evan's way?

Perhaps.

"You have something in your hair," he said.

"Do I?" Evan felt behind his ear, seemingly totally unsurprised by that. "Rosemary. It must have gotten tangled in there when I was working in the greenhouse this afternoon. Here." He dropped the stem by Brendan's half-empty glass. "For remembrance."

Brendan liked the clean, verdant tang of rosemary better than he had Magnus' rum. Lifting the sprig to his nose, he took a deeper sniff. "Thank you, but I can honestly say this isn't the kind of arrangement I'm likely to forget."

Griff, who Brendan could already tell was the sort of man who'd never found a chair he couldn't lounge in, kicked back and grinned at him, the same sort of fierce, edgy angle to his lips that Brendan had noticed before. "Memorable," he said. "That's a start."

"You'd know," Brendan said before manners caught up to him. "Here. Don't say I never did anything for you."

He felt under his seat, and tossed the battered cowboy hat he'd fetched and carried all the way from the hospital to Griff, who caught it with a pleased noise and settled it promptly on his head. Not a lot of men could wear a hat, rather than the other way around, but on Griff... Brendan's mouth went dry.

Good job, well done, he congratulated himself. *First you take a shine to Evan, and you pick now to notice the way Griff fills out the shoulders of that chambray shirt? And those jeans... Oh, for God's sake. Leave well enough alone, man!*

Evan—hopefully, please God, misinterpreting—laughed at the look on Brendan's face. "I don't mind being noteworthy, either," he said. "Have you eaten yet?"

"Was I supposed to?" Brendan *had* noticed almost half of the plaza's occupants busying themselves with clinking silverware, but he hadn't really taken in the details. Now that he did, the bright red of boiled shellfish and the brilliant yellow of corn caught his eye. The smell made his stomach rumble. He blushed. "There's your answer. It's just that I didn't know..."

Why he was even there, his mind supplied. What the point to this was. Invite him for drinks—and dinner, apparently—when he'd made his grand introduction by hitting on one half of a solid couple? Who *did* that?

Griff, for one.

Brendan watched in fascination as Griff lifted one hand to summon a waiter. "I do like a hungry man," the roughneck said. "*Garçon!* Boil for three, and make it snappy. I've got an appetite tonight."

* * * *

"My story? Not much to tell. I moved here after the surgery, as soon as I could." Evan broke kernels of corn off the cob he held loosely. He didn't care for meat in general, but he liked the taste of the spices and the flavor the gleaming red crawfish loaned everything else in the boil. He popped a bite in his mouth. "It was the last place I'd been before things got really bad where I was happy. I told myself I was going to get well, just so I could come back for a visit. And then I never left."

Across the table from him, Brendan nodded with the distracted manner of someone wholly caught up in a story. Evan liked the way he paid attention. He enjoyed watching Brendan eat, too, arching his eyebrows with surprise at the heat of the spice, and the way his lips reddened, and the neat deftness of his hands in peeling open crawfish.

See? Evan encouraged him mentally, gladder with each fraction of tension Brendan lost, a tightness he was almost sure Brendan didn't know had burdened him, weighing down his shoulders. *See? We don't bite.*

Well, Griff might. But only if you ask him nicely.

Evan sincerely hoped that Griff would put two and two together about his own interest in Brendan soon. Griff's delight in Brendan couldn't have been more obvious to everyone *else*, what with the way he kept giving the good doctor full body scans and cracking a grin whenever he managed to take the man off guard.

"Have you been to the hot springs yet?" Evan asked, leaning across the table to touch the back of Brendan's wrist. Light and easy did it.

"There are hot springs here?" Brendan asked. A wisp of dark hair fell over his eyes.

Evan itched to nudge it back into place. He folded his hands demurely instead, and as he'd thought, Brendan's gaze followed his movements. "Mm-hmm. I think that's how the town got its start. The hospital, too."

"Some gold miners who decided they could make better money keeping clean rather than digging in the dirt," Griff put in. He nudged Evan's foot with his under the table. "They've got a couple of the old signs in the town museum. 'Come try the miracle waters' and all that. They don't advertise these days. The locals would rather keep it local."

"Huh." Brendan returned his attention, pensively, to pulling a new potato apart. "I didn't know there were hot springs in this part of the country."

"There aren't, except for this one."

"Have you been in them?"

"Once," Evan said thoughtfully, remembering. "I don't know about miracles, but I left feeling pretty good. And isn't that the whole point?"

Brendan chuckled quietly and touched his fingertip to a flake of parsley that'd fallen on the tabletop between them. "Fair enough. And... Forgive me, but your deciding to move here... It was that easy for you? You liked it, and so you came, end of story?"

Evan raised one shoulder. "It wasn't hard. I think life's usually complicated enough without deliberately trying to make it that way."

"Says the one who's had a secret tucked up his sleeve since Wednesday," Griff muttered.

Evan elbowed him gently. "Shush. You're enjoying yourself."

"He's not wrong," Griff admitted with a devil-may-care grin. Enjoying himself, no matter what. Griff dipped half a crawfish into a decimated cup of melted butter then dropped the morsel in his mouth, making *yum* noises and licking the shining juices off his fingers. Watching that, Evan had to hold back a laugh.

Watching Brendan watch him, lips parted slightly, made Evan need to hold back something else.

Though—he wondered—if he did cut straight to the chase, reach across the table, and draw Brendan to him for a kiss, would that make the situation simpler or not?

Probably not, he decided with a twinge of regret. Griff would get the point, but Brendan would be more likely to cut and run. Better to let things unfold more naturally.

At the same time, that didn't mean he couldn't lend them a hand getting started—and he had an excuse right at his fingertips. The last finger of cool, clear water from the springs they'd just mentioned went down sweet and fresh. He rattled his glass to show its emptiness and stood, using Griff's shoulder as a booster. "No, don't get up," he said to Griff's questioning look. "I feel like stretching my legs. I'll get us all refills. Griff, keep Brendan entertained, would you?"

It wasn't quite the same as locking them in a closet together, Evan thought, but it might work in a pinch. They'd see.

Griff shook his head as Evan traipsed off without a care in the world. Across the table from him, the good doctor looked startled. "Was it something I did?"

"What? Nah. He does that. Gets an idea into his head and goes straight into action," Griff said. *Just as well, come to think of it.* "Your turn now. Satisfy my curiosity. What brings you to Blue Creek and St. Hawk's?"

"It's not complicated," Brendan said, keeping his eyes on Griff. "An oncologist I worked with spent a few weeks here doing clinical trials, and she came back looking like she'd been to the Virgin Islands. I thought, my God. I'd like to try that for myself."

Griff grunted. "Yeah, it's a good town for that. You find what you were looking for?"

"Not yet." Brendan ran the pad of his thumb around the rim of his glass. "The jury's still out."

"Don't wait too long. If things don't happen, try making them happen," Griff advised. He checked over his shoulder to see if Evan was out of earshot. "While I've got you alone…"

Brendan frowned. "All right…"

"Evan," Griff said. "Everything as it should be with him? He doesn't tell me anything much more than he has to when it comes to the, you know." He drew a line down his chest where Evan's surgery scar would be. "He always tells me he feels fine, but what I know about medicine you could fit into a specimen cup with room left over. So."

"I'm not really the best one to ask." Brendan toyed with the tines of his fork as he answered. "Dr. Kelly would know the nitty-gritty. I only ran a check-up, and the nurse did most of the work."

"From what I've seen, they mostly do," Griff said with a shrug. "Still, they're not here and you are."

Brendan sighed. "As far as I can tell, he's in fantastic health," he said. "Better than most men his age, I'd bet. He works as a gardener, doesn't he?"

"Yep. His greenhouse is his pride and joy."

"All that fresh air and sunshine and exercise would do anyone plenty of favors. If he's careful and if nothing happens, he could outlive either of us."

And thank God for it. Griff let out a long breath and nodded. "Good. That's what I wanted to hear. Don't know what I'd do without him, but I have a feeling it probably wouldn't be pretty, and it'd finish with somebody getting tossed into jail. Probably me."

Brendan shook his head once. "I don't understand."

"Don't you? Hell, it's not complicated." Griff stretched his legs into the space Evan had left behind. "Me, I'm a bad man from way on back. Oh, I see the way you look at me, like you want to ask if Evan knows. He does. I grew up rough, is the long and the short of it. I know myself, and what I'm best at is getting into hot water. If it weren't for Evan, I doubt I'd try. He makes me a better person, or at least he makes me want to put in the effort. And he gets me the way most people don't. So that's that."

Finished, Griff linked his hands loosely across his lap to sit back and get a better look at how the good doctor took that little speech. *Not bad.* Soberly, but that seemed to be his nature. He did clean up pretty, though, didn't he? Take off the white coat and he had a pair of shoulders that a quarterback could be proud of. Strong arms filled out the light sweater he'd wrapped himself in, something made in soft-looking yarn that variegated between gray and white with dark speckles like cinnamon dashed over cream.

Griff leaned to the side to get a better look at how Brendan fitted into his jeans, and whistled under his breath.

"Glad you approve," Brendan muttered behind his own nearly empty glass. He blushed straight after, but he didn't duck his head and turn away, and Griff liked his spirit all the better for it. "Listen. I hadn't meant to bring this up, but I might as well."

This ought to be good. Griff fished a sprig of mint out of his glass and twirled it at Brendan between thumb and forefinger in a *well, let's hear it, then* gesture.

Brendan met his gaze as a man should. "I don't know why Evan invited me, except that as far as I can tell he's genuinely that sweet-natured."

"Not wrong," Griff said. "And?"

"And, he's yours," Brendan returned calmly. Only the white of his knuckles gave his true feelings away. "I still don't know what's going on inside *your* head, but I didn't come tonight to cause trouble. I'm asking you plainly if you want me to leave."

Griff's contrary nature always had led him around by the balls. He kicked his legs forward, sprawling wide and lazy. Evan called that a surefire tell, swearing that when Griff was most interested, he looked least likely to move. Sleeping Tiger, Snoozing Dragon. "Now, why would I want that?"

Frustration brought a brighter spark of life to Brendan's face and made his accent burr-r-r. Damned fine-sounding. "Because if you weren't here, I would still be interested in him," he said. "And even with you here, I'm tempted. Is that plain enough?"

"It'll do." Griff enjoyed teasing this man more than he'd thought he would. "You don't think I'm pretty?"

"Of course I do, I'm not—" Brendan shut his mouth with an audible *click* of teeth. He exhaled. "And that is not something I'd meant to say. If you're kind, you'll pretend it never happened."

Oh, Griff thought as the engine inside his head *finally* started ticking over.

"Back," Evan announced from behind him. He eased drinks full to the brim onto their table as deftly as any professional waiter, though with a twinkle in his eye Griff would bet astronauts could see from space.

Evan, you sneaky son of a gun. I see what you mean now. Right in front of my eyes.

"Oh, thank God," Evan breathed as he took a seat and curled up with one foot beneath himself. "I wasn't sure what I'd have to do if you didn't get there soon."

"You think you're clever, don't you, darlin'?" Griff asked quietly as Brendan tried to bury his thundercloud of emotions in a fresh glass of red, red wine.

"Yes, I do," Evan murmured, one soothing hand warm on Griff's thigh. "He's exactly what we've been looking for. Are you with me?"

"Since the physician can't heal himself," Griff said. He tipped back a hearty swig of his refill with a satisfying clatter of ice cubes. "All right, darlin', you started the music, so I'm gonna call it your dance. How do you want this to go?"

Evan winked at him. "Just follow my lead."

Evan hadn't chosen the Palomino at random. Griff loved the food, but Griff would chow down on a block of newsprint if it came with enough butter and salt. The views through the floor-to-ceiling windows would take anyone's breath away, but if he wanted to take in the great outdoors, he preferred to *be* outdoors. Any bar and grill or just plain bar might have done, except for one thing—live local music on Friday nights.

And he'd timed his exit and return just right.

Pleased with himself, he tilted his head to catch the first warm-up notes of the band. Not one he knew, but he'd idled by the low-rise stage while watching Griff work his magic from afar, and the peek he'd gotten at the band's set list suited him down to the ground. They'd start off fast and hard, and moving to that kind of music would be like falling into bed after going long enough without it to be *hungry*.

Brendan must not have noticed the musicians setting up. He pricked his ears, and almost seemed to slump. At Evan's curious gesture, he explained, "I'd hoped to have a word with you, but they look like they're going to be loud."

Evan kept a straight face as Griff nudged him in the side. He nudged back. *Don't you worry, I've got it covered.*

"You can still talk to me," Evan said to Brendan. He slid his chair back and stood. "Any time you want. Music doesn't last forever, and I'd rather enjoy it while I've got it. You could enjoy it with me, out there. I'd like that."

Griff coughed to cover the chortle Evan *knew* would have popped out of him.

Brendan blinked those huge dark eyes of his at Evan.

Poor guy. Evan's heart softened. He really wasn't used to this at all, was he? He took both of Brendan's hands in his and pulled gently, coaxing the good doctor to his feet. Just to be on the safe side, he held on to the right even when Brendan was fully upright. "Come on. Let your hair down tonight. You'll like it once you try it, I promise."

"That's not what I'm worried about," Brendan muttered. He caught up his drink, spilling a few drops over his hand and down his wrist, and tossed back a deep enough gulp to make Griff give him an impressed tip of the hat. "Tonight, that's... You're sure?"

"There's nothing to doubt," Evan said. Behind his back, he tossed a quick gesture to Griff, which he hoped Griff interpreted correctly as *Give us a minute, and then you can play too.* Then, he tugged at Brendan's hand. "I want this. Come with me."

* * * *

The Palomino didn't have a dance floor as such. They did understand that music played loud and skillfully would get people on their feet, and a gaggle of servers had finished clearing out a group of tables and chairs just before the band started. Even so, the patch of empty floor had filled itself up again just as fast. It'd be standing room only, with use of elbows required.

Evan didn't mind. He liked the feeling of being surrounded, enveloped by humanity. People were beautiful creatures, only most of them never figured that out. Too busy trying to one-up themselves, or too convinced they never could, and they wasted so much *time* they could spend living instead. Not him. He'd learned that lesson.

Brendan hadn't. He looked about as comfortable as a long-tailed cat in a roomful of rocking chairs, but at the same time he didn't make any excuses or try to cut and run.

Evan decided he'd take that as a positive sign.

He touched Brendan's shoulder lightly to show him where to stop, then angled in front of him. The band's bass player had a wicked way with the notes, winding them sinuously around one another, and the drummer kept a beat as steady and chest-deep as a heartbeat. He never bothered counting in his head—just let the sound control his hips—but it usually worked out.

And he wasn't stupid. He knew what it looked like when he raised his arms and closed his eyes. How the light jersey he wore clung to his chest and rode up over the waist of the jeans Griff had made him promise to never, ever throw out. The way his hair moved with him, curling against the line of his throat. He could feel Brendan watching him. Sense how much he liked what he saw.

Good.

"I haven't danced in years," Brendan warned—but he wasn't that bad, actually. He made the effort. And while he might be out of practice, sure, a little unpolished, but give him enough time to become comfortable with his own body, and he'd leave Evan in the dust.

Evan leaned in close, his lips brushing Brendan's ear. "What did you want to talk to me about?"

"Nothing," Brendan said shortly. "It doesn't matter now."

Oh no. He wasn't getting out of it that easily. Not now that Evan was *sure* of him. Evan took Brendan's wrist in a careful bracelet hold, two fingers at his pulse. Beating like a trip-hammer, far more so than was natural for a healthy man doing nothing more than dancing. "But it does matter," he said, pressing the tip of his nose beneath Brendan's ear. "Tell me."

Brendan flinched as if Evan had touched a live wire to his spine. "It can't matter. You're here with Griff, and I'm not— I won't— Let me go. Please."

"Why? There's no need, Brendan."

Brendan was stronger than he looked, and his muscles were hard when he took Evan by the shoulders and pushed him to arm's length—but his eyes were wild, and from the looks of him, he'd come to the fine edge of what he could tolerate. "I won't be made fun of, either," he said. His words were harsh, but his voice pleading. "What are you up to?"

Griff, who'd come up from behind while Brendan wasn't paying attention, put his arms around Brendan's waist to hold him in place. "Nothing," he said on Brendan's other side. "Except for exactly what you're trying not to think."

Brendan stilled, then wrenched his neck to try to look back at Griff. "What—?"

Griff clicked his tongue. "Hush, now. You know." He'd already caught the beat, and moved with the music. Careful not to spook him again, Evan took Brendan's hips in his hands and guided him to the beat. Sandwiched between them, Brendan couldn't help but rock to the same rhythm.

He closed his eyes once as a shiver ran through him. "Why?"

Evan approved of his moving on from *what*. "Because we like you," he said, before touching his lips to the hollow of Brendan's collarbone. "Because you're handsome, and kind. Because you're new here, and it's a good place. Because we have done this before, and we know what we want. Because it feels good. Just because. Isn't that enough?"

"Beats the hell out of a welcome basket," Griff chipped in.

Brendan laughed, short and out of breath. He shook his head.

Griff moved in. He slipped one hand beneath Brendan's shirt, easing the edge of the fabric up with his thumb. His sun-darkened skin looked burnished against the fairer stretch of Brendan's stomach. "Just to make it clear, I'm all on board with the plan." He eased Brendan's hips tighter to him.

"God, you're hard." Brendan groaned. He bit his lip. "It can't be that easy."

"But it is," Evan said, firmly now. "Do you want it? Say yes or no. That's all you have to do."

Chapter Three

Brendan hadn't noticed before how the lowering lights of the Palomino were just like stars. Or was that his vision? He'd fallen dangerously quickly under their spell, and now... But now...

Do it quick, before you lose focus.

"Before I answer, there's one thing I didn't tell you," he said, steady and firm as he could. "Mostly because I didn't think to, and that's no one's fault but my own. I assumed you'd know. Now I wonder. You do realize I'm not here for keeps, don't you?"

He could tell from the way the man stilled that Griff had not. *Damn.* He exchanged glances with Evan, who'd started to frown but wasn't piping up.

"I'm a substitute," Brendan said. "I'll only be here until Dr. George comes back from sympathetic leave. I should have made sure you knew that. I'm sorry."

"Well, now." Griff narrowed his eyes, as if in thought. Beside him, Evan laid a light touch on the man's shoulder. Encouraging or discouraging? Brendan couldn't tell.

"Might have been good if you'd said something about that before," Griff drawled. "So. This would be a one-time thing?"

Brendan made himself nod. "I wouldn't have let it get this far if I didn't think you were on the same page." His cheeks burned with embarrassment. "Do you still want it? Me?"

"Hell, Doc, that's not in question," Griff said with a snort. "Question is, do you want us? All cards on the table, now. I'm willing if you are."

And Brendan...

Was there a reason why he *shouldn't*? They were solid, Evan and Griff. He wouldn't get between them. But to take that which they freely offered... Better than a gift basket, Griff had said. An unconventional welcome from two odd but endearing men, one he'd wanted right away, and one he was—despite himself—growing to like more than was wise.

Just once. Yes. He could do that.

Brendan opened his eyes and let his focus settle on Evan in front of him, while Griff blanketed him from behind. "All right," he said, his voice rough. "Where?"

The touch of Griff's lips, of his stubble, made Brendan's nape tingle. He turned his head, offering more skin.

"Don't know about Evan, but I'd like to see you in our bed. That sound like a plan? Good. My turn to take the lead now," Griff said.

"Where?"

"Home," Evan whispered in Brendan's ear as Griff kissed him. "Come with us. We'll show you the way."

* * * *

Griff didn't kiss Brendan again until they'd shut the door of their home behind them. Evan had taught him how anticipation made delivery all the sweeter, and he suspected Brendan had a fair amount of tension built up that needed a good hard release.

Brendan groaned low in his throat when Griff finally took pity, and took a double fistful of Griff's overshirt to grab as he leaned into him, into his kiss. The man had a natural gift for this. Maybe a hair awkward, but only from eagerness and hunger. It'd go to a man's head.

True enough that he'd hoped for more than one ride on the carousel, but he was certain Evan had his back. They'd make it work. And besides, who knew? Might be they could entice the good doctor into coming back for seconds.

Evan pressed tight to Brendan from behind. Griff kept firm hold on Brendan, one hand at his waist and one at his nape, keeping him steady and kissing him through the startled flinch when his sweater bunched — Evan lifting it from behind to get his hands on soft, smooth skin.

If he'd thought Brendan's eyes were wide before... Now, the black almost swallowed the irises.

He let Griff hold his weight. "What's he...?"

"Undressing you. He likes it. I tell him sometimes he must have had a previous life as a pole dancer," Griff told him. He moved to brush his thumbs over Brendan's cheekbones, keeping him occupied so Evan could strip that man as bare as the day he'd been born. He could tell Evan enjoyed the view with equal pleasure. "So far so good, Doc?"

Brendan's laugh was breathless, more so when Evan eased the trousers off him. "Good. This too. This is..."

"Isn't it?" Griff teased.

"Very," Brendan said. He lifted his head to return Griff's kiss. "God, yes. More."

"That's what we like to hear," Evan said. He rested his chin on Brendan's now bare shoulder, conveniently close enough to kiss, and why not?

He could feel Brendan's dazed attempt to study them at a cockeyed sort of angle, and better still, his small sigh when he pressed his head to Evan's and parted his lips, listening to them taste each other.

Griff thumbed a drop of kiss-wetness off Brendan's lip. "You like that too?"

Brendan made a move Griff thought was a nod. "You don't have to ask."

"But we want to." Evan took Brendan by the wrists and walked backward, leading him, giving him a sideways view of their bed. Seeing what he intended, Griff swept a double armful of the neck and back pillows Evan liked off the mattress, clearing the way before he started to shimmy out of his own jeans and shirt.

At that, Brendan gave him a wide-eyed look. Then a longer, more uncertain glance at Evan. Reminded of who had prior claim on what, Griff wouldn't doubt. He kicked his jeans away to land wherever they pleased and touched a fingertip to Brendan's lips. "Shush now. C'mere. I promise it'll be good. And don't you worry about Evan. He isn't feeling left out."

Left out? Not at all. Still at Brendan's back, Evan could guide him where Griff directed the lot of them. He sat on the edge of the bed — far back, knees fitted to the mattress, and spread his thighs wide to pull Brendan down in a comfortable seat between them. "No protests?"

"None," Brendan breathed.

"Good." Taking care to be sure Brendan could see, Evan teased his way down from waist to hip and curved inward to drag his fingernail over Brendan's engorged cock. He splayed his fingers wide then shaped a cup over Brendan's cock, stroking the way he thought Brendan would like best. Not too hard, but nowhere near gentle.

"You like that?" he murmured near Brendan's ear. "Tell me."

He could only just see Brendan's face in quarter-profile, but could tell when Brendan's lips parted and his eyes hooded. "You really don't have to ask."

"But I like to." Evan nudged him, gently. "Well?"

"Answer the man, and you'll get a prize." Griff folded neatly down in a kneel, hands on Brendan's knees to push them wide enough to allow Griff's broad shoulders room. Almost too far — he wouldn't be used to the stretch — but with a promising result. His cock jerked against Evan's hand, slickness beading at the tip.

Griff had noticed. "Like it rough, hmm?" he asked, lifting Brendan's knees over his shoulders. "Not too much at once if you want to be able to walk tomorrow?"

Brendan rolled his hips, nudging his way ever more firmly into Evan's hand. "I want to feel it tomorrow."

"Don't worry about that. You will. You'll feel it for days." Evan switched to his knuckles, dragging them lightly over the goods. He nuzzled beneath Brendan's chin, nipping at the smooth skin. "Griff's planning to suck your cock. Will you let him?"

Griff blew a long stream of warm air over Evan's hand and Brendan's cock. "Look at you. So hot for it you're leaking. What do you think, Evan? Think he tastes sweet?"

Evan knew a cue when he heard one. He lifted his hand to his mouth and tasted. "Salty. You should try him."

Brendan shuddered and swore. "Either stop making me nuts or do something about it," he said, so very hard, so very eager.

"It's not all up to me." Evan returned his focus to Griff, who nuzzled the insides of Brendan's thighs. Beard burn for sure. He doubted Brendan would mind. He certainly had no plans to. But— "You need to say it now. So we're all sure. Do you want this? Last chance to back out."

"No," Brendan said, so softly Evan barely heard him. His gaze said what he didn't, hunger and yearning fast overcoming all else. "No stopping now."

"Then we won't stop." Evan wrapped his hand around Brendan's shaft. Nature had designed him in the right proportions. At a guess, Evan's narrow hand would cover exactly the length Griff couldn't comfortably take in his mouth. "We'll take good care of you."

Brendan parted his lips to moisten them. "Yes. God, yes."

Evan held Brendan close and still when Griff took him into his mouth. He seemed slimmer and lighter, every wrack and tremble threatening to rattle him apart. "Shh," Evan soothed, threading his fingers through Griff's hair to guide him. "Go slow. Gentle."

Griff did. Evan knew very well how gentle Griff could be when he wanted, how quick and clever his tongue on the short flicks, how lush and lavish in the long, slow licks. Brendan wrenched at the waist and pushed at the both of them, forward and back. "Stop." He exhaled a gasp of breath. "Ever since the bar— If you don't, I'll—"

"Be kind," Evan said in an undertone. He didn't think Brendan noticed.

Griff read him loud and clear. He drew away, licking his lips. "Supplies under the pillow?"

"Only what you want to use," Evan cautioned before Brendan could question him.

Brendan laughed drunkenly. "All of them?"

Griff snorted. "Trust me, it wouldn't be a challenge." He nodded to Evan. "Down on the bed, both of you."

Evan knew Griff's shorthand well enough, and his agility extended far enough to grope Griff—to give his heavy, swinging cock a long, luxurious tug—as between them they eased Brendan down on the bed. Each chose a side to lie on, bracketing him. Griff kissed him, sealing Brendan's mouth. A signal that it was Evan's turn again.

One more in the plus column for Brendan—he accepted, without question, the arrangement, his only confusion a perturbed lack of focus in choosing which of them to look at, which only made Evan smile. They'd solve Brendan's problem for him.

Griff edged back to make room for Evan to slip over and halfway across the top of Brendan's slim body, streamlined in shape save for the heft of his cock. He and Griff were both growers, and Brendan a shower, but he'd firmed up sweet and strong. Eager, too.

"What are you...?" Brendan tried to sit up and look.

Evan, with Griff's help, nudged him back down. He could rest on his elbows, Evan decided, but no more than that. Evan slid down Brendan's firm thighs and calves, savoring the friction of his own aching hard-on against Brendan's leg then the sturdy duvet. Only when he'd positioned himself exactly so, and blown a cool stream of air over Brendan's cock, did Evan look up at the dazed young man through his eyelashes and ask, "What do you think I'm doing?"

Taking my turn would have been the right answer, but Evan didn't give Brendan the chance to speak. Brendan smelled of soap and salty musk. Cleanliness came next to godliness for him. Evan liked the effort, at least the first time around. Time enough later to show him the value of quick and dirty, the taste of sweat and heat.

He stopped to kiss the inside of Brendan's thigh, strawberry-pink from Griff's five o'clock shadow, bent his head then took Brendan deep. Perhaps too deep for a man not used to it on a regular basis. Griff had to hold Brendan down gently but firmly when he shouted and arched up. Needing to take such care could become an addiction. Almost as potent as the hesitant hitching of Brendan's hips. Evan ached with the need to let Brendan have his way, but even so, face-fucking without practice wasn't on the menu.

Later, Evan thought. He rested his hands on Brendan's hips, a gentle request to lie still, and drew the man as deep as he could, pulled back with a wet suck, then pushed forward again, hollowing his cheeks.

Griff shifted up. His blunt finger traced lines on Evan's cheeks. Evan could feel both men watching him, avid, hungry, fascinated in different ways. Brendan with amazement. Griff, because he swore and proved every time they played with a third that he couldn't get enough of the sight of Evan with his mouth full of cock.

Brendan moaned, head back, breathing in sharp, shallow gasps. It seemed almost too much of a struggle for the man to bend forward and watch, but he tried. His movements nearly matched the pace of his breathing, ragged and out of sync, surging forward, falling back. He reminded Evan of the waves.

"You can feel me too, can't you?" Griff asked Evan, his voice dropped in pitch to midnight bass. He ran the pad of his thumb over the corner of Evan's mouth, catching the saliva that slicked Brendan's cock. "Feels good, yeah?"

Brendan shook his head, helpless to speak if Evan were any judge. Even without his mouth full, Evan wouldn't have managed it. Only Griff would never shut up.

Evan managed not to laugh out loud, but only just, and the vibrations were going to undo Brendan. Evan wasn't much better off, and had to stop and take hold of his cock and squeeze at the base. No way was this going to be over just yet. He drew off, leaving Brendan's swollen member slick with spit and salty pre-cum, straining toward his mouth, not willingly but for the lack of air. If he didn't he'd come all the same.

"You were right. He's sweet," Evan told Griff. He almost wanted to send Griff in for another taste, but caught himself in time. He wanted to know the full flavor of the man, and only a little more would get him there. Brendan's balls, well-shaped as any Evan had ever seen, tightened when he palmed them. Eager, so very eager, and almost there.

Stop. Stop now.

"He could finish you this way," Griff said. He'd curled up tight to Brendan's side, hand on Brendan's tight stomach, teasing him. "Or you could try the rest. Your call."

Brendan groaned and ground the heels of his hands against his forehead. He writhed between them, a clumsy yet still sensuous stretch, and reached for them in uncoordinated turn. "I don't know," he said. "No. Yes. I do know." He tried to spread his legs, wanton as a wild creature, but his gaze was steadier than it had any right to be. "I want it all."

"Will you let Griff do it?" Evan asked. He could top, but he'd much rather enjoy the view. And if Brendan could handle Griff with no holds barred, then they'd be onto something good indeed. "He wants it. I see the way he watches you. He wants to fuck you."

A moan escaped Brendan. "I — yes. Please. That."

Evan nipped his earlobe. "Good man. Such a good man. Take care of him, Griff. Do it right."

"Don't have to tell me twice," Griff said. He ran a hand up Brendan's chest. He'd gone heavy-lidded with desire, and hot with eagerness. "I'll show you how it's done."

* * * *

And he did. Naked on his back, his ass wet with lube and his thighs raw with friction, Brendan could only cling to them as Evan and Griff carried him away on sensation after sensation, one blurring into the next, hotter and higher, until —

"All right?" Griff asked, a solid, exciting weight draped atop him. "Need to hear you say it, Doc."

Brendan took his nape in hand, and bit at the man's mouth. "Do it. Do it now, God, please."

He couldn't find a real grasp on Evan, but Evan provided one for him. He took hold of Brendan's cock, stroking him in counter-rhythm, whispering things that made no sense but curled hot and stinging as the rasp of a dragon's tongue. His curls, wet with sweat, tickled Brendan's chest, but they were good for hanging onto — and Evan liked it. He purred and rumbled something that sounded like approval, leaning up, his sleek tongue stroking as deep in Brendan's mouth as Griff's cock in his ass.

Griff grunted with the sound of all things amazing and pushed deep, faster now. Brendan shuddered, feeling too large for his skin, as if he'd split open. He'd had sex before. Who knew how many times. It'd never mattered. Not like this. Griff hit every spot he hadn't known could be a pleasure point, and Evan's lips parted as he watched them. He rolled his hips, rubbing against Brendan's thigh, slick wetness between them.

They *fit*, all three of them.

"It's all right," Evan said, kissing Brendan everywhere he could reach. His hand never ceased to move, and so neither did Brendan's, even if all he could manage was clumsy petting. Griff fucked him harder now, his balls slapping Brendan's ass in a way he wouldn't have thought could do such *things* to his head. Made him—drove him. His mind didn't drift away so much as it *snapped*, his eyes shutting so tight he saw sparks of color against the backs of his eyelids, and his muscles howled at him with the force his orgasm made punching its way out.

Evan would have fallen back if Brendan hadn't found, from somewhere, the strength to tug him closer. Griff was still hard in him, not done yet, and so that meant Evan wasn't either.

"Finish with him," Brendan ordered, staring Evan in the eye.

Evan laughed under his breath.

"What'd I tell you?" Griff asked, sounding bizarrely proud. "Keep on helping Evan. I like the looks of that."

Brendan reached for Evan, despite the whirling in his head. Fuck, but he couldn't think straight. He could only hope he got it right when he tugged at Evan to encourage him. The angle was almost awkward, but he must have hit Evan where Evan liked it. Cum not his own spurted over Brendan's stomach, thick and hot, dribbling down his hipbone. He pressed his forehead to Evan's and breathed for him, with him.

Griff sped up, harder, deeper. Brendan cried out, not in pain but with shocked pleasure—he'd already come but it was no less good. It was *better*, somehow, this knowing that Griff wanted him and liked him so much he'd go after his own this way, without mercy. He thrust back, silently offering more—all Griff wanted—and kissed Evan in the way Evan had taught him, with affection and care. So strange how they went so well together...and somehow, not strange at all.

Griff's short nails dug in when he came with a roaring growl.

"Not done yet," Evan murmured, moving slick and quick. "Never went soft, did you?" He took Brendan in hand, twisted that odd wrist, *curled* his fingers, and—

Brendan could barely breathe or look down in shock at the jerk of his cock emptying again. "Christ," he gasped. "Oh Christ."

Griff slipped out of him. It hurt, but not in a way Brendan minded. He liked having the pain to show for the gain, and he forgot about it when Griff kissed him until his thoughts went shadowed and fuzzy.

Brendan covered his eyes. Breath came back with a lusty gasp. "Jesus," he said. "Jesus Christ."

"Well, fair enough," Evan said, holding back his amusement. *Almost* holding it back. "That was your second coming."

Brendan groaned. He could still feel Griff's cock as clearly as he did Evan's mouth, even though the men themselves now lay on either side of Brendan. Hot, sweaty bodies molded to his, stroking each other and him too. He felt as if he'd swallowed the sun and the rays beamed out of him. It wasn't logical, but somehow that didn't seem to bother him now.

"You were right," he said at last. "Better than a welcome basket."

Chapter Four

The next morning came far too early. They usually did.

Experience had taught Griff that the best souvenirs always took a day or so to show up. Griff stretched his arms out before him, fascinated, on his amble from bedroom to kitchen. He followed his nose, twitching like a hound's at the scent of bacon sizzling and the sharp tang of oranges. He tied the drawstring of his sleep pants into a double knot as he went to keep from tripping over their ragged hems. They were his favorites, a Scottish plaid pair that'd seen him through his last year of high school clear to now. He'd lost track of how many times Evan had threatened to cut them up for dust cloths or just burn the damn things when he had his back turned, but always laughing longest when he made the direst promises.

He had it good with Evan. God, he knew that much for sure.

Case in point — the man cooked meat for him that he wouldn't have gone near otherwise. Evan, who'd stationed himself far enough back from the range to avoid bacon spatters and wrinkled his nose at the toothsome contents, looked up with relief when Griff stumbled in. "You're walking like you're still dreaming. What's —? Oh."

Griff held his arm up. Hard to see clearly just yet, but he figured he'd have a real bracelet around his wrist later. "Not too shabby, huh?"

Evan snorted quietly, and turned in three-quarter profile to show Griff the love bite darkening his clavicle, then back to lower the waist of his yoga pants and display its twin on the point of his hip bone. A pretty sight, no doubt about it, but not one Griff enjoyed more or less than the trailer of honeysuckle Evan had wound crookedly around the crown of his head. "More like what happens when a tornado meets a volcano. I didn't expect that. Did you?"

Yes and no. Griff couldn't see the marks of fingernails on his back, but he relished the low burn whenever his muscles moved beneath the tender skin. He took the thick ceramic mug of coffee Evan pushed his way, sweetened with raw honey, and buried his face in the steam for a tongue-scalding, head-clearing chug.

He licked his lips, chasing the drops, then let Evan steal the mug back from him even though the roar of caffeine had already gone a good way toward easing the growling throb growing in his head. Hell. Better take some aspirin and hope he could ward it off at the pass. Last thing he wanted to deal with was a migraine.

"Guy's got some passion to him, no doubt about that," he said. "The way I see it, he's either been saving that up for years, or he ought to be taking care of business more often than 'just the once'. Am I right?"

"I don't think you're wrong, no," Evan said slowly. He clicked the stove off, pushed the pan of bacon to the back of the range, and sank into a chair on the sunlit side of their kitchen. "But I guess that's all it can be. Just wondering, and idle questions. For us, I mean."

"It's what he asked for." Old habit brought Griff down in the chair opposite him. Neither matched, but both were equally well loved.

"Mmm," Evan voiced noncommittally. He plunked the mug of coffee between them and swirled his finger around the rim. "That's what he *said*, sure. I just wonder if..."

Yep. Thinking the same thing. "We did agree," Griff pointed out.

Evan cut him a faintly annoyed glance. "I know that. I'm not planning to shadow him and tackle him when he least expects it."

Griff snorted. "Good, because I kinda think you'd set yourself up for an epic fail. You are many things, gorgeous, but sneaky ain't one of them."

"Ass." Evan swatted at Griff, then settled with his fingertips lightly dancing over Griff's wrist. "I wish it was different. I will say that. And that I wonder why he wouldn't even leave the option open for 'more'. I don't think it's what he wanted." He made a sideways slicing motion with one hand. "I'll leave it there—as long as you admit it, too."

Griff raised one shoulder. So maybe he did wish the grand finale hadn't gone down the way it did, but what could he do about it? Life went on.

So would they.

* * * *

Darry, as it turned out, had a three-day stretch of time off coming to him. Brendan couldn't tell whether disappointment or relief dominated his head when he checked the nursing station and found it conspicuously empty of the massive jokester. Sure, Darry would have teased him without mercy and probably had something to say about cutting off his nose to spite his face—and he wouldn't have been wrong—but it wasn't anything Brendan didn't already know.

Even if he'd chosen not to listen to himself.

Besides, it was his business. No one else's.

And if he spent more time than he should measuring the marks Evan and Griff had left behind in a mirror and in his memory, that was his affair too.

He'd get over wanting them. It'd be for the best. It *would*.

And if he told himself so enough times, the lesson ought to stick.

"Dr. West?" Magnus, in his professional role of physician's assistant, rapped on the side of the bathroom door. He was a looker, wasn't he? Tall and lean, wiry with whipcord muscle, and boasting a slow, lazy grin that coaxed a return smile from Brendan before he knew what his face was doing.

"Just a second, sorry." Brendan worked the paper towel dispenser with the point of his elbow, and patted his hands clean, calming himself from high alert to no-threat. Magnus looked too relaxed for any major emergencies. He lifted his chin at the man while wadding the towel to throw away. "What's up?"

"The sky and stock prices," Magnus replied with a wink so broad that advertising agencies could have rented out space, but only for adult merchandise. "Also, the big boss wants to see you when you've got a minute. I was passing by and I don't mind carrying messages."

"Nice of you."

"I'm a nice guy," Magnus agreed. Nice, yes, and straightforward. The up-and-down once-over he gave Brendan lacked any subtlety, and yet...it didn't offend. Too open for that, somehow. "If you don't know where his office is, I wouldn't mind walking you there, Brendan. Dr. West."

Brendan couldn't help laughing. "God, does that work on anyone?"

"Every now and then," Magnus agreed, undeterred by being caught.

Brendan hesitated, almost tempted by what Magnus clearly had on offer. His long limbs suited his torso, and his face, and the sparkle in his eye promised nothing but a good time. Absolutely the kind of guy best suited for a vacation fling.

Nothing at all like Evan's quiet beauty. Even less like Griff's rough-edged charm, but... He doubted Magnus would *mind* being a first step. And if he was going to get over Evan and Griff, he had to start somewhere.

"Something in the water," Brendan murmured.

"What?"

"Nothing." Brendan made his choice, and tried not to regret it, either for his sake or for Magnus'. He took a deep breath and said, "So. Are you only passing by, or could you be convinced to stay while I take a break?"

Magnus raised one eyebrow. "Well, then," he murmured, giving Brendan a more thorough once-over. "If that's how it is, I could be convinced to loiter a little longer."

* * * *

Evan absently pocketed the bottle of aspirin he'd picked up on his way through their home, and had almost forgotten about once he'd set foot inside his greenhouse. *Would you look at that?* He couldn't be sure from where he stood on the ground, but he thought a hummingbird had made its nest at the topmost angled panes. Tiny jewel-like wings flashed in the same sun that made it impossible to be certain of its nature.

Beautiful, though.

He shaded his eyes to watch the bird as best as he could. Movement made him aware, briefly, of the fading ache from his — their — one night with Brendan.

"Chick-chick-chick," he clucked to the bird, who ignored him.

It wasn't their first rodeo. That hadn't been a lie. They'd gone in with the same motivation, mostly. Someone they'd liked, who hadn't minded the looks of them either, and who wouldn't push past the lines they were always careful to draw early on.

They'd skipped most of that with Brendan. Mostly because Evan had had too much fun teasing Griff. Probably a mistake.

Maybe that was why he'd slipped beyond the boundaries so easily.

Hard to say.

The hummingbird, which might just have been a common jay, rattled its wings against the glass and let loose with a warbling trill of song that brought a bright smile to Evan's lips. He knew from the feel of that particular smile and the way it changed his mouth that it was the one Griff called his favorite. He'd told Evan so just yesterday morning — said it while sprawled carelessly, artlessly in bed before dawn, his hands on Evan's bare hips, guiding Evan through riding him as if he was one of his beloved motorbikes racing toward the finish line.

Evan had more recent tender spots and the memories to go along with them than Brendan, and yet...

Wait. Was that a hornet? Or a yellow jacket, maybe.

He took three steps back and narrowed his eyes at the roof. Damn it, that *was* a papery nest tucked up there, far too close to the bird. That wouldn't do. He liked bees for their honey, but wasps and he didn't get along. They had their place in nature but they were territorial and could be cruel. Leave them alone and the birds wouldn't come back.

Better do something about it. Evan rubbed his chin as he studied the angle of the roof. He *could* climb it, if he wanted. It wasn't so very high to the top of the greenhouse. No more chancy than clambering up to the roof of their home, and he'd done that the Christmas before last to hammer down icicle lights as a surprise for Griff. That'd worked.

Although if he cast his mind back, he could still hear Griff yelling at him for taking that kind of risk. He'd made the windows rattle, then they'd very nearly broken the bed frame afterward.

Maybe not a good idea to climb, then. Griff would do it, if Evan asked him sweetly enough, and Evan never really had to try. Came naturally.

Would Brendan climb, if asked? Evan couldn't be sure, and he let the sunlight bathe him while he rolled the idea over. *Yes*, he decided eventually. *He wouldn't want to at first, but he'd be curious enough to try after he'd taken some time. And he'd want to do it so I wouldn't have to. He's like Griff, and not at all like Griff, too.*

Birds and bees were easy, when it came to challenges. Doctors, somewhat more difficult. Was there anything to do about the Brendan problem, really?

Evan sighed. He wasn't sure. He didn't think so.

But he doubted that would stop him trying, either. In some ways, he and Griff could be a little too much two of a kind.

* * * *

"Hey, wake up!" A rough hand jostled Griff out of a half-waking, half-sleeping doze at his workbench.

He blinked, but the blur that'd accosted him didn't resolve itself into a clear image. Didn't matter. He still knew the voice. "Jesus, Rafe. Give me an attack, why don't you?"

All bark, no bite. Usually. They all knew it. The tattooed rapscallion gave him another shake. "You want an attack, finish falling asleep and go face first into an engine," Rafe said in an undertone. He looked rough, but he had the heart of a marshmallow. "Or are suspension systems suddenly that boring?"

"Yes. Give me something with some meat to it."

"You've got plenty of meat waiting for you at home. Pay attention to the poor engines. Make some pretty swans out of these ugly ducklings."

Griff snorted as he sat back. *Hellfire.* He liked Rafe, at the best and the worst of times. Half Native, half Mexican, thirty-odd years old, all confidence. Nobody could spin a dirtier story or tell a joke so ripe it'd turn the air blue.

He could have done without the sass at the moment, but beggars couldn't be choosers.

"You got any aspirin?" he asked, digging one knuckle against his temple. So far he'd done a decent enough job keeping the migraine at bay. It'd sweep back in if he gave it even a second's window of opportunity, and man, he had too much on his mind for that.

Evan, for one. Always Evan. Sometimes he'd sit awake at night and draw around the scar down his chest, the first thing his gaze had been drawn to when he'd pulled the tow truck up to the rattletrap VW Bug he'd somehow driven himself all the way up the California coastline without crashing to his death. He'd had his shirt off and had planted himself on the hood to get some sun. That scar of his had stood out a mile.

He hadn't scowled or scolded at Griff for staring. Had just cracked one of those sweet smiles and asked if he could help.

Griff liked carrying around those pictures in his head. Only thing was, here and lately they'd joined up with the bare smattering of Brendan-memories and doubled down across the background of his thought, and he wasn't much of a man for introspection. He left that to Evan whenever he could.

So why he kept closing his eyes and circling around the question of Brendan like a hornet around a glass-encased Popsicle was anyone's guess.

He'd been nice enough not to say Griff's past put him off, but...

Fuck it, anyway. *Let the man have his peace. He made himself clear.*

"No aspirin, sorry," Rafe said. He didn't move on, as he normally would. That was the deal. Give Griff a hard time, sure, but keep walking. He stayed there instead, head cocked, frowning at Griff. "You okay, G? You look kind of—"

"What, hungover?" Griff put in before Rafe could extrapolate. Be the last thing he needed, for him to land a lucky shot. He added a dash of camp to the work, or what Evan would call camp, rubbing his temples. "Shut up."

That did the trick. He couldn't see Rafe clearly but he could very well imagine all the tumblers slipping into place, and his hoot of laughter sealed the deal. He thumped Griff on the back once, good and hard. "Don't drink so much during the week next time, idiot. Stay awake and I'll see what kind of painkillers I can rustle up in the boss' office."

Griff breathed a grim sigh of relief when Rafe ambled away. He'd make up the lie sometime. Evan and his odd sense of justice allowed for misdirection when there was no other alternative but for fists to start flying, but restitution needed to be made. Maybe he'd bring bagels the next time he had a morning shift.

For the moment, he pounded back another swig of coffee long since gone cold, gave his head a good hard shake, then focused on the pile of greasy engine parts scattered on the workbench. They wanted to fix a shot motor? Man, he'd give them the finest damn repair job this side of the Pecos.

At least that was something he could do right. Evan would say otherwise, but Evan was too kind for his own good sometimes.

He checked his phone, frowning. No messages so far today. Odd. Unusual, for Evan.

Wonder what he's up to?

* * * *

"You may think you have everyone else fooled, but it's not working on me. Good morning, by the way."

Brendan checked his watch. "Four-thirty, this says," he remarked as he closed the file he'd tried and mostly failed to occupy his mind with. Nothing earth-shattering. Hints that the flu season would hit harder than usual this year, which had led to his wondering if Evan would need extra protection, and if Darry hadn't distracted him just then he might have rummaged out his tablet and started researching Immunosuppressants versus H1N1.

He rubbed his face instead, and found more stubble there than he usually liked. He couldn't remember shaving since Friday, a full week ago now. Good God, what he must look like... It was a wonder the nurses hadn't ganged up and shaved him yet.

Darry rubbed a knuckle over his whiskers in passing. "What, are you trying to join the club now? And morning, afternoon, it all blends together after a while." The big man gave a philosophical shrug as he sat in a task chair at least two sizes small for his bulk. He didn't seem bothered by the creak of the bolts, but focused dually on shaking packets of sugar into the takeaway coffee he'd brought and in keeping one eye on Brendan.

Not, it would seem, likely to wander off any time soon. Brendan still couldn't tell if that was a relief or a frustration. "You were just on vacation. Shouldn't you be less resigned to your existence?"

Darry chuckled. "Three day leave isn't a cure-all."

That sounded more serious than anticipated. Brendan sat up straighter, already sliding into what he imagined Griff would tease him for as *doctor mode.* "Anything the matter?"

Darry waved him off before he could start. "I'm fine, don't worry about me." He tapped coffee off the pen he'd used as a stir stick and pointed the business end at Brendan. "Word is that while I was away, PA Magnus made his move."

"Ah," Brendan said. He sat back. The emergency department of St. Hawk's wasn't often busy at this time of day, and at the moment he decided to be grateful for that. "Forgive me, but that matters—why, now?"

If Darry noticed any of the prickles in Brendan's tone, they didn't go any further than skin deep. He raised one sturdy shoulder in response. "I don't have anything against him. He's decent enough. Has enough notches on his bedpost to slap a frame around and call it postmodernist sculpture, but…"

"I did notice that," Brendan said. "It's fine, Darry. I'm not looking for much more than casual, to be honest. He's diverting."

"If you need a diversion."

"And why shouldn't I?" Brendan replied calmly, warding off the doubt that niggled beneath his skin when he thought of Magnus. They'd not gone beyond flirting as yet, but even so, Brendan had to put his back into summoning up more than basic interest in the man. He'd be a catch for anyone who had the time, patience and inclination to tame him, but…

Brendan's taste ran more toward the impossible. Any day now, he expected, he'd admit it to himself— but today wasn't that day, and he could carry on fooling himself if he liked.

Or, he could put Darry out of his misery, and by nature Brendan wasn't a cruel man. He stole Darry's coffee and took a sip. "I want what I can't have," he said. It wasn't anywhere near as good as Evan's tea.

"The sooner I get past that, the better off we'll all be. You can't argue with that, Darry, no matter how much you might like to try."

Darry shot him a dark look, but sighed. The air went visibly out of his sails. "You're sure?"

"Yes." Brendan nudged him with the toe of one shoe. "I've been meaning to ask. Why get so involved in everyone else's love life? Why not cast a bit of concern on your own? You must have someone."

He knew the moment he'd said it that he'd made a terrible mistake.

Darry didn't reply. Not so much as a backward glance before he'd taken his coffee and stood, back turned to Brendan, walking away.

Damnation. "Darry, wait," Brendan said, standing to jog after him before he could make his escape from the nurse's station, where all good doctors lurked when not occupied with patients. No one willingly spent time in their offices, not even at St. Hawk's. "I'm sorry. I didn't mean—"

He'd just caught up with the man in front of the emergency department's sliding double doors, and put a hand on his elbow to stop him. "Hey. Calm down. What's going on?"

Darry wouldn't look at Brendan. He did open his mouth to answer, but was looking away, through the bay of the doors. Brendan followed his gaze.

It gave him a perfectly framed view of a car slaloming sideways into a parallel space, whoever was driving lying down on the horn.

"Help!" a man shouted before they'd so much as killed the engine—no, not just a man. *Evan.* He stuck his head and arm out of the window to flag them down. "Jesus Christ, whoever's in there, someone *help.*"

Chapter Five

Brendan took the sidewalk at a run, instincts firing before the rest of his head had a chance to catch up. He could hear Darry following fast behind him, nearly on his heels. Even so, Evan had wrenched open the back seat door before they reached him and started trying to coax Griff out of his huddled slouch on the seat.

He didn't appear to be having much luck. Griff's sub vocal growl rattled against the windows of the car. Bizarrely, Brendan noticed it was a 1970s vintage VW Bug with sunflower decals on the bumper. Had to be Evan's. It looked like his style.

"No, don't try to move him," he warned Evan, giving Darry a silent signal to put himself between Evan and the car. No matter how well-meaning friends and family might be, directly underfoot was never the place for them during triage. He couldn't blame Evan. He'd feel the same way. He *did* feel that way now. His hands didn't shake, though. Thank God for training.

He could *just* about see Griff properly in the dimmer light of the car. He sat hunched over himself, arms around his head. No blood. *Good.* "What happened? Griff, can you tell me?"

Griff muttered something. Brendan couldn't make it out.

"He's been talking, but it hasn't made any sense," Evan said, reluctantly stepping back behind Darry's strong arm. "We were supposed to meet around three to run a couple of errands. When he didn't meet me and didn't return my call, I went looking. The guys at the garage say he clocked out around two, but when I went around to the parking lot he'd tucked himself up in the back seat like that. I think he'd been there all along."

Brendan exchanged glances with Darry. "Does he get headaches?" he asked Evan.

"Sometimes." Evan speared one hand through his hair, sending it up in spikes. He'd never looked anything but calm and cheerful before, but now he'd gone pale with worry. "He thinks I can't tell when they're getting bad. I knew he had one coming, but… Not like that."

Ahh. Now it made sense. "Migraine?"

Griff muttered again and gave them a small, ragged wave.

Relief made Brendan's knees turn to jelly. Migraines were the definition of misery, but not the end of the world. This, he could help with. He gave Darry another direction-filled gesture, and the big nurse proved his worth by damned near reading Brendan's mind and doubling back for a wheelchair.

"All right, you big dope," he said, partly to Griff and partly to Evan, who from the looks of him needed reassurance nearly as much as Griff did. He laid his hand on Griff's knee and squeezed, giving him something to focus on. "Hang tight. We'll get you taken care of."

* * * *

Brendan hadn't had cause to treat a migraine during his time at St. Hawk's, but Darry — all business now — led them to a triage room with no windows. He helped Brendan ease Griff onto the exam table, which would have to double as a bed for the moment, disappeared, and returned with a diffused nightlight that plugged into a wall socket.

Enough light to see by. Hopefully not too much. Though he'd been lucky enough never to suffer one himself, Brendan suspected Griff's pain threshold would best be described as ridiculously high. For him to go down like a felled log, well. Agony wouldn't be too strong a word.

Brendan kept Griff's eyes covered with one hand while he spoke in low murmurs, winkling the information he needed out of Griff, when Griff could talk, and out of Evan when he couldn't pick individual words out of Griff's muttering.

He thought everyone in the small and crowded room breathed as deep a sigh of relief as Griff when Darry slid a needle into the man's vein to deliver a shot of painkiller.

"God *almighty*," Griff breathed through lips that'd gone dry and cracked. Bitten, Brendan decided, making a mental note to get some balm on board when Griff could tolerate even its non-taste. "Fuck me."

Evan snorted. He stood close enough to Brendan for Brendan to feel the tremors in his limbs. "Cursing like a sailor. He's already feeling better."

"Fucking fucked-up fuck," Griff muttered. "Balls."

"Now that's the kind of love they ought to put on greeting cards," Darry said, his thunderous baritone quieted to a low rumble. He patted Evan on the shoulder. "Come on. Doc's just about to kick us all out of here so Griff can get some rest and let the meds work."

Evan's head came up in surprise. "But I—"

Brendan could fill in the rest of that sentence. *Don't want to leave him.* "He's not wrong," he said, with a glance up at Evan that he hoped would reassure the man. "Rest and quiet and a chance to catch his breath, that's what he needs most. Go and get a cup of tea from the cafeteria, or have a walk around the gardens."

"Start on the mountain of paperwork for this visit, you mean. I know the drill." Evan caught his lip between his teeth. He rolled his shoulders forward, likely testing the strength of Darry's grip and whether or not he could change Brendan's mind. "But..."

"Go on," Griff said, his voice barely a rasp. He'd loosened his fists, though, his knuckles no longer white and bloodless from being clenched. "Chocolate doughnut. Get me one."

"Yeah, no. Not gonna happen." Evan took Griff's hand and kissed the back. He held it to the side of his face as he asked Brendan, "Will he be okay?"

Doctors knew better than to ever, *ever* make that sort of promise. Brendan opened his mouth to tell Evan as much.

It wasn't quite what came out. "Unless I'm needed on another emergency, I'll keep a watch over him myself," he promised, deliberately ignoring the sharp rise of Darry's eyebrows. The big man would have all sorts of things to say about that later, no doubt. *So be it.* "And if anything happens, I'll let you know. You have my word."

Which would—on any other day, in any other place—have been the end of that.

Not so in St. Hawk's.

Griff waited for the door to shut behind Evan and Darry, and for Brendan to sit beside him, before he cracked one bloodshot eye and breathed out an echoed sigh of his usual devil-may-care chuckle. "Not bad, Doc."

"Rest and quiet," Brendan replied. He stood to check the IV line. "Do you know what that means, or should I get a dictionary?"

Griff chuffed quietly. "Nah, I'm good." He snagged the cuff of Brendan's coat. "Hey. Look at me?"

Trapped, and neatly, too. "Stubborn, stubborn man, aren't you?" Brendan asked. He should hush him. No one needed to carry on a conversation mid-migraine. But he fell quiet, and he let Griff take hold of him without a fight.

"Better," Griff rasped. He lifted his chin, and he did not let Brendan's coat go, but wound it tighter in his fingers. "Got something to say to you. You willing to hear me out this time, darlin'?"

* * * *

"He's in good hands," Darry said, oh so casually placing himself between Evan and the exam room, closing the door behind them. "Doc might be new around here, but he knows what he's doing. I'm not the only one who's noticed how he fits in."

Evan tried to smile for him. He could see the concern just below the surface of Darry's bonhomie. The big man had a good heart. "I know. You don't need to play barrier. I've been here before, just…"

"Mostly on the other side?" Darry filled in for him. "I figured."

Evan touched the tip end of his old surgical scar, the half-inch that showed when he wore his collars loose or low. "Mmm. Is it always like this out here? If it is, I think I need to do up some written apologies for a few people."

"You're what we call a good patient. But yeah, that's about the size of it on the outside looking in. From what I've seen." Darry patted him on the back again, a monster-truck-sized love tap. "Go get that cup of tea and settle your nerves. I'll set you up with all the paperwork and have it waiting by the time you get back. If anything happens, I'll come and fetch you myself."

But for now, clear out, was what Evan supposed to be the subtext there.

At least he did know the way to the cafeteria. By heart, even. If he chose to go there.

He started walking in that direction, for a start. If he changed his mind, no one would chase him down unless he tried to sneak through the air ducts into Griff's room. Which Griff would do if the tables were turned, no doubt about that. The thought made Evan chuckle under his breath.

He'd be all right, even if Brendan didn't want to say so. Understandable. It'd only take one time promising a thing that couldn't be delivered before anyone would learn to pull their punches. As long as Evan could read between the lines, he could live with that and when a man like that gave his word, you couldn't ask for much more.

But if *more* was what you wanted...

They'd been good together. They'd *fit*. The more Evan saw of the man, the more Brendan convinced him he belonged with them. A third who could keep the balance and watch out for both of them when they got themselves in trouble, and who wasn't too proud to play when they tickled him right. It would work, it *could* work, but if wishes were horses...

I think I'd still wish for him, warts and all.

"Brendan," someone said to his left. "Have you seen him? Dr. Gabriel asked for him in his office almost an hour ago. For the second time. You did give him the message earlier, didn't you?"

Evan slowed his amble and pricked up his ears. One advantage to being quiet was the ability to hear far more than people realized, and to observe even more. *Dr. Gabriel, hmm?* Evan had met St. Hawk's chief operating officer once, at a county picnic. Good guy. Wound a little tight, but he had a ton of responsibility on his shoulders and no one to share it with.

It'd been a secretary who asked, a cheerfully tousled kind of guy who looked like he'd be fun to play poker with. He'd pulled up short to ask the question of a physician's assistant Evan recognized, but didn't know personally. He'd never quite trusted the guy — Magnus, was it? Too good-looking.

Magnus didn't stop, and the secretary had to trot to keep up with him. "Not sure, sorry."

The secretary sighed. "Not as sorry as I'll be when I have to tell Gabriel his pet project ditched."

"Pet project?" Magnus said with a laugh. "That's a new one. He's cute enough. I passed the message on. Whatever he's up to now isn't my problem, is it?"

"No? Because I've noticed you giving him the eye, even if he hasn't. And I know how you are about attaching yourself at the hip to hot new doctors," the secretary pointed out, dodging in front of Magnus to break his gait. "And I am using 'hip' as a polite metaphor."

Evan liked the secretary's style. He couldn't say he was too fond of Magnus' knowing grin.

"Dirty mind you have there," Magnus said, raising one eyebrow. "Look, I saw him, I spoke to him, and I could have done more—he seemed willing—but I'm not a supply closet sort of man. I'm taking him out on Friday. Come Saturday morning, you can feel free to give me all the winks and nudges you want."

"Sure of yourself, aren't you?"

"Shouldn't I be?" Magnus asked just a hair too confidently. "Tell you what, I'll step down after I've finished rounds and see if I can't rustle him up."

"Uh-huh. And after you're done, then you'll send him to Dr. Gabriel?"

In answer, Magnus winked.

Evan rolled his eyes. Good lord, he hoped Brendan had better taste than that. *And good luck, if Griff's well enough to give you the runaround.*

The thought made him laugh out loud. God, as soon as Griff felt better, Brendan had better watch out. There was nothing like the burst of adrenaline after a good scare to loosen inhibitions. He'd bet his last dime Griff would have decided to draw a line in the sand and, as soon as he could string a handful of words together, meant to get some better answers out of the good doctor.

And more power to him.

* * * *

Griff tapped the face of his watch. Though he couldn't hold his eyes more than halfway open without even the soft glow of the nightlight being too much, his head didn't feel like a punch bowl stuffed with lava anymore. He could focus. Could think. Maybe more clearly than he had done, trying to be a decent man instead of himself. Trying to think instead of do what he did best—act. "Thirty minutes, Doc," he said. "I'm still here. Time to make good on your half of the bargain."

Brendan, standing well-distanced at the sink where he'd planted himself after making the bet Griff couldn't lie still and let himself recuperate that long, sighed and crossed his arms. He couldn't fool Griff, though. Griff could see the reluctant smile tugging at the corners of his lips. "You're a stubborn man, Griff."

"It's been said," Griff admitted. He blinked. His eyes felt gritty, dry, but he'd done worse.

Brendan made a *hmm* noise. "How often has this happened before?"

"You mean the whole threesome thing? Less than a dozen, more than half a dozen."

"Jesus." Brendan's eyebrows shot up. "I meant the migraines, but... Jesus. With Evan, or before?"

"Hell, life before Evan mostly blurs together." Griff waved a hand. His teasing wasn't up to snuff, but he'd get there. "With Evan. All of them."

He watched Brendan digest that, passing through surprise to awe and back to doubt. "I don't... Forgive me. It's just... I've never known a couple like you before."

"Never will again, either. God broke the mold when he made us."

"That I'd be willing to believe." Brendan cleared his throat. "And the migraines, Griff?"

Griff made a hopefully noncommittal gesture. "Not often. Had 'em bad when I was a teenager. Maybe once or twice since then. This one's your fault, you know."

And there went the cartoon blink of surprise again. "Excuse me?"

He didn't look offended, only startled, so Griff elaborated, "I've had more on my mind than usual." He pointed directly at Brendan to make sure he picked up on his meaning. "Can't seem to stop chewing you over."

"God, now I feel like a dog biscuit."

Griff laughed. He winced and made himself stop, but honestly and truly, he did feel better. "What? It's true. Same goes for Evan, only he wanders around muttering to himself and I mostly go out and tear up junkers to clear my head. Hasn't worked too well. Wonder why?"

Brendan didn't say anything. Not at first. He pulled the rolling stool out with one foot then sat, tenting his fingers beneath his chin. Even then, when he opened his mouth, no words came out.

Griff would beg his pardon later, but just then he saw an opening and he meant to take advantage. "So. I guess it's not been just us, now. Has it?"

"No," Brendan said. "It hasn't, and I think you knew that before you asked."

"Touché." That was one thing Griff would have to admit he'd liked about the man from day one. Lay down a gauntlet, and he'd pick that bad boy up straightaway. Maybe he needed the challenge. Griff would have to keep that in mind. He watched Brendan for a long moment, making sure of him, before he reached out and took the man's wrist in the circle of his fingers. *Pulse is going like a war drum.* "You might as well talk to me now. I'm not too crazy about the idea of finding another reason to make a race for the hospital, but if need be I'm not above it. And the things I would like to do to you, once I've got this damned IV out of my hand... Mmm." He lowered his eyelids to half mast, watching Brendan from beneath his lashes, well aware of what that would do to a man. "I've had this picture in my head of you on your knees with Evan in your mouth, and me in Evan. He'd like that. Bet you would too. Or the other way around. I could go down on you for hours. Lick you open until you're begging to get fucked."

"*God.* Stop."

"Why?" Griff cast a glance below Brendan's belt. Looked like the start of something promising there. "Looks to me as if you like it."

"Too much. Griff, you are a bad man," Brendan said, wide-eyed and pink-cheeked. "I have a point. Let me get to it. You're a very bad man, and Evan is a very good man. Maybe too good. Almost innocent. Don't give me that look. I know exactly what he did in bed with me. I was there, after all." His cheeks flamed up a darker shade of rose. "What I mean is that he's untouched by life. All he's been through, and he's not bitter at all. Do you know how that sets him apart?"

Griff met his gaze and held it. "More than," he said. "And I'd do anything to keep it that way for the rest of his life."

"Then you see," Brendan said. He dislodged Griff's hand to hold both of his palms up. "And how's that going to last with me wedging myself in the middle?"

Wait. Was *that* it? "Good God," Griff said. "Fuck me. Uh-uh. If you're using that as an excuse —" And he was, Griff could see that all over his face now that he knew where and how to look— "Think again. We invited you. How's that getting in between us?"

Brendan looked like he desperately wanted to argue the point, but he held back. After a moment, the fight seeped out of him. He rubbed at his forehead. "Okay. That's... I suppose that's fair enough."

"Damn right." Griff shifted his head, glad the triage table tilted at an angle so he didn't have to strain his neck to keep watching Brendan. "I told you before, now. We like what we like, and what we like right now is you. Me and Evan both."

Speak the devil's name, and he would appear. A gentle rapping at the door announced Evan's arrival. "Did Darry let you in?" Brendan asked. "It's all right. He's better now."

"Evan, take his hand before he takes a run for it," Griff directed. He closed his eyes only just long enough to keep them from drying out, and dragged them open again to see Evan taking him at his word. He shut the door and planted himself between it and Brendan.

"Don't scare me like that again," he told Griff.

Griff raised himself on his elbows. "Not planning on it." He lifted his chin. "Doc and I have just been having an interesting chat. I was gonna try and tease him into giving us another shot. What do you say? Are you in?"

"I'm in," Evan said, no hesitating, so quick that even Griff blinked. "Come what may, I'd like to see what we could make of this, Brendan. I want to see you with Griff again. To watch you, this time. Give us until New Year's to change your mind. Only as a friend, if that's what you want. We can make that work. Just don't shut us out."

Hang on a minute, there. Just friends? Griff started to protest, but despite what others believed he did know how to shut his mouth when the situation called for it. He could see the surprise at war with the doubt in Brendan's face then the reluctant relief — and the turn that came when he raised an eyebrow at Griff. "And you? Could you live with that?"

Griff rubbed his chin, knuckling the stubble on his jaw. It wasn't ideal, but... Hell, he'd done more with less. It helped that he knew how to read Evan, and right now Evan's entire body language broadcasted a message tailored for Griff alone to notice. *Give him time. He might come around if we're patient. I'm willing if you are.*

Want to?

"I'll be just your friend, if that's what you really want," he said, offering Brendan his hand. "As long as you know you're free to change your mind absolutely any time you please, it's a deal."

Brendan blew out a long breath, but he took Griff's hand for a good firm shake. "Deal."

Griff doubted he believed himself, but that was all right. Promises were like pie crusts sometimes, weren't they? Made to be broken.

Sometimes with a little help.

Chapter Six

Three weeks left to go before his time's up. And where are we?

Griff stood behind Brendan. Close behind. At a guess, Brendan would calculate he'd kept one generous inch of distance between them. He could feel the body heat blanketing him. Far enough to claim he was behaving himself. He guided Brendan's arm with three fingertips on his wrist, drawing it back next to his body then out to its fullest extension.

"This one's for all the money," he said, mouth almost but not quite touching Brendan's ear. "Sink it home, and look at what you stand to win."

"Ten dollars Griff found in one boot and a celebratory round of devil's wings," Evan said from the round-topped bar table five feet behind them.

Brendan chuckled as Griff dropped his predatory pose and shook a warning finger at him. "It's for honor and glory. Chicken wings are icing on the cake."

"New number one on the list of things I never thought I'd hear anyone say," Brendan murmured.

Griff flicked his shoulder—but leave it to him. He could turn any sentence into pure innuendo. "My mouth is a gold mine. You've just barely tapped the surface." He chuckled, seeming pleased with himself, when Brendan caught his breath, and wrapped Brendan's fingers more securely around the steel-tipped throwing dart. "Bullseye. Bet you can do it."

Brendan hadn't played darts since college. Standing in the almost-circle of Griff's arms, the cheerfully boisterous, neon-lit bar and grill they'd decamped to and all the cares of adulthood faded away to a time where things were... He didn't know the right word. *Simpler*, maybe. He closed his eyes and breathed in the rich spiciness of Griff's aftershave. Griff's hair tickled his neck, making him want to tilt his head.

"Take the shot," Griff said, guiding Brendan's arm.

"Griff," Brendan replied quietly. "Mind yourself."

"Me?" Griff bent his head, nosing at Brendan's nape. "I'm not doing anything but giving you a hand."

"It's more than that, and you know it. Stop teasing." Brendan opened his eyes and let the wishful thinking drain out of him. His shoulders lost their tension, and his feet felt flatter against the floor. It would already be hard enough to leave in three weeks without adding another stone to the load he carried.

He took the shot.

"Son of a..." Griff stepped back, forgetting himself for a moment. He narrowed his eyes and jabbed a finger at the dartboard. "Bullseye. You hustled me!"

Evan dissolved into laughter and put his head on the table.

"I thought you said you hadn't played since—"

"I did." Brendan put more space between them with the excuse of needing to retrieve their handful of darts. "If you assumed I wasn't any good at it now or then, that's your business."

"He's got you there." Evan's face was rosy from laughter. He beckoned to Griff. "Fair and square. Nice work, Brendan."

Brendan carefully dropped the darts in the middle of their table, next to a platter of decimated wing bones half drowned in sauce so hot his fingertips and lips still tingled. *Friends.* On the surface, on paper, he supposed it would seem to others as if they'd made the transition.

In real life, well. That was a different story. But he couldn't say no to at least giving it a try. They did that to him.

Or maybe it was the town of St. Hawk's, with its sky that went on forever, and a sense that anything could be fixed if you only had the right tools.

Brendan bit at the inside of his cheek. What had to be, had to be, and he covered anything else either Griff or Evan might have picked up on in draining his glass. He worked the crumpled Jackson laid on the table out from beneath the salt shaker that'd held it pinned down and waved the bill at them. "Next round's on me. I think I have time for one more."

"Right," Griff said. He and Evan exchanged glances while Griff visibly—from Brendan's perspective—clamped his jaw on what he really wanted to say. Behaving, for a given value of *behavior* and *Griff.* Give the man credit for determination. He restrained himself to exhaling and propping his chin on his hand. "You're meeting Magnus here at eight. Almost forgot."

No, he hadn't. But Brendan couldn't help admiring his moxie.

Nice try, Evan thought sympathetically. He made room for Griff at his side, nudging his bar stool closer and patting the wooden chair top. When Griff slouched down and put his elbows on the table, Evan rested his hand on Griff's back. While the line between frustration and sulking could be a fine one, he thought he knew which side Griff came down on. Evan knew his man, and rested sure in the certainty that after having come around Griff would stay there, convinced Brendan was right for them, and they were right for him.

For that matter, Evan thought the same. Only Brendan still held out.

"He's stubborn," he said simply to Griff. "We just have to keep trying. That's all."

Griff dealt Evan a baleful look that Evan let slide off his back as easily as a drop of rain. "Magnus," he said in deep disgust. "Magnus. What kind of name is that, anyone?"

"The one his parents gave him, I suppose."

Griff huffed. "You're no fun."

"Liar, liar." Evan rubbed a light circular pattern on Griff's back and watched Brendan at the bar, waiting his turn for two pint glasses filled with dark stout and one with pear cider. Most watering holes in St. Hawk's knew him from his daily rambles around town, and the ones he liked best kept his favorites in stock.

Magnus, though. Evan shook his head. He was all for living and letting live, and for giving Brendan enough room to work off all the steam of his objections, but… Griff did have a point. "He's about as unlike us as possible," he said after a moment's consideration. "For what it's worth, I think that's the only reason why Brendan gives him the time of day."

Griff eyed him. "That's your best shot at being comforting?"

"I didn't say I was trying to comfort you." Evan knocked their elbows gently together. "Only trying to explain. Brendan isn't a stupid man. He knows what Magnus wants."

"Cheap sex."

"True. The kind of one-night stand that happens on vacation."

"Seems to me most people end up regretting those kinds of overnighters," Griff grumbled.

"They do." Evan tweaked his ear. "That's why I don't mind letting it happen. I figure the worst that happens is he gets a basis for comparison. No insult to Magnus — well, much — but how can we help but come off looking better after that?"

Griff snorted, but Evan could see the grin tweaking at the corners of his mouth. "And they say I'm a bad man."

"I learned from the best." Evan carried on rubbing Griff's back, and keeping an eye on Brendan. "He will too. Give him time."

"You're that sure?"

"No." Anything could happen. As unlikely as it seemed, Brendan and Magnus might hit it off. They could be soulmates. Stranger things had happened, and likely would continue to as the world kept spinning on. He'd do what he could to influence its trajectory, yet even so... "I just don't see any point in not hoping for the best. Do you?"

Griff made an odd, disgruntled noise, but the grin had fully bloomed. He took Evan's hand and lifted it to his mouth, pressing a kiss against the knuckles. "Never change, you."

"Not planning on it." He knew how to be faithful.

He wasn't sure how, unless something big happened, but if only they could coax Brendan into seeing it their way...

* * * *

Round ordered, Brendan tucked his wallet away in his jacket pocket. He'd been watching the pair of them out of the corner of his eye. He didn't think they'd picked up on his surveillance. If so, Griff at least would have been shooting those come-hither looks his way, and Evan wouldn't be a hundred percent wrapped up in the man.

God, that sounded jealous, didn't it? Brendan clicked his tongue chidingly at himself. Jealousy didn't enter into the equation. It was more a sense of knowing what he was missing, by his own choice, but he could only take that and use it to strengthen his flagging determination. Stubborn, they called him? Rightly so.

Because every time he saw a moment like that pass between them, he understood that while they might want him, they would be fine together long after he was only a fading memory in St. Hawk's. They didn't *need* him.

And it was better that way. For all of them. It *was*. He had only three weeks left in his stay — two weeks and six days, if he counted tonight — and after that, Dr. George *would* want the return of his job. There would be nothing left for him but to go back, and to leave one thing that could have changed his life would be bad enough. To let things get out of hand again with Evan and Griff would make it all the worse.

Ergo, Magnus. Brendan sighed. He'd liked the man decently well before Griff had put his two cents in, but all Magnus wanted was a good hard fuck. If nothing else, Brendan had to appreciate the simplicity of his approach.

He glanced around the bar, but didn't spy Magnus' distinctive hungry-wolf presence. If he hadn't been absolutely certain the man wanted to tap him like a maple tree, he'd have wondered if Magnus meant to show.

"Two beers, one cider," a bartender called, waving a coaster to grab Brendan's attention. "And a Screaming Orgasm."

He'd said it with a straight face. Brendan had to give him kudos for that despite his confusion. "I didn't order one of those."

"Bought and paid for by the gentleman down at the end." The bartender nodded at the far side of the bar.

Ah. Magnus. Early, which Brendan supposed was all right, but when he scanned the area he didn't see his fellow doctor. "Did he leave?"

"Bathroom, I think." The bartender armed spiky bangs out of his face. He had a slightly rough, wholly approachable look to him. "I'd take it, even if you're not interested. Nothing wrong with a free drink. *Carpe vino.*"

Carpe vino, indeed, Brendan thought with a mental shrug. He tried to adjust his grip for four instead of three, but preoccupation made him clumsy. He grabbed too quickly for the drinks, and sent them sloshing very nearly everywhere. In his rush to right them, his elbow jarred against that of a man who'd seated himself at the bar and, until then, had been staring at his half-empty pint glass with the deep fascination of a man who hoped he'd find something besides dregs at the bottom. "Damn it! Sorry about that. Did I get any on you?"

Luck was on his side. The man had raised his arms quickly as a set of wings and slid as far back as the bar stool would allow without falling. A few drops spotted his slacks and his tie, but he hadn't gotten drenched. That was the good news.

The bad news? Brendan recognized the man as soon as he turned his face. "Dr. West," his boss said, remarkably calmly. "I hope you're better with patients than you are with beverages."

Brendan spared a moment to be glad Griff wasn't there. He'd have laughed himself silly.

Evan would have put his arm around Brendan's shoulders and hugged him.

"Dr. Gabriel," Brendan said, resigned.

He'd admired the chief operating officer of St. Hawk's Medical from afar before they'd met. Considerably afar. Though even bigger and broader than Darry, Dr. Gabriel took the opposite approach when it came to personality. Cool. Calm. Couldn't be ruffled or flapped, and wouldn't know an antic if it did the chicken dance on his head.

He hadn't realized before tonight, in the kinder lights of the bar, that Dr. Gabriel could give Magnus a run for his money when it came to good looks. Dark skin, the sort so rich in hue it almost seemed to have purple undertones, a smooth goatee so neatly trimmed it reminded Brendan of velvet, and wide, intelligent eyes rimmed with black lashes.

And a sense of humor, it appeared.

"No need to look at me as if you're wondering whether you should pack up your office now or in the morning," Dr. Gabriel rumbled as he flicked a few drops of beer off his fingers. "I'll consider it a sign that I've had enough."

Brendan kept his head high. "I'll be glad to buy you another—"

"Thank you, but no." Dr. Gabriel accepted a handful of napkins and an apologetic grimace from the bartender. As he wiped his hands, he nodded to Brendan. "Just as well. We never did manage that meeting a couple of weeks ago."

Oh shit.

"Had a busy day in emergency," Brendan said. Lord, how this would make Griff howl when he heard the story. "I'd thought your secretary would reschedule."

Dr. Gabriel rolled his eyes. "Office assistant. And I'll have to speak to him about that, though I wouldn't suggest losing any sleep waiting. It wasn't anything that couldn't keep." He folded his hands loosely on one knee and gave Brendan the sort of once-over that, while it held no heat or interest, missed absolutely nothing. "Three weeks left, as I understand?"

"Yes, sir."

"Mmm." The noncommittal noise gave no hint as to its deeper meaning. "Come and see me next week, if you would. Call my message service to set it up, not my office assistant."

"I didn't mean to get him in trouble—"

"He seems to manage that just fine on his own." Dr. Gabriel laid his fistful of napkins on the bar, stood then straightened his tie. "If you'll excuse me?"

Damn. Brendan hadn't had much occasion to cross paths with Dr. Gabriel's assistant, but he'd liked what he'd seen of the guy. Flighty, yes, but genuinely sweet.

Looked like it might not be a good idea to get on Dr. Gabriel's bad side.

Wonder what he'd have to say about Brendan's hooking up with a patient? *Jesus. Maybe I should try that Screaming Orgasm after all.*

"Now that's an interesting look," Magnus said. Though Brendan hadn't seen him coming, he touched down as lightly as a sardonic butterfly. "You haven't touched your drink. If you keep ignoring the cocktails I've bought, I'll start to wonder if you want to be here."

"Magnus," Brendan said—stupidly, he knew. His heart had jumped into his throat when he registered the man's presence. "I wasn't sure you were the one who'd sent it."

"Me, and no one else," Magnus replied. He pushed the sticky-looking glass closer to Brendan. "Go on. The taste grows on you, I promise."

Brendan doubted it, but made his lips form a noncommittal smile.

Magnus was...not what Brendan would have gone for, if he'd been looking for anything long term. Magnus was the instant gratification of the dating world. Sex, and nothing but. Cheap flirtation that came easy and shut the door behind itself on the way out.

Like fast food for a hangover, Brendan thought. And he'd thought he wanted that, or that he could make do with it, but...

"I can't do this," he said, pushing the drink away from him. "I'm sorry. I just can't."

* * * *

"Where do you think he's going?"
"Not sure. He doesn't look happy."

"Huh," Griff grumbled. He leaned to one side to better keep an eye on Brendan, and on Magnus, who'd taken off while looking deeply offended — if not ready to call it a night. More like he meant to regroup before he'd try to twist Brendan's arm. Maybe a difference of opinion over what they wanted to drink. Magnus had made a beeline for the bartender, anyway.

Arguing not five minutes into their date? Not a good sign.

"Think he needs a hand?"

"Yes. I also think he won't ask for one." Evan pressed their shoulders together until Griff gave in and turned to look at him. He'd stuck one of the complimentary parsley sprigs behind his left ear — to match the curled bit of basil caught at the back of his head, Griff guessed.

"Don't tell me. I'm obsessing?"

Evan held his thumb and forefinger a few centimeters apart. "A little, maybe. You're in good company, but..."

Griff propped his cheek on one hand. "But?"

Evan nibbled at his lip and looked down at the table, drawing patterns in spilled salt. "I wonder exactly how much you're not going to like watching him leave with Magnus when they get around to that," he said. "If it's about equal to the way I think I'll react, then I'd as soon not have a front row seat. We know it's going to happen."

"Might not," Griff argued, partly thanks to his contrary nature, and part... Hell, he didn't know. Wishful thinking.

Evan laid a hand on Griff's cheek. "Might not, but probably will," he said frankly. "Which means we can either go tackle him at the bar — and he's a proud man, so I'm not going to recommend that—or we can cut our losses."

"You really want to do that?" Griff frowned. "You changed your mind about wanting him?"

"You know I haven't. He's special." Evan raised one shoulder. "But the only other option I'm seeing is waiting for Magnus to go get his car, and waylaying him in the parking lot for a private chat. By which I mean fistfight."

Griff perked up.

Evan rolled his eyes. "I wasn't serious."

"I might be." Griff eyed his glass and the tiny puddle of beer still in the bottom. He shrugged and tipped it back. Barely enough to wet his tongue. "He never did bring us that round back."

"I think they got spilled," Evan said.

"So? The bartender knows how to refill glasses, and I'm thirsty. I can take care of the beer situation without mounting him."

"Can you?" Evan shook his head, but he scooted his chair far back enough that Griff would have room to slide past him. "It's just—" He stopped. Tapped a light staccato burst on the tabletop. "I wonder if we're doing the right thing. He made his decision. We had agreed to honor that. Is it fair to any of us to change our minds now?"

"No," Griff said. He didn't need time to think about it. "It was a dumb decision. His and ours. I'm not giving up that easy. You know me. Besides, it's like the saying goes. There's nothing fair about love and war."

"Tomorrow's another day," Evan said. "I won't give up if you won't."

"Sure I can't do something dumb instead?"

"You could. I don't know if you'd be happy with yourself."

And the thing was—he didn't have that wrong. He knew Griff far too well.

Griff, on the other hand, knew the kinds of things the sorts of men he used to run with would do to stack the decks their way. Magnus might have all manner of polish on the outside, but on the inside?

Men like Brendan wouldn't know that. They might even do something so thoughtless of the consideration that they'd—for example—leave a cocktail glass fully unattended on the bar while they borrowed a dishtowel from the beer jockey and knelt to wipe up spilled lager before anyone could slip. While Magnus took a second amble past the bar, past the drink.

Griff knew he wouldn't be able to prove anything, but he'd swear he saw the glass move as if someone had added a little extra bonus in there. God *damn*.

Magnus had disappeared by the time Griff made it there in half a dozen great big strides and knocked the glass off the bar. He'd keep. Brendan wouldn't. "What the hell, Doc? Don't you know any better than that?"

Brendan, underneath the overhang of the bar itself, startled and nearly slipped off his heels.

Griff caught him. "You okay?"

Brendan's eyes had gone wide. "Christ, you nearly gave me a heart attack."

"Better that than a roofie."

"*What?*"

"Damn it, stand up so I can talk to you without shouting." Griff took Brendan's hand and helped him to his feet, more gently and with less bite than all his bark would have indicated. "Don't you know not to leave an open glass out?"

"I—what?" When it sank in, Brendan's creamy skin faded to skim-milk pale. He put a hand over his mouth. "Oh God."

"Did you drink any of it?"

Brendan licked his lips, but thank the baby Jesus, he shook his head. "No. I would have, but the beer was drying sticky on my shoes. I thought I'd take care of that first."

"And you'd better be glad you did," Griff said. His heart thundered in his ears, and his hands shook with the reaction. "Man, I tell Evan he needs a keeper, but *damn*."

Evan had joined them, and he gave Griff his waist and shoulder to lean against and steady himself on. "I saw," he said. "Brendan. Are you all right? Do you want us to go after him?"

"What? No." Brendan blinked those impossible eyes, the fans of lashes sweeping his cheeks. He hadn't gotten his color back yet, but when he blinked again it returned in a rush. "No, let him go. If you hadn't stopped me…"

"Yeah, well. I'm good for something after all. Hurray for me." Griff hadn't let go of Brendan's hand yet, and he didn't want to. Evan, attached to his side, wasn't pushing for it. He'd laid a hand on Brendan's shoulder, and turned his face with two gentle fingers under the chin to study him for what, Griff didn't know. Shock, maybe.

They looked fine together. Even now. Gold and cream and sable, and Griff could no more help wanting that than he could have chosen whether to cut off his left hand or his right. *Damn all stubborn men's pride, anyhow.*

Or maybe…

Brendan hadn't let go of him yet either.

Griff chose to take the chance. He replaced Evan's fingers with his own, and when Brendan turned his head in surprise Griff was there to change fingers for mouth. He couldn't taste anything but spice and beer on Brendan's mouth, and he checked pretty damn thoroughly.

Brendan's eyes were all pupil when Griff stopped to let him breathe. "I…"

"Uh-uh," Griff said. He didn't mean to allow any argument this time. "You. Home. With us. *Now*."

Chapter Seven

Last chance, son. Either take it and make it – or break it.

Griff barely listened to himself, though he knew he needed to. He'd made it from bar to car and from car to front steps, Evan on his heels and Brendan marched along in front, before he lost his grip on the tangled threads of *want* and *wish* and *need*.

Brendan made a startled sound as Griff pushed him against the wall, beneath the lamp that glowed warm and steady beside their front door. Yet, though his eyes went wide in their customary surprise, his lips fell apart and color heated his cheeks.

Those lips needed to be kissed, and Griff might not be the best man for the job but anyone else who wished to apply could damned well get in line. His body pressed flush against Brendan's, a solid line of man joined at chest and hips down to their tangled feet. His wrists fit well within the circle of Griff's hands as he stretched them over Brendan's head and pushed them hard to the wall.

"Griff," Evan said quietly behind him.

He knew what Evan meant. Evan had no problem with PDA, but the sensible thing would be to *not* spook Brendan off by taking him right there on their front steps.

See above, with regards to not listening to himself. Brendan's mouth was warm, wet and sweet, tasting of beer and spice. He opened when Griff growled the demand, parting those plush lips wide for Griff to slide his tongue inside—and when Griff let go of his wrists, he didn't lower his arms.

Evan exhaled quietly in Griff's ear, then laid his head on Griff's back. *It's your move*, the gesture said. *Even if I think you're being rash, I've got you covered.*

Good man. It gave Griff the bump he needed to push past the first kiss into a second. To tilt Brendan's head back and allow him the room to press rough, messy bites down the side of Brendan's neck. He worked his hands between Brendan and the wall, then between Brendan and his now-rumpled slacks, inside to take a double-fisted hold on smooth skin and sleek muscle.

"All right?" he asked between abandoning Brendan's neck and choosing a new spot below Brendan's ear.

"God. Very all right," Brendan said. He sounded fucking well wrecked. When Griff looked up at him, he hadn't closed his mouth, damp and red from kissing. He licked those lips once, and though he had gone pale he'd gone hard in feature and harder at the groin. He slid his feet apart, a deliberate invitation for Griff to get a knee in there, a plea for Griff to give him something to grind against. When Griff didn't do as he'd been told right away, Brendan lifted his chin. "I said it's all right. Do you want an invitation now?"

"No." Griff took Brendan's nape in hand and spoke from bare inches away, almost nose to nose. "I want more than 'all right'."

"Then try this." Brendan raised his hips, working them forward to rut against Griff.

Damn, but it almost worked, too. Griff shook his head and didn't let go. "Uh-uh. This is how it's going to work. I have no fucking idea what you're thinking right now, but that's all right. You're here. You get one chance to walk away."

"And if I don't?"

There was something pleading in those ridiculous eyes that Griff knew he couldn't interpret. Evan might have been able to, but all Griff could manage was to work with what he'd been given. "One night," Griff said. "If you're here with us, right now, then be here. No questions. No doubts. Put your back into it and make it worth everyone's while."

Brendan's pupils had dilated while Griff issued that series of rough, sex-edged whispers, until now they were almost all inky black with a ring of dark blue. "And after that? Tonight? Tomorrow?"

"That's up to you," Griff shot back. "If this is all you think it can be, then be gone by the time the sun's up. Otherwise…"

"Otherwise, stay," Evan said, joining in at last. He pressed a soft kiss to the back of Griff's neck, then put a hand at his waist and moved forward to take Brendan's face in the other hand. "Stay forever. If you choose. Just like Griff said. It's up to you."

All true enough.

Which didn't mean Griff wasn't going to do every damn thing in his power to tip the scales in their favor.

"Well?" he asked, biting the corner of Brendan's mouth. "What's it gonna be, Doc? Anything you want."

Evan could tell from the look of the doctor that he had no idea. *Better help him.* "It's all right," he murmured, pressing his lips to Brendan's shoulder. "Whatever you want, and however it needs to be. Trust us. I've got you." He laid his hand flat on the bend of Griff's elbow, stopping him from his eager reach toward the promise of the hardness still there in Brendan's slacks.

Griff looked back at Evan, puzzlement written across his face along with the fire and need that parted his lips and lidded his eyes halfway open.

Evan shook his head at Griff and kept a firm, restraining grasp on Griff's hand.

Griff frowned. Not quite a scowl. "What?"

"Shh. Follow my lead, this once." Evan took Griff's hand in his and helped him drape his arm around Brendan's chest. Easy, easy, easy did it. He kept Griff there, chafing his skin and moving his hand slowly but firmly. All the while, he rubbed Brendan's back and kept his lips at Brendan's neck, beneath his ear and at his temple, keeping him distracted.

Evan guessed there were those who would think of Griff as stupid for having grown up rough, as he put it. They'd have been wrong. Griff only ever needed to be taught a lesson once. Evan leaned across Brendan and kissed him, catching his lips and Griff himself by surprise.

Good, yes, just like that, don't stop now.

Evan thought he understood. Griff tangled his fingers in Evan's curls, tugging them. Evan bit his lip in return. Fine by him if Griff played rough here. Griff growled playfully, bit back, and bit the point of Evan's chin. *You can play rough with me, but take it easy on Brendan tonight. Gentle, gentle, gentle.*

"All right," Griff said. "Your game, your rules."

That deserved a reward. Evan tilted his head to give Griff all the access he wanted to his mouth. Which he took, no hesitation. *Good.* Let Brendan work up an appetite, watching. It'd take the two of them to settle him, and Evan could just hope Griff understood, now, what it'd take to catch and to keep Brendan for always.

One way to find out.

There was a score in encounters like these, and Griff was well aware of what it should be. Roughness, grabbing and taking, that was what Griff understood and the moves he knew by—maybe not heart, he guessed, not as Evan would interpret it, but as close as a man like him got.

This, now, this was different in ways Griff couldn't begin to explain, not even inside his own head. A kind of different that made Griff want to close his eyes so it'd seem to last longer. Drink it deep, and drain it dry one sip at a time until he could hold no more.

Evan took care of them both. Griff watched him as he took the knee of Brendan's leg and guided it outward, giving Griff room to get in between. No need to guide Griff—he'd always sprawled as a matter of course, making ready access to any who cared to take advantage.

Brendan swore when Griff got a hand around his cock. Shouted loud enough to startle a nightingale hidden in the trees outside. The bird shrieked at them as it burst into the air, its wing beats heavy as horse hooves.

Griff didn't think Brendan noticed. He'd clamped his mouth shut and curled back, tight against himself, gritting his teeth right away against letting anything else escape—but he didn't have Griff fooled. *Poor bastard, and then some,* Griff thought. Needing so much he didn't dare reach out a hand to take.

He looked to Evan for help. Evan didn't look back. Too busy guiding Brendan onto his side and coming in from behind, arms around him to pin him down but also to shield him at the same time. Brendan shoved back, but Evan could surprise a man with how strong he was when he chose to be. The turn he took exposed the front side of Brendan to Griff.

Griff moved in and took Brendan by the free arm, moving Brendan as Evan did, bringing Brendan's hand down to cover his groin. Hard, oh hell yes, hot as a fire you could beat steel down with. "You want this? Show me."

Brendan closed his eyes tight, but by damn. He straightened his hand, long and slim, then cupped and pressed down to give Griff what he needed.

Better. Much better. Griff rocked slowly into that touch, and this time when he tried to take hold Brendan hissed between his teeth and allowed it. "There you go," Griff said, nice and easy but with no more hesitation. As long as he took care, they'd be all right.

First time for everything, Griff guessed. And he couldn't stop this anyhow.

Griff guided Brendan with a hand on the back of his neck, pulling him close enough to kiss. "Yeah?"

"Shut up. For God's sake, shut the fuck up." The words were sharp and startling, but Griff couldn't think on them when Brendan twisted his hands in

Griff's hair and jerked him with a stinging prickle-pain close enough to have his way with.

"Christ," Griff said, breathing the word out. His grasp on Brendan flexed. "Evan, give a man a hand here, would you?"

Evan heard and answered. He surged up as high as he could go and while still holding Brendan in place. He met Griff's mouth with his and held him there. Goddamn, but Evan kissed like no one else on earth. When Evan kissed him, Griff forgot anything else was close to mattering. And yet, with Brendan beneath them, and both their hands on the skin they bared by shoving his shirt up together, he couldn't forget Brendan either. Not for one second.

Together, they managed to get the three of them inside with the front door shut snugly behind them, and stopped to breathe only when they had to. Evan settled behind Brendan, still in charge, and laid his lips over the hammering pulse beneath Brendan's jaw for a count of three to make sure Brendan and Griff both knew that.

"Gonna treat you right," Griff promised. He spoke in as close to a whisper as he could, each word a warm stream of air against the crux of Brendan's neck and shoulder. He moved, and didn't stop, undoing belt and button and easing the zipper open.

From his place behind Brendan, Evan held him tighter and encircled Brendan by the waist. Griff had Evan's scent now too and he could hear the noise Evan made, a groan, and he could feel the movement of their legs. He almost scrambled back up, wanting to see Evan rubbing up against Brendan, and see how Brendan looked when he couldn't resist how good that'd feel.

Better not drift off point, though. Best to keep Brendan in the moment. They had not come this far to stop now. He didn't want to.

Griff had impulse going for him. Imagination, too. There was a way.

He telegraphed everything to Evan until he could no longer see Evan's face, making his way on a slow slide down Brendan's body until he reached that hardness he craved so much his mouth watered with the need to stuff himself with cock. As soon as he could, Griff pressed his face to Brendan's inner thigh, rough enough to make the both of them crazy with the heat and pressure of breath, tasting copper and sweat and man. Brendan's cock jerked against Griff's cheek, his lips, as Griff eased it free and couldn't help but taste him on the way. Slow laps and flicks of his tongue, seeing what Brendan liked.

"Stop." Brendan dug a painful claw-grip into Griff's shoulders. "Too much, Griff."

Griff heaved out a breath and laid his head to rest by Brendan's side. "Then what do you want?"

Standing just inside the bedroom, Brendan wet his lips. He could have this. If he wanted it. They needed it. It didn't matter if he did — that he did was...

Fuck, he couldn't think. Brendan could only want. He pushed his shaking hands between them, not daring to use them on zips and buttons stretched tight over easily-damaged flesh, but kneading to make them gasp and break apart and remember him.

Slowly, slowly, Brendan crossed to the bed and crawled over the mattress to lie on his back. He beckoned, relieved when they followed and climbed up on either side of him. When he was sure he'd riveted their attention, Brendan had the words he needed ready. "You let me do my share," he said, making sure Griff understood, that he saw it in Griff's dark eyes and the half-drugged dip of his head that he agreed. A hint of Griff's wicked grin lifted the right corner of his mouth. Playing, still playing.

But that was who he was. Brendan didn't want to change him. The end would come soon enough and after that...

Fuck it—he wouldn't think about it. Not now. Not when he'd sacrificed almost everything to taste this for a few stolen minutes. He kneaded over their cocks and hoped they'd understand what he wanted.

To see.

No words needed—they got the idea. Fast. Above him, Brendan could sense, then feel, then hear Griff taking quicker measures to free Evan, and Evan doing the same for Griff.

Then he could see each take the other in hand. They looked different, Griff's cock heavy and uncut— Evan's longer and with a swoop of a bend up, so that it slapped his belly and Griff's hung weighty between his legs, jutting out of his jeans. Evan gave an impatient breath that almost made Brendan want to laugh, and he would have if he hadn't had to swallow back too much saliva.

He could do this. First Evan, because that was just how it had to be, awkwardly tugging his jeans and boxers down till they slid free of his small, tight ass and slid to mid-thigh. Evan made a noise again, a quiet groan, and though the sounds of Evan and Griff's wet kissing, deep and too eager to be neat, never stopped, Evan found Brendan's shoulder with his hand and squeezed. Kept him there.

Griff wasn't shy about wanting both of them. When Griff growled again and tried to grab Brendan by the wrist, there was a certain strong pleasure in knocking Griff aside and doing the work himself. Same differences there—Griff's body built on squarer, more solid lines, a body made for hard labor and rough play.

And once they were both free, above him, Brendan could not make himself stop from reaching to take both in hand, the angle wrong to do more than lay on pressure and thumb the swollen, wet heads. There was power in the way they broke apart, Griff swore, and they both went to brace themselves on one arm to breathe.

It wouldn't last. It couldn't. That wasn't how the world worked. But until it ended, there was nothing else in the world that mattered—and God, hadn't there been enough off kilter about this night that it couldn't last longer than it *should*? He ached and he burned, too, needing to let go. Not wanting to, not yet. Fighting hard, like if he had the strength of will the sunrise itself might just hold off until it had to burst free.

"Hell yes," Brendan heard Griff whisper behind him, rough-raw as unrefined molasses, before Griff was on top of him—and he was a fast learner, it seemed. He must have remembered Brendan's hot spots, and used them now. He knew how hard to push and where to stay clear even when his hips jerked with the need to get closer. His chest heaved and Evan bit his lip white, not giving commands any more, just hanging on.

And so it came down to him, Brendan saw.

It didn't stop him this time, even if it should have. No turning back now. Brendan dragged his nails over each man's hip.

They let him, and more. Evan slipped above Brendan, and nudged Griff down. Brendan had a wet mouth and a hot, clever tongue teasing his cockhead, and a cock dark with need of attention nudging at his own lips. He'd never even dreamed of being stuffed like this, but *God*, what a rush.

No stopping now. They had to bend and stretch awkwardly, the three of them, but bend they did, Evan with quick fluidity, Griff eagerly and Brendan clumsiest of all, ease of skill versus rusty unfamiliarity. Neither was better than the other.

And they never stopped, touching urgently now, too hungry for sense, and what was the point in sense anyway? Sweeping it with his tongue told Brendan it was Griff's cock in his mouth and Evan's nimble tongue tormenting his. Griff tasted spicy like cinnamon and raw like whiskey. Griff, already wanting to move, pushing his hand beneath Evan to knead his ass, frustrated that there wasn't more he could reach.

The tightness and squeezing shocks to his balls came so much sooner than Brendan wanted, and long, long after he thought he'd be able to stretch it. It still wasn't enough. He dug his nails into Griff's hips, deep enough to leave pale half-moon marks.

A little longer. Please, that's all I ask for.

Evan came with a sigh, and Griff with a satisfied, chest-deep growl, and Brendan with a sense that it'd happened far too soon—though they must have been in bed together for nearly an hour by then. A year would have been too soon.

Brendan let Griff's cock slide free on a gasp and a groan, and butted his head hard to Griff's stomach. *It's too soon.*

But the thing was… He'd had his share. Any more would have been asking for heartbreak—if it wasn't far too late already. And if it was, then every moment spent with them would be one too many.

He started to speak.

Griff stopped him. "Don't," he said, wrapping himself up in Evan, and letting Evan wrap Brendan up. "Just close your eyes and rest for a while. Think about what you want. Tell us tomorrow. Deal?"

Brendan closed his eyes and nodded.

* * * *

Griff knew he ought to have been wholly unsurprised when he woke to find himself and Evan alone in the bed big enough for three.

Ought to have been, but wasn't.

He let his head fall back on the pillow that still smelled of Brendan, landing with a *thud* and a growl, his mood souring from just-awake to snarling and dark. *Damn it!*

They'd lost him.

Hell, he hadn't even left a note, had he?

Chapter Eight

He should have left a note. Too late to go back now, though. Brendan sighed and tried to straighten his hair, which refused all attempts at control. The exterior matching the interior of his head, he supposed.

Brendan had arrived at Dr. Gabriel's office earlier than he'd intended. No reason not to. He hadn't managed any sleep after leaving Evan and Griff's the night before despite his best intentions. *Best intentions.* Wasn't there a saying about the road to hell being paved with those?

He pinched the bridge of his nose and tried to massage away an incipient ache behind his eyes. He'd done the right thing. He was sure of that—he had to be. If he let himself start thinking beyond the *now* with either of those two, he'd…

He'd…

To hell with it, and we'll all be better off. Brendan lifted his chin to Dr. Gabriel's secretary slash office assistant, whatever his true title might be. His nameplate read

Devon Jones. "Devon," he said, choosing the best of the options at hand. "Dr. Gabriel told me to —"

Devon, never without a smile, didn't disappoint now. He shook curls out of his eyes and grinned at Brendan. "Yep. He'll probably turn cartwheels over your actually showing up. Oh crap. I didn't mean like that. Not to say you're flaky or anything, I just. Wow. I should stop talking."

Griff would love this guy. Brendan wasn't anywhere near good enough to tease him properly. "It's all right," he said. "Is he inside?"

"Yep!" Devon chirped, apparently all forgiven and all forgotten from where he stood. "He'll know you're here. The door on his office is thin as a saltine. Just go ahead and knock."

Brendan hesitated. "Do you know what he wants?"

"Nope, sorry. Worth more than my job to answer that one, and I'm usually on thin ice as it is." Devon winked at him. "But I think it'll be okay."

So he said. Brendan eyed the door. In his estimation, there would only be one reason why Dr. Gabriel wanted a one-on-one with him, and it wouldn't be to ask him his opinion of the new scrub tops some of the nurses sported. More likely, to discipline him for fraternization with patients.

That was fine. He'd earned his scolding. As long as it didn't touch Evan, or affect the care he received, Brendan could live with taking a licking.

Head up, shoulders squared, he stepped past Devon to knock at the dragon's door. *Here goes nothing.*

* * * *

"There you are."

Brendan looked up—and up some more—to find Darry peering down at him. "There," he said. "Near. Far."

"Wherever you are," Darry replied. He made a face. "Now I have Celine Dion stuck in my head. Thanks for that."

"Any time."

"Scoot over," the gentle giant ordered him—and gentle or not, whenever a giant expressed a desire that room be made for him, a wise man would obey orders. Brendan budged sideways on the steps of St. Hawk's Medical Center to give Darry enough wiggle room to sit next to him even though he'd had plenty. Even sat together they wouldn't block access. Space wasn't so much the point as was a gentle order to stop chasing his own thoughts around his head and let someone else in.

Despite carrying an oversized travel cup in each hand, Darry sat with more grace than most men of his size would be able to manage. "Let's try this again," he rumbled, nudging one of Brendan's hands with the smaller of the mugs. "Here. As in, this is for you. Take it before I burn my fingers."

Brendan made a noncommittal noise. His stomach didn't care overly much for the idea of anything hot and acidic, but it would be rude to turn down a well-intentioned gift, and it'd take a crueler man than him to disappoint Darry. He cracked the lid off the mug, sniffed, and sneezed in surprise at the scent of paprika and chives. "This isn't coffee."

"Pfft. The last thing you need is more caffeine," Darry said. "Potato chowder. Not your standard breakfast fare, but it's getting close to noon. Unless I miss my guess you didn't stop for breakfast and you were going to blow straight through lunch. Am I right?"

"You're not wrong," Brendan said. He tried a sip of the soup. Smooth, hearty, and the paprika loaned it a warmth that tingled gently on his tongue. "It's good." Another swallow soothed the rumbling in his stomach. Brendan rolled the mug, watching bits of potato float to the top. "Has the gossip already gone around, or are you just a considerate guy?"

"Six of one, and half a dozen of the other," Darry replied.

Easy enough to read between those lines, Brendan supposed. Gossip, but filtered through the delivery of a kind man. "Who are you dating right now, Darry? I've never asked, but I hope they know how lucky they are."

He knew he'd made a mistake when Darry winced.

"Damn it. I'm sorry," he started.

Darry cut him off. "It's all right. I don't talk about them much. Thing is, I know better, but... Well. The heart wants what it wants, doesn't it? Even if the head disagrees."

"The soup really is good," Brendan said. He couldn't tell if Darry wanted him to ask, or... "Married?"

"In his heart, I think," Darry replied, mug of soup mostly forgotten in his hand.

Brendan gestured to the hospital in silent question. "Did it happen here?"

"What? No, no. He's still alive and kicking." Darry made a wry face. "He and his new wife have been married almost a year now. She's a little slip of a lady, as unlike me as a human can get. The worst of it? I've tried, but I can't even hate him. I don't think I'm built that way."

"Damn."

Darry made a brush-it-aside gesture. "I'm moving past it, or trying to. Distractions help. Hence my getting over-interested in *your* love life."

"Ahh. Now it makes sense." Brendan sent a gentle elbow sideways. He drained the mug, and turned it around in his hands. "So you've heard everything. What do you think I should do?"

"Wrong question." Darry took the mug away before Brendan could mangle it. "And it's not my job to answer it."

"What were you just saying about over-involvement?"

Darry chuckled. "That's me. I own my flaws. Do you?"

"I burned my bridges pretty thoroughly with them. I'm not sure they'd give me another chance even if I did ask."

"A hundred percent sure?"

Brendan shook his head. "Sure you don't want to help?"

"Oh God, yes. Which is why I won't. Honestly, though, I don't know what the right answer would be. You're the only one who has to live inside your head with the choice you make. But I guess..." Darry clinked the mugs together. "Whether you stay or go, you have a friend. That's not a bad place to start."

"A friend who brings soup," Brendan said. He knocked shoulders with Darry. "No. It's not bad at all."

Darry thumped Brendan's back, then used him as a brace to stand with. "For what it's worth, good luck."

Brendan watched him go. The soup had gone a long way toward making him feel almost human again. He blew out a long breath and rubbed his face briskly.

Then, he closed his eyes and turned his face toward the sky. Occasional shafts of light had begun to break through the dark clouds that'd hidden the sun all morning, and he wanted to feel the warmth on his face. Even the St. Hawk's sun seemed different. He'd noticed that from the start.

As if what had been impossible could be done, here.

A longer, leaner shadow fell across him. "I didn't touch your drink," Magnus said.

Brendan cracked his eyelids halfway open and sighed. "I'm pretty sure you didn't, no. You can tell by the way you didn't get a call from the police."

Magnus chuffed. "Thanks for that. You'd seemed awfully convinced at the bar, though."

"Emotional overload," Brendan said thoughtfully. He copied Darry's brush-it-aside gesture. "Look, I'm giving you the benefit of the doubt. Try anything funny, and you won't be happy you did."

"I figured." The left side of Magnus' mouth twitched in a rueful sort of way. "How are you now? You look all right, but are you?"

Brendan took his time in answering. "I don't know," he said at last. "Maybe. I think I'm getting there."

"Any chance that—"

"Good God," Brendan said, the laugh jumping out of him. Magnus wasn't a bad sort. He had to admire anyone with that much tenacity, anyway. "No. I'm flattered in a weird sort of way, but no."

"I had to try." Magnus held out his fist for Brendan to touch knuckles with. "Take care of yourself, Brendan. I'll see you around, all right?"

Brendan opened his eyes fully, and looked down at the valley, at St. Hawk's, and at the mountains rising tall behind Blue Creek. He could hear the hospital living and breathing at his back, could taste fragrant spices on his tongue, and he knew then what he wanted to do. "I'll be here," he said. "Come what may."

Though whether or not he would be there alone, well... That, he'd find out.

* * * *

"Ouch!" Evan slapped at his neck. The yellow jacket that'd stung him evaded his blow and buzzed away, the angry sound its wings made as grating as a file rasping on steel. Evan sighed as it disappeared among the thick leaves of the tomato stakes.

There had been and would be no talking to Griff until he calmed down. Even good men had their rough spots, and Griff's were at least identifiable. Evan knew him better than the man sometimes knew himself. Right now his pride was as bruised as the skin on a windfall plum. It'd take a while for him to recover.

He could wish he'd never brought Brendan to Griff's attention in the first place. They might all have been better off. He'd been sure Brendan would come around, but —

The yellow jacket made another pass by Evan's ear. He dodged just in time to avoid a second sting, already thankful enough for one day that he wasn't allergic.

As he watched, the insect rip-sawed its way toward the roof of the greenhouse where the papery nest clung stubbornly to the rafters. Where there was one, there would be hundreds, all of them ready to wage war against something so simple as the freedom to pick and eat a tomato right off the vine.

They were only doing what nature had shaped them for, and Evan wasn't often given to temper of his own, but everyone had a last straw that could snap.

Evan found a broom lurking in the corner of the greenhouse. Must have left it there after cleaning up some spilled potting soil last autumn. He stretched as high as he could go on his tiptoes, but it wasn't a big broom. The bristles came a good foot short.

So, that wouldn't work. He could hear Griff shouting at him now — well deserved, too — about what the hell made him think knocking down a hornet's nest would be a good idea. Evan laid the blame on his out-of-sorts mood.

Finding his smudge pot took more work, but he supposed it was just as well. The smoke did the job it was meant to, and watching the nest slow to torpid sleepiness soothed Evan's ruffled feathers. He breathed in, tasting the herbs he preferred to tobacco leaves, and let the tension ease out of him.

There was always a way. Sometimes it took more work to find than others, but they could get there in the end.

He found an old kitchen chair tucked behind one of the raised beds, one he remembered perching on while doing the fiddly work of transplanting seedlings. When he poked at the struts, they creaked but didn't give way. It might not last any longer than the time it took him to remove the wasp nest, but at least then it would be done.

Maybe he'd call Brendan later and ask him to go on a walk, Evan thought as he situated the chair beneath the nest and stood carefully, balancing himself. And maybe he'd drag Griff with him.

Yes. That'd do, for a start.

Careful not to tip over, *careful-careful-careful*, Evan stretched to reach the nest.

As soon as he'd taken care of this, he'd start damage control on the men...

* * * *

The underside of an old Jeep made for a decent den to hole up in and lick his wounds, but the fumes played merry hell with Griff's headache.

Laid out flat on a dolly, Griff rubbed at his temples. This one had grabbed hold early in the morning, and he'd known it'd be a problem when the first cup of coffee had gone down sweet and hot but hadn't helped either the sullen throbbing in his head or the blackness permeating his mood. Not a migraine—he didn't think it was, anyway—but that didn't make it any more pleasant.

Hell, he'd half torn Evan's head off for no more than trying to help. Times like those, Griff figured it'd be best to cut his losses and go burrow up somewhere until he'd worked off his temper. Trouble was, when the *mad* got to him, he usually didn't have the sense to slink away. If he didn't have the garage, God knew what he'd have gotten up to, trying to wrestle his upset into submission.

Why weren't they good enough for Brendan? What in the hell did a big city have to recommend it that he and Evan couldn't match and trump right there in Blue Creek and at St. Hawk's, where Brendan had loosened up enough to laugh, and play darts, and fuck without holding back?

Griff applied a wrench to a stubborn bolt in the Jeep's engine. Let him suit himself, then, he muttered inside his head. *Goodbye, and good luck.*

Bam! Bam! Bam! Whoever was there meant business, and since their first attempt apparently hadn't done the job, now they seemed intent on rattling the door straight out of its frame.

God damn it. "Evan, get the fucking door, would you?"

No answer. Figured. At least Evan had finally gotten the hint that the best place for him to be just then was somewhere else. Griff growled as he kicked the rolling dolly he lay on out from underneath the old Jeep then wiped his hands on his coverall, and stalk-stomped to the garage door.

As soon as he'd shoved it open, he wished he hadn't. The sun chose that moment to send another spear of light down through the mottled murk of sullen gray clouds, straight into his fucking eyes. Griff growled as he flung up a hand to cover them. "Whoever the hell this is, it'd better be good."

He blinked his eyes open when they didn't answer, and although he maybe should have expected it, he wasn't at all prepared to find Brendan standing on the doorstep, caught up stiff between knocking on the front door and staring at him.

Not staring. Watching. Whatever. Wasn't that much of a difference between the two.

Griff fished a cleaning rag from his right front pocket of the coverall, stiff with old grease but still usable, and rubbed it over his hands. "What are you trying to do here, Doc? It's easier to huff and puff if you want to blow the whole house down."

Brendan made an odd, half-aborted grimace. He pushed his hands into his pockets. "I was beginning to think you wouldn't answer."

"Would have served you right if we didn't," Griff pointed out. He tossed the grease rag over his shoulder. It'd served its purpose, but it might not be salvageable this time around. Evan would know — if Evan wasn't currently planning to string him up by the short hair for being an ass. "Doc. Brendan. What do you want?"

"To see you," Brendan said after far too long a pause for Griff's liking. He looked rough, red-eyed and rumpled. Worse than he had the morning he'd come by for coffee, and it'd taken Evan almost half an hour to get him to admit he'd spent the night stitching up a kid who'd taken a beating from his so-called father. Like the world was a shitty place but the first people he thought of for comfort was them.

Made Griff want to let go of his frustration — and because he was a contrary son of a bitch, that only wound him up tighter.

"You've seen me," he said. "Now what? You made yourself pretty damn clear, Doc."

Brendan's throat worked as he swallowed. "I know. I did."

"Well? What, then?" Griff's temples pounded in time with his words. Low key but aggravating. His heart might never have needed fixing or replacing like Evan's, but it couldn't take much more of this. "Changed your mind? Again?"

A muscle jumped in Brendan's jaw. He shook his head, mouth already open to say something Griff knew would piss both of them off.

"Cat got your tongue?" Griff goaded. "Man, either spit it out or be on your way."

"If you give me half a chance, I will," Brendan shot back. His ridiculous eyes went wide, same as they always did when Griff riled him up enough to speak without thinking.

Griff remembered how soft those thick, sooty lashes were against his skin.

Two-thirds of the fight seeped out of him. "I'm listening," he said, leaning his shoulder against the garage door. "Just say it, and be done. I've got work to get back to."

"I need to say it to Evan, too."

Sounded like an apology in the making to Griff, who screwed his face up dubiously. Hell. Evan would want to hear it, though. "He's in the kitchen, or was the last time I checked. Evan!" he shouted over his shoulder. "Evan?"

No answer. Brendan stood up on tiptoes like a kid trying to peer through the big bay window. "I don't see him."

Where the hell had he gotten to? Griff cocked his head to listen for the sounds of Evan puttering around, and heard nothing. "He didn't go anywhere, I don't think—"

They both heard it at the same time. Griff knew they did. The sound of dry old wood splintering, *crack!*—a startled yell—and the heavy, meaty thump of a body hitting the ground hard, fast, bad.

Panic might have started Griff charging forward faster than a match to kerosene, but it was Brendan who took the lead. He didn't need directions—he knew their house, their home, as well or better than the Los Angeles apartment where he got his mail, but couldn't say he'd *lived*.

He knew their house as if it was his own.

Through the kitchen, where Evan held sway and Griff jumped to. Down the corridor to the left, where Griff had gone to his knees for Brendan. They hadn't cleaned away the scuff marks his boots had left on the wall. Out of the back door, pushing through hanging pots that, though empty, still smelled sharply of peppermint and lemon verbena.

Into Evan's greenhouse, with Griff running, swearing, at his heels. He broke the tricky latch off the door and shoved Brendan forward. "Don't know where, maybe over by the window with a crack in it—" he started to say.

He hadn't needed to. Brendan could triage an emergency waiting room with one sweep. He could find one man.

Evan sprawled on the floor next to the pieces of a broken kitchen chair, one leg splintered messily into sawdust and shrapnel, the rest leaning in a drunken tripod. Not unconscious, thank God. Struggling to push himself up on his arms—but not having much luck.

"Son of a bitch," Griff growled. One shot from his shit-kicking boots crashed the remainder into kindling. "Evan? Darlin', what the hell were you—?"

He went to his knees beside Evan, trying to help him up.

Brendan shoved him aside. "Stop. Griff, *stop*. He can't breathe. Give me some room."

"*Shit*." Griff often claimed he didn't have the sense to come in out of a storm, but he knew enough to let go of Evan and shift back on his knees. "Fix him."

"Trying to." Brendan didn't like the looks of Evan's color, far too pale, his lips not yet tinged with blue but getting there pretty damned fast. Broken ribs? Could be. Likely not. He didn't cry out in pain nor was he trying to guard his chest. Brendan touched the old surgical scar then tipped Evan's chin up to try to catch his focus. "Evan? Can you hear me?"

Evan's eyes had gone out of focus, but they moved in response to the stimulus. His forehead puckered, and his lips parted. He covered Brendan's hand with his own and shook his head, wild, confused. It wasn't the heart. Brendan could feel it thumping under his palm, fast enough to indicate panic, but not erratic. *Then what…?*

A yellow jacket buzzed past, the angry sound loud and hostile in Brendan's ear. He looked up —

"Griff? Kick that damned chair into matchsticks," he said. He took Evan's chin in two fingers and weaved with him, letting Evan track him. "Calm down, Evan. You'll catch your breath in just a second. It'll hurt, but I'm here, and I won't let you stop breathing again. Okay?"

He wasn't sure Evan had heard him. Not before Griff knelt behind the man, sturdy and strong at his back, and put his arms loosely around Evan's waist. "You better know what you're doing, Doc," he muttered over Evan's shoulder, glaring.

Brendan didn't need to be told what was at stake if he got this wrong. "I'm right. I'm sure of it," he said to Griff. "Slap him on the back. Gently. Mid-chest."

Griff growled something that might have been a prayer or a curse or a mixture of both, pressed a messy kiss to Evan's nape, and for once in his life did as he'd been told.

Brendan was ready for it when the temporary paralysis let go of Evan's chest and the first breath hit him harder than a fist to the ribs. A horrible sound, and followed by Evan's groan of pain — but he could make noise now. The second breath went in rattling and out with a wheeze, but the third wasn't quite as bad.

"I will fucking well kill you myself if you do that again," Griff said, arms loose but knuckles white. "You want to let me in on what the hell just happened, Doc?"

Brendan's knees gave way and dumped him from crouch to ass, wobbly as a newborn foal. He pressed his hand to his mouth to stifle a whoop of relief. "He must have landed on his back. Temporary paralysis of the diaphragm. He got the wind knocked out of him. You'll want to take him in for X-rays at the least to be sure nothing's fractured, but other than that he should be okay. I promise."

He covered his face with his hands, meaning to steal a moment to wrestle some control together.

Would have worked if Evan, whose airflow still rattled, hadn't kicked him in the shin.

Griff laughed, rough and just the other side of the line from tears, intermingled with warnings and promises to roast marshmallows over the fire he intended to make of that poor kitchen chair, and—

And Brendan knew. Understood, inside himself, what his decision would be.

What it should have been all along.

"Griff," he said, reaching for the man's hand. "It'll all be okay. He's safe, and I'm here. It's all right. Do you hear me?"

Hell. Oh, hell. Griff had to let go of Evan, because the doc had a good idea there. Dropping back flat on his ass in the crumbles of dirt that strewed the floor of the greenhouse was about the best plan ever, and a good thing too. Griff couldn't have held himself upright for another second.

He kept his eyes on Evan, drinking him in greedily. He'd leaned forward when Griff had let go but braced himself on one arm. His breathing sounded like an asthma attack, but each one went in easier and came out with less fuss.

"You've damned nearly got a salad's worth of green caught in your hair. Don't you ever, ever scare me like that again," Griff said. He didn't sound any too steady himself, but when Evan looked over his shoulder at Griff with an attempt at one of his prettiest smiles curving those lips, that was all the medicine *he* needed. "Thought it was the heart. Swear, I thought you were having an attack."

"Me too," Evan said. Rough, but ready. He put two fingers to the side of his neck. "Come here. Feel. Steady as ever."

Griff found he could move his limbs after all. He pressed his lips to the beating pulse at Evan's throat, and rested his head on Evan's shoulder. Evan tipped his head to the side, leaning it against Griff's, holding him there home and safe.

Which gave him room to look at Brendan. The good doctor hadn't budged further from his sprawl than necessary to crook the leg Evan had kicked. He was still pale, with white lines of stress showing at the sides of his mouth, but starting to come around.

What the almighty hell they'd have done if Brendan wasn't there... Griff had to swallow down a sour, spiky clot of fear. He didn't want to think about it, but he couldn't help the horror-slideshow that slid past his mind's eye. Hadn't been the heart, but what if he'd done the wrong thing and Evan had panicked himself into an attack?

Man alive, Griff's heart couldn't take that. Nor could Brendan's, from the looks of him. His shoulders jerked as *he* breathed, and the way he watched Evan...hell,

Griff knew that face. He saw one almost exactly like it in the mirror every day.

He pushed Evan's hair out of his eyes, then bit at the skin of one knuckle.

Evan laid one hand on Griff's knee. He nodded once, barely an incline, but enough for Griff to know he'd come back and was ready for more.

"Brendan," Griff said. "Doc. You with us?"

The question brought Brendan's head up sharply. Griff watched him try to moisten his lips. "I'm here," he said. "They offered me a job."

And—that wasn't what Griff had expected. "Say again?"

Brendan laughed, breathless and just a hair wild. "I've been playing tag with Dr. Gabriel for weeks now. Just never in the same place at the same time. We finally caught up to each other this morning. He called me into his office. I thought it was to tell me Dr. George had decided to come back early, so thanks for your help, we'll see you when we see you."

"It wasn't?" Evan asked. He covered Griff's hand on his chest with his own, and used Griff for leverage to sit up straighter.

"No." A bark of laughter escaped Brendan. He shook his head as if he still couldn't wrap his brain around the notion. "Dr. George is coming back, but there's a Dr. Sinclair who's leaving. Everyone who isn't too busy ragging on St. Hawk's for being the 'hippie hospital' is playing the cutthroat game angling for a job, but he asked *me* if I wanted first crack. Said the work I'd done here was as good as any interview process."

"Can they do that?"

"He's chief operating officer for the entire system. I'd say he can do what he wants." Brendan dragged a hand over his face. "I told him I didn't know what to say. But I..."

The hell he was going to wriggle away again. They *needed* him.

Wanted him.

Loved him, come to that. Cared for him, not the same way as he cared for Evan, but with a sudden, deep certainty that'd taken its time growing and burst into bloom beneath his nose. Nine weeks' germination, point-nine seconds of fruition, or however Evan might put it. Evan knew, of course. Would have known all along and played it close to the chest.

"What are you going to do?" Evan asked, sounding almost like his old self again.

Brendan shook his head wordlessly. He looked from Evan to Griff and back again.

Though Griff had no clue, Evan seemed to understand. He sat up a little straighter still. "What do you want to do?" he asked. "It's your life."

"And yours," Brendan said. "And Griff's. I..." He pressed his hand to his mouth, then took it away. "I want to stay. With you. Both of you. But I swear to God, I don't know how you could think about giving me another chance now. That's why I came here. I didn't know what to say. I still don't, even now that you've heard it all. I'm just me. You're just you. Tell me what to do. Tell me if I can stay."

Evan's limbs were still shaky, but they held him up well enough to lean him forward, and to lay hands on the good doc. One on his knee, and one on his chest. Brendan blinked at him in that way of his, the startled cartoon blink that had been the first clue that he was someone Evan could care for as much as Griff, if in his own way.

A man who had saved his life. Maybe literally. Maybe not.

A man in a million, and not one to carelessly cast aside. God bless Dr. Gabriel.

He touched his fingertips to Brendan's mouth, and felt his own curving in a relieved smile. "Stay? What makes you think we were ever going to let you go?"

Brendan came unstrung. He might have fallen if Griff hadn't come around to brace him up. That was, Evan thought, the best thing about coming in threes. Always someone to guard your back and have your front. "Which means don't you fucking dare say no," he told Brendan. "Just you try to get away. I'll tie you up and sit on you if I have to."

A burst of laughter brightened Brendan's face to no end. "Kinky," he said. "You really…"

"We really," Evan said. He touched his lips to Brendan's, and let Griff do the same. They were covered in smears and crumbs of dirt, and all three of them had greenery stuck in their hair. It was nothing like Evan had imagined, but so much better. "And you really. It's a done deal now, Brendan. You're ours."

Chapter Nine

Griff pushed Brendan backward onto the bed.

Startled, Brendan landed with an undignified yelp, but it pleased Griff no end to see the surprise shift just as quickly to delight, and the yelp to a breathless bark of laughter. He feasted his eyes as Brendan laid his head back on the mattress, parallel to the mismatched pillows Evan insisted on piling up. "You've been wanting to do that for a while, haven't you?"

Griff tapped the side of his head. "Smart man, Doc."

"Then why didn't you before?" Brendan asked of Griff, while he watched Evan take the slower road down to lie at his side. He reached out with one hand to patter his fingertips lightly over Evan's chest.

Evan favored Brendan with one of his sweetest smiles then tipped his chin up so the man could be properly kissed.

Griff whistled quietly to himself. Maybe Evan was onto something with that whole *I like to watch* business. Just another thing that made Brendan special. He made Griff want to see all the sides of a question.

Evan cut Griff a heavy-lidded, knowing look as he began to pluck the buttons of Brendan's shirt open, kissing the smooth skin beneath. He took one of Brendan's dusky nipples in his teeth and bit while sliding his hand lower, down below Brendan's belt and under his slacks.

Holy hell, now that's a pretty sight.

"You're welcome to join in," Brendan said, still short of breath, still glowing with delight.

"Mmm." Evan nuzzled under Brendan's pectorals. His bronze curls spilled over Brendan's chest like sunbeams cast in metal some bright and shining metal—and his hand never stopped working below the belt. "Did you see his balls, last time, or the first time? They're full. Heavy. Soft. Come and see."

"That means 'I second the motion for you to come play'?" Griff asked.

"It means you have a big, big mouth," Evan said demurely. "Which is useful for more than talking. Get down here. I've got a front row seat, and I'm going to make good use of it if you don't."

He would, too. "Mind if I level the playing field first?"

"Mind, no. Encourage, yes." Evan rolled away from Brendan with one last kiss, and lay with his head tucked on Brendan's chest. Brendan slipped one hand behind his head to cradle it in. Both turned their attention to Griff—and it had never been like this with any other third they'd picked up over the years.

Guess this is what it feels like to finally get it right.

"Go ahead," Brendan said, gaze hungry-feeling as it ate at Griff. "Let me see."

And what could he say to that besides yes? Griff skinned off the comfortable old plaid he'd worn to work in, still smudged with engine grease, and the singlet he wore beneath it—a new one, soft ribbed cotton that clung to him as a second skin. Brendan made a soft, choked noise as he watched.

Evan winked at him. He rose gracefully, as was his wont, to his knees and reached for Griff, helping him, guiding the singlet over Griff's head and coming in fast to press his hot mouth against the crux of Griff's ribs. The touch of a quick, agile tongue against his skin made Griff suck in a sharp breath. He pressed his hand to Evan's nape to hold him there.

Brendan wouldn't be left out, though. He rose behind Evan, clumsier but no less eager—and reached out to catch Griff by the hip. He flicked open Griff's buckle and drew his zipper down. "Less clothes," he said, his voice gone rusty-raspy. "For all of us."

Evan chuckled. "You heard the man," he said, digging the point of his chin into Griff's navel. "Better hop to it."

* * * *

All of the pillows had scattered to the floor, and they'd churned the sheets into a terrible mess. Clothes had ended up tossed absolutely everywhere, one of Brendan's shoes leaving a mark on the wall where Griff had thrown the thing.

Evan loved it.

Laughing, he opened his arms for Brendan, guiding the man down on top of himself with Griff not far behind. They weren't too heavy for him, not with Brendan braced on his arms and Griff on his knees. When Brendan kissed him, his mouth tasted of Evan's cock, salty-musky-bittersweet. Evan lifted his head for a better angle, meaning to chase the taste on Brendan's tongue until he'd licked away every atom of the flavor.

Brendan moaned. He pushed one leg between Evan's, the smooth, hard muscle of his thigh giving Evan something to rock against. Still hard. He'd had the sense to order Brendan off before he came. Blowjobs could be heaven and Brendan gave as much pleasure with his mouth as Griff did, but Evan thought he was in the mood for something...more, tonight.

He nipped at the fullness of Brendan's lower lip and laid his head back, still chuckling under his breath. "You like that?"

"You and Griff both say he's the bad man, but I think he taught you a thing or two." Brendan dropped his head to Evan's chest as he caught the slow, lazy rhythm of Evan's hips. "*God*. You're killing me here."

"Good." Evan reached past Brendan to Griff, beckoning him closer. "Tell me how you want it. Both of you. Use your words."

Griff and Brendan scoffed at the same time. Evan dissolved into mirth.

"The looks on your faces," he chided, one hand plucking at Griff, and one sifting through Brendan's well and truly tousled hair. It was the strangest thing, but he felt as if he was swimming through champagne. Bubbly, golden, not enough to quench his thirst, but plenty sufficient to whet his hunger. He lifted his chin. "How do you want to do this? Whatever you want, it's yours. I'll give it to you."

"Damn," Griff said. He cupped himself, rubbing. Evan knew what that felt like, to want so strongly that there was no keeping any hands off. "Doc, you're not wrong. He's gone evil. Your call, but make it quick, would you?"

Evan cocked his head to one side, considering Brendan as Brendan braced above him. He could see the thoughts play out like quicksilver and sparks over the good doctor's face, even as they faded from overload to awe in a handful of seconds. He traced the edge of Evan's old scar and shook his head, seeming lost for words.

That was all right. They'd come with time. Evan kissed Brendan more sweetly this time, slow and thorough, not stopping until Brendan had found his rhythm again. "Or I could suggest something," he said.

"Or that," Brendan agreed in a rush. He bit his own lip before Evan could do it for him, and when he brushed his fingertips against Evan's cheek, Evan thought it was with a sense of wonder. "Why was I so stupid, for so long?"

Evan's patchwork heart thumped in double time. He caught Griff's eye, and noted with satisfaction the same thoughts and feelings fleeting over his face too. Pleased, he laid his head back and braced both hands on Brendan's chest, making sure Doc listened to him as he said, "Because you're human, but it doesn't matter. We got there in the end. I know what I want, and how I want it. Griff, help him."

He hadn't had to ask. Griff already had Brendan in hand.

They fit together, Evan thought. They looked right, and they were beautiful to watch as *they* kissed, hands at hips and fisted in hair, drawing each other together and down, onto their sides facing Evan.

They belonged. Still, and always.

"Do you trust me, Doc?"

Brendan did, but he wasn't so sure about his ability to speak. He managed some sort of sound that made Evan laugh quietly against his chest and Griff chuckle behind him.

"I'll take that as a yes." Griff kneaded Brendan's hip, helping to guide his leg up. A good thing, too. Brendan knew he wouldn't have made it on his own without Griff's strength and Evan's kindness. He wondered how he had managed for so long.

They had lost time to make up for. Starting now.

"Just like that," Evan murmured. He replaced Griff's hand with his own, working Brendan open with slick fingers. Brendan's cock bumped against gentle Evan's thigh, making him shudder and moan between clenched teeth. "Better hurry, Griff. He's not going to last."

"This time," Griff said, hand busy between his legs, slipping on a condom. Brendan felt the man's mouth at his nape, hot breath and lips shaping half-formed words. Then he slid inside on one smooth thrust, and didn't stop until he'd bottomed out. "Oh, *fuck*."

"That's the idea," Evan said. He traced Brendan's face, and though Brendan couldn't keep his eyes open long enough for a good look, he knew — could tell — how the man watched him. He nudged forward, taking Brendan's cock and his own in his hands. "Help me out here."

"Really won't last long — *Oh, God,* don't stop."

Evan's laugh echoed in Brendan's ears. "Then don't last," he said. "Wrap your hand around mine — like that — and we'll see if we can beat Griff at least."

"Not — likely."

"Try anyway," Evan said. He nodded at Griff. "Go, darlin'. Make it count."

And Griff did. God, did he ever. In another time, with a clearer head, Brendan would have admired the iron control it took to keep a steady pace, and would have teased him for the biting grip he had on Brendan's deltoid. "Feel good," he said, a low rumble at Brendan's ear. "Feel so damn good."

"Not so bad yourself," Brendan managed. His memory hadn't exaggerated Griff's skill, or the girth of him that was *almost* too thick to manage, but stopped just short of the line. He couldn't fuck quickly, but he could give it to Brendan good and hard, jolting him forward into Evan's eager arms.

Brendan cried out when he came, the orgasm an electric surprise. Evan caught the cum on his palm, and the cry in his mouth—and Brendan returned the favor a moment later when Evan snorted, shook his head, and sighed his way through the climax.

"I win," Griff said behind Brendan—and he had, but not by much. He clamped down on Brendan's hip, hard enough Brendan knew he would have a mark to remember this with, and emptied himself with muttered swearing that would have turned the air blue if it hadn't already been filled with the fugue of sex and breath.

"There," Evan said. He draped one arm over Brendan, his reach long enough to allow him to idly stroke Griff. "That's what I wanted."

* * * *

Sleep came neither as quickly as Brendan had imagined it would, nor as slowly as he'd guessed it might, but at its own pace. He drifted, safe between Evan and Griff, their scents of engines and herbs mingling with Brendan's tang of hospital-clean and coffee.

Griff had draped one arm over Brendan, while Evan cozied in and wrapped him up from the other side. Brendan toyed with a hand that rested at his side, not sure which man it belonged to, but content with either. With both. He pressed his nose to Evan's scar then touched his lips to the old mark.

Behind him, Griff mumbled something sleepy-sounding, and resettled his head. "All good, Doc?"

"Better than," Brendan replied. "Darry's never going to let me forget he was right."

"He's a smart man," Evan said contentedly.

"Mmm." They weren't wrong. Brendan exhaled, letting go of the rest of his cares, and sensed the drowsiness growing ever deeper. "I want to be part of the group handing out sparklers at the Festival."

Evan chuckled.

Griff poked him. "That's next year, Doc," he rumbled against Brendan's nape.

Brendan closed his eyes, content. "So it is."

"And are you still going to be here?" asked Evan. Not as if he doubted the answer.

Nor should he have.

"Yes," Brendan said, feeling the rightness of his choice deep down. Bone-deep. Heart-deep. "I wouldn't miss it."

"And why is that?" Evan asked, nosing sleepily at Brendan, a light counterpoint to Griff's idle stroking of Brendan's side. Everything he'd never thought he wanted, and everything he needed. "Go on. I know the answer, but I want to hear you say it."

"Because," Brendan said, tasting the savor of each word. "My wish came true."

GIVE CHASE

Dedication

With thanks to S.J.B. for his input.

Prologue

Isaac Paliades pushed through the partially open door to the plaza of the Blue Creek Hotel ballroom and out into good clean fresh air. He drew a deep breath into his lungs then let it out in satisfaction as his eyes adjusted to the light of the moon and stars. "Aha. There you are."

His associate Dr. Declan Day sat—or sprawled, rather—on a low bench just past the doors, half in shadow and half in the rich light spilling from the crowded celebration behind them. Lean and dark and hungry-looking, he raised a half-empty glass to Isaac. "Here I am, and there you are, yourself. Don't feel like dancing, or are you too buzzed to keep a beat?"

Music from the party thumped on inside, violin and strings abandoned for a disc jockey and a bass beat a few hours ago. No one could party like an MD with a chance to let his hair down. Breaking ground on a new family medicine department of St. Hawk's Medical was as good an excuse as any, and better than most.

"Buzzed on two glasses of boxed wine? Well. Two and a half," Isaac said, lifting his glass for Declan to see. "I'm not that much of a lightweight, and that's my jam going on in there. Trust me, I could shake a booty if I wanted, but I've chosen not to inflict my dancing on them. I deserve a medal."

Declan's shoulders had started to shake with amusement before Isaac had finished that little speech. "God, you are ridiculous."

"Only when I'm feeling no pain."

"Mmm." Declan tilted his head back, visibly assessing Isaac for signs of truth-telling or falsehood. "I'm not sure if you should be like this more often, or never at all."

"Split the difference down the middle and go for sobriety. Mind if I sit?"

Declan gestured at the corner of bench he hadn't taken over, just about wide enough for one-third of an ass, and parted his lips in a lazy tiger's grin at Isaac. "Be my guest."

"Or maybe not," Isaac conceded. The long plaza railing that faced the bench hit him right at the hips. Good for leaning and perching, and with two glasses of oaky burgundy warming his blood, he was in the mood to linger a while longer.

Declan watched him, one eyebrow arched. "Lightly buzzed, and you think sitting on a fence above a ten-foot drop is a good idea?"

"I won't fall."

Declan wrinkled his nose then gave a fatalistic shrug and a quirk of the lips that he hid behind the rim of his wine glass. Which was a shame. The man had a mouth like a kiss waiting to happen. "Suit yourself, big man. If you do tumble down and break your crown, I'm not cleaning it up."

"Fair enough." Isaac swirled the inch of wine left in the glass he'd brought with him, watching the light dance invitingly on its surface. "So here's what I can't figure out. You fought like the devil was on your tail to get the family medicine department up and running—"

Declan made a disparaging noise.

Isaac didn't let that stop him. He wasn't finished. Nowhere near it. "And you're not even family medicine. You're sports medicine." He used his glass to point at Declan. "But it mattered to you, enough to make enemies and to burn twice the recommended daily dosage of midnight oil. I know for a fact they want you on all the cool committees now."

Declan raised one shoulder, looking for all the world as if he couldn't possibly be less bothered. "It's not a big deal, Isaac. What else do I have to do, anyway? Let it go."

Convincing on the surface, but the thing was—Isaac knew a mask when he saw one. What he couldn't figure out was why Declan wanted to wear one. Why he seemed to feel he needed it. It wasn't a thing Isaac could let go of. It was what made him a good doctor, that drive to keep digging until he struck gold or answers.

"You say things like that, and it makes me wonder why I have this nagging feeling that there's an ocean of things you're not telling about yourself."

"That would be because there are," Declan said.

The man had courage, Isaac would have to give him that. "That's going to bite you in the ass someday. You do know that?"

"I'm aware."

"And yet you keep on keeping on. Which makes me wonder," Isaac said. "Why is that?"

Declan didn't blink. "Because those things are private. They're mine."

Okay, fair enough. Isaac conceded the point with a tilt of his glass. He knew that wouldn't stop him asking, but to be fair, Declan would be well aware of that too.

"Ten bucks says you end up dancing before the party's over," Declan said, looking deliberately away from Isaac. "And if you do, I call the right to take a video on my phone and make you Internet famous by morning."

"Be my guest." Isaac raised his glass to his lips and tasted the wine. "So if I go back in, you're planning to follow? Because that's another thing that interests me. Why you ducked out of the party you should be swanning around as king of."

Declan said nothing. Nor was he likely to. He rarely did about the things that mattered.

Isaac sighed. He swung one leg, idly kicking the railing he leaned against. He wasn't worried for his safety. Built tall and strong and kept lean from his daily jog around the perimeter of Blue Creek—he and Declan often crossed paths—he wasn't any worse than warm from the wine, and besides, he doubted that Declan would let him fall. They teased and bickered and pulled each other's pigtails, but he'd always had a sense of certainty that Declan would have his back if the chips ever really started to rain down.

He hoped Declan knew the same went for him. Hard to tell.

Isaac liked the way Declan watched him from his shadowy corner. His dark hair had fallen over his forehead as the night had gone on, and he'd undone both the top button of his shirt and the knot of his tie. Left open, they framed a smooth column of neck and throat beneath a strongly pointed jaw. He had a way of keeping his face still even in repose that helped make him a difficult one to read. Isaac had liked the looks of Declan since the day they'd met at St. Hawk's, both green newcomers hired on at nearly the same time, neither of them at all prepared for the vibe of the laid-back mountain hospital. Both in love with the job, and so very alike that Isaac supposed it was only natural they'd get along like cats and dogs.

Even if they both enjoyed their private battles, Isaac wished it could be different. The things he'd like to do with Declan out in the open... *Mmm.*

Declan loosed a small bark of a laugh. "Might want to cool it with the bedroom eyes unless you want me to take advantage of them."

Oh really? They hadn't gone there yet, not in almost a year of knowing one another. Danced around it, sure, but never stepped over the line. He swallowed a mouthful of wine to cover his surprise. The warmth tingling on his tongue gave him the spark of courage to answer the way he'd wanted to most. "And if I did? We're in the same boat, you know. Why try and row in different directions?"

Was that a laugh? Could be.

"Because we are what we are, Isaac," Declan said. "I don't know about you, but I've never given up without a fight in my life. I wouldn't know how to start making it easy for either of us."

Probably true.

One tiny drop of wine glistened at the bow of Declan's mouth, and Isaac abruptly wanted nothing more than to touch his tongue to the plush velvet of the man's lips. It must have shown. Declan's lips parted, and in the depth of shadow that limned his face he took on a new aspect. *Hunger.*

And why not? Isaac deposited his glass on the rail, uncaring if it fell or stayed there until dawn, and pushed off. Momentum carried him forward. One step, two steps, three, to the bench without stopping until he stood in the vee of Declan's sprawled legs.

Declan watched him through a gaze not quite shuttered enough to hide his interest. "The look on your face..." he said. "It's a bad idea. I know it and you know it. And why now?"

"Because I'm not quite drunk," Isaac said, brushing his fingertips along Declan's jaw. "But I'm closer than I have been in months of you looking at me like you want to eat me alive."

"It isn't just me."

"Acknowledged. But let me tell you something—buzzed doesn't mean my judgment is impaired. I know what I'm doing." Isaac raised his chin, knowing he would look halfway cocky and halfway dangerously open. "So? Are you in or are you out?"

"It won't fix anything," Declan pointed out. "Might even make it worse."

"That's pretty much the way life works." Isaac pressed a fingertip to Declan's lips. "Shh."

"Uh-uh. If you want to shush me, come here and make me." Declan took the tip of Isaac's finger briefly between his teeth, wet heat and sharp edges encompassing him for one lush moment. "If you think you can."

Isaac didn't answer right away, and not in words. Declan had taken a wide seat, but his hips were narrow and his joints clearly loose with teasing and alcohol. No trouble at all to slide onto Declan's lap, one knee at either side of the man's thighs, and bend to see if he could taste the tang of the wine on Declan's tongue.

Declan held himself so carefully still that Isaac knew it wasn't just him. "You're sure about this?"

"Sure enough," Isaac said, fascinated by how their lips touched when they spoke. "I swear I don't understand you, Declan, but I'll kill myself trying if that's what it takes."

"Uh-huh," was what Declan said. What Declan *did*, now. That was another story. One arm stole around Isaac's waist, pulling him closer, tighter, hard against him. He shifted up and hissed when Isaac slipped one hand beneath the buckle of his belt and wrapped his fingers tight around the shaft without word, without warning. His fingers found their way into Isaac's hair and gripped hard. "*God*. You drive me crazy too. Just so you know."

Yes and *no* fought a brief, fierce battle on Isaac's tongue. In the end, he kept them both locked away, and pushed his breath into Declan's mouth instead. He wasn't sure, but he didn't want to let that matter anymore.

He had no idea what would happen next, but he'd have this at least. Even if it was just the once…

Chapter One

And *once* was all they'd had. *Once* seemed as if it was all that would ever be. They were what they were. Maybe Declan had the right of it, and maybe their separate paths never would fully merge into one.

And if that was the case... Well.

"You look like you've had a fun night. Anything interesting?"

Isaac glanced back over his shoulder to find Dr. Gabriel not quite hot on his heels, but making decent time. Not a lot of people 'got' their chief operating officer's deadpan sense of humor, but he tickled Isaac's funny bone. Gallows humor was a must for surviving the field of medicine. "And then some. The stories I could tell, God. You?"

Dr. Gabriel winced. Tall and built on stern lines, he seemed sober to most but once you knew how to read his small tells and giveaways, a world of expression opened up. "Teenagers out too late with booze."

Isaac made a noise of sympathy. He'd been elbow-deep in the aftermath of that particular combination more times than he cared to remember. "Knife fight," he offered. "And a baby with a fever of a hundred and two."

"So, business as usual."

"Pretty much." The employees' only side door of St. Hawk's tended to stick and scrape in extra-cold weather. Isaac wedged the stubborn metal beast open, propped it with his hip, and stuck his head outside to drink down a deep draft of the icy January frost.

Mmm. Bliss. So good after a night running from trauma to trauma in the Emergency Department. Isaac draped himself over the door's crash bar and hummed a deep, quiet moan.

Dr. Gabriel chuckled at the sight he must have made. "Enjoying yourself?"

"Only a little." Isaac shivered with yearning pleasure as the cool breeze kissed his cheeks.

"Uh-huh. If I could please my dates 'a little' like that, I'd have the reputation of a sex god." Dr. Gabriel made a show out of eyeing the gym bag Isaac carried, and the pair of athletic shoes tied together by their laces that hung around the crook of one elbow. A grin tugged at the corners of his mouth as he shook his head. "Running in this weather. *Tch.* Better you than me."

Isaac hummed noncommittally as he savored the moment's worth of standing still, letting the cold wash him clean. Declan was already waiting for him on the sidewalk outside, just like always. Every morning after every night shift since July, they'd gone for a run together. Isaac wasn't sure if it was Declan's way of keeping him at arm's length but within his line of sight, or if Declan had another motive in mind. The man could be a mystery. Either way, Isaac enjoyed it. On a good day they were evenly matched. Though Declan had the long, lean legs of a natural runner,

Isaac's broader shoulders hinted at his deeper reserves of stamina.

Days like this, he felt as if he could run forever.

Thinking about keeping pace with Declan brought a frisson of heat back to Isaac's blood despite the cold. This, yes. This was what he'd needed all night long.

Dr. Gabriel eyed first Isaac then Declan. "The man who never gives in and the man who never gives up. How's that work, again?"

Isaac blew out a breath. "Got me. I can let you know when I find out."

"Better you than me," Dr. Gabriel said. He clapped Isaac firmly on the back. "Tell him I'm still waiting for an answer about his spearheading the new family medicine committee, if you can remember that while you're out there. Unless you'd care to take a look up at the sky, realize we're about to get at least three inches of snow dumped on us, and come to the Whistle Stop for a cup of coffee like a sane person."

"I'm not sure 'sane' enters into it." Isaac returned the slightly too firm pat on the back with interest. "And I don't think I could stop, even if I wanted to. When people say running is an addiction, they're not wrong."

"I've heard the same thing said about sex," Gabriel mused. "That's the problem with putting too many stubborn people in one place. We never know when to give up, no more than we know when to give in."

He wasn't wrong, for sure. Which was at least half of the problem. One taste wasn't enough. Isaac wanted more.

He left Gabriel behind at the doors, not wanting to risk Declan deciding that he wasn't going to join him. He hadn't yet lost the warm springiness in his calves from a night spent mostly on his feet, and he liked it that way. He jogged the few yards from St. Hawk's to the low-walled sidewalk lining Hawk Drive, and dropped to one knee to undo the laces on his work shoes. He'd pack those and his work clothing in the bag, drop it in his car on their way past, and change again when their route brought them back to St. Hawk's.

He took a thoughtful peek sideways and found Declan already looking back at him, a deliberate sort of devil-may-care glint in the doctor's eye and a rakish grin turning his mouth into a wicked temptation. Like magnets that should be drawn together forever fighting opposite poles, there was at least six degrees of sliding separation between them. Someday one of them would find a bridge. Isaac hoped it would be him, but he'd give it no less of a thumbs up if it came from Declan.

"At long last," Declan said, words richly laced with the sort of challenge Isaac could never say never to. "I'd started to wonder if you'd show."

Safe behind his careful shield, one he'd built layer by layer, Declan watched Isaac lift his pointed chin. Nothing got his motors running like a challenge, and the dare made the deep green flecks in his hazel eyes shine.

"I figured I'd give you time to psych yourself up," Isaac fired back, brisk and warm as coffee with a shot of whiskey tucked inside. "Of course, if you don't want to..."

"Keep dreaming," Declan shot back, because that was what was expected of him. Not because he wanted to. Not as such. Every time Declan earned one of Isaac's cheeky grins, a sense memory of what those pretty pink lips had looked like stretched wide around his cock rose up from the depths of his mind and knocked him sideways.

Even in the bitter cold, the thought drew a dark, sweet ache to his groin that made him grunt. To cover his lapse, he pretended a fascination with the horizon while Isaac changed his shoes, peeled out of his tie and button-down, and tugged a hoodie on over the T-shirt he'd worn beneath that. Several months had gone by since the sweltering Blue Creek night when they'd let a few glasses of good wine, a full moon and leftover adrenaline get the better of them, and Declan hadn't forgotten a moment. Nor had he stopped wanting to do it again. Nor had Isaac, at least as far as Declan could tell.

Some things chance and circumstance had chosen for them. Some, not. He'd made his choices. So had Isaac. Now they could live with them.

Declan noted that Isaac had finished his wardrobe adjustments. Relieved, he stamped his feet on the sidewalk. He needed a damned good workout on a morning like this one, too cold to be safe and too charged to be still. "I'm headed down Maple and across the park. Should be mostly empty — of people — right about now." He rolled his head to crack the stiffness out of his neck. "If you're up for it. Are you?"

Isaac's lips parted in appreciation. He'd know the route by heart, loaded with hills and sharp curves — everything they both loved best. "What do you think?"

In answer, Declan let the energy coiled up waiting in his calves burst out of him and propel him forward. No need to worry about leaving Isaac behind. He hadn't gotten more than five lopes away before he heard a second set of light, quick footfalls following fast behind him.

Just what the doctor ordered. Adrenaline spiked as Declan let loose with a wolf howl. *Game on*.

* * * *

Declan wished he could keep his eyes closed as he ran. He took a chance on a few steps with his face turned toward the pale winter sun. The air might be cold, but if he concentrated on the sun he could almost imagine it was summertime again. Warm nights filled with the song of cicadas and grasshopper choruses and fireflies dancing in drunken patterns against the night sky. Frosted glasses dripping with condensation, whether liquor or sweet iced tea. Summer had always been his favorite.

Summer looked good on Isaac. Declan remembered how he'd watched the man through the length of that whole conversation at the hotel, tracking the beads of July sweat on honey-brown skin from his nape to the hollow between his collarbones. It always was the littlest things that tipped a man over the edge. He'd chased them with his tongue, salty-sweet.

"Not going too fast for you, am I?" Isaac called back.

Declan flipped him off. Perverse bastard, he took it as a sign of affection. Nothing squashed that man, Declan thought in a mix of skepticism and amazement. If anything could, he hadn't come across it yet—and he'd done some hunting. The only thing that stymied him was stonewalling, and Declan didn't delude himself that would work forever.

He never could decide whether he wanted that, or not.

Hell. If he let Isaac inside his defenses… Declan put his head down and lengthened his stride to come abreast with the man. *If* he let Isaac get to him, Isaac wouldn't stop with just answers to just questions, no matter how private they were. How little Declan wanted to think about the things Isaac wanted to know. It wouldn't be enough. There was always more. He'd want it all. And Declan would want to give it to him.

Sometimes he was more tempted than others. God, it'd be good to rest. Just lay his head down for a while.

But want it though he might, he couldn't make himself take it. He'd tried.

Just wasn't built that way, he guessed.

At least they had this, yeah? The running. Neither of them had deliberately chosen a route, but without discussion or doubts they'd combined the better halves of their respective favorites and made the Frankentrail work for them. Started off easy enough, down the sidewalks in the mostly flat part of central Blue Creek. Loops and figure eights around St. Hawk's. Just enough to get them warmed up.

Then, the good stuff. Hills with steeper and steeper slopes, stretches without sidewalks but *with* rough, untended shoulder, and back into the city where flights of stairs seemed nearly to line whole streets. The effort robbed Declan of breath and made his calves burn as if they'd been lashed with nettles and thorns deep inside the muscle. Salty-stinging sweat dripped into his eyes. Isaac went tight with concentration, a pretty picture no matter who did the looking, stubborn as hell and not going to be stopped as long as Declan kept pace. Then, just when Declan thought there was no way he could push himself another step, everything went loose and springy as rubber bands, all of it working together. Felt like flying. *Fuck, yes.*

Declan couldn't help it. He raised his face to the sky and let out another baying yowl.

Oh, so that's how it is, is it? Isaac let rip with a wildcat's howl in answer. If Declan wanted to play, at least he wouldn't have to play alone.

He saw Declan look back over his shoulder, alight with exertion and adrenaline. They'd reached a quieter street than the ones that surrounded St. Hawk's, halfway between residential and commercial, almost empty of any other life. The snow that'd threatened had begun to fall when Isaac hadn't been paying attention. Snow was, in his opinion, a good backdrop for Declan. Isaac enjoyed the sight of the light, airy snowflakes that dusted Declan's dark hair as they fell unheeded on his head, shoulders and hands gone pale with the cold. When framed against the iron-gray sky of a snowy dawn, the pale blue of Declan's eyes snapped and sparked electric-hot.

Isaac could blame the sight before him for missing a step, and perhaps he should have, but he wouldn't have been alone. He crashed to his knees with a cry of equal parts frustration and alarm.

Declan turned in a tight half-circle and loped back to him. "Careful!" He flexed his hands as he came to a stop. Isaac knew the impulse to help, trained into every medical professional until it became second nature—or was supposed to. He'd seen enough of Declan in action to be sure with him that it wasn't an act. He scanned Isaac quickly, but efficiently, from the top of his head to the soles of his shoes. "Anything broken?"

"Nothing but my pride," Isaac admitted. He held his head high, meeting Declan's gaze. "Give me a second."

His defiance drew a smile to Declan's face. "You are one stubborn son of a bitch, aren't you?" he asked with a sharp bark of a laugh. He offered Isaac a hand to help him back on his feet. "Take a licking and keep on ticking, don't you?"

Isaac laughed out loud. *Oh, really. You think so?* There was only one possible answer for that, to Isaac's mind, and without taking the time to think it over, he cut loose his caution and let Declan have it.

Declan grunted in surprise and satisfaction when instead of backing down from the teasing, Isaac came to his feet in a rush that startled him into taking two steps back, almost into a crackling bush edged with prickly leaves. A good idea, extra points there, but the execution lacked style. His foot slipped on a few drops of body-warmed snow and sent him heavily forward, landing body to body with Declan all in a rush.

Declan had good reflexes. "Careful," he said, hands moving automatically to catch and guard. "Don't want to hurt yourself."

"I'm always careful," Isaac said. "Shouldn't I be?"

"Not always," Declan replied. "And should you? You tell me."

Pressed so closely together, he could feel—was abruptly, utterly aware of—the lean strength that made Isaac's body thrum with tension, of the skill in his dexterous hands at Declan's hip and shoulder... And of the hardening cocks trapped between them. Not just his. Declan's breath caught in his throat, a cold swallow that burned his lungs.

He watched, mesmerized, as Isaac licked his lips with a quick stroke of his pink tongue. Try as he might, he couldn't interpret the look etched deep in the man's gaze. "One of these days..."

Declan swallowed hard. Isaac wasn't wrong. Maybe sooner or maybe later, one of them would break. And wouldn't it be interesting to find out what happened next?

"One of these days," he said, gaze fixed on Isaac's mouth. His pulse thump-thump-thumped in his ears, and he knew that if he tilted back his head then Isaac's hand would tighten around his nape. That he would bring his mouth down to cover Declan's—and that once he'd started, he might not stop. Bad idea. Terrible idea.

God, yes.

And once more, anything could have happened.

And this time, anything did.

A noise. A quiet, unexpected sort of sound in this empty neighborhood and on the lonely street. Declan stopped, still, and put a hand on Isaac's chest to push him back when he would have opened his mouth in a question. "Did you hear that?"

Isaac's forehead furrowed. "Hear what?"

Had he imagined it? Maybe. Declan shut his eyes, listening for all he was worth, and—

There. Again. He turned his back on Isaac, pushing himself forward on legs that protested all this stopping and starting and told him in no uncertain terms how they weren't at all happy with the punishment. He ignored them, and dropped to his knees by the edge of the bush. The roots and branches were a few months' overdue for winter trimming back. Probably why it'd been chosen.

When he pushed an armful of winter foliage aside, there it was. Nestled between the roots, wrapped in a blanket that might have been pink once upon a time, long since washed to a dull rose gray. Crying louder now, shrill and scared, after the cold air had disturbed the box it'd been tucked into.

God *damn* it.

Isaac rested his hand on Declan's shoulder to get a better look over him, and went still. "What the…?" he said, jagged with surprise. "Declan, that's a newborn."

Chapter Two

"Very newborn," Declan said, distantly surprised at how far away his own voice sounded. Isaac's question had seemed to come through a tunnel, wisps of sound ghosting at his ears. "Still has vernix on her."

"A couple of hours old, if that." Isaac crouched beside Declan. He kept his hands off, but Declan could see the lightning speed of analysis in the quick flicks of his assessing sweep over box, blanket, and baby. "My God, Declan. What is this?"

Declan's temper sparked off a warning. "What do you think it is? Hide and go seek? Might be. She's a little young for it, but everyone says you should start early."

Isaac sat back on his heels, hands up. "Okay, okay. Dumb question. I get that. This doesn't happen every day." He rubbed at his mouth. "Thank God it doesn't happen every day. I just..." He ran out of words.

The doctor inside Declan noticed that Isaac had gone pale with the shock of the surprise, more so than the chill in the air. He wondered if he looked the same, ghostly white and almost pale blue. Probably not.

Isaac's translucent skin gave away everything he thought, and everything he didn't know he felt. Always had been an easy read. Not like Declan — and Declan had always meant to keep it that way. Only Isaac had a way of sneaking through the cracks in the walls no matter what.

Declan shook his head hard. *Focus.*

Isaac hadn't noticed. All his focus went to their foundling. "Jesus. If we hadn't heard her…"

"But we did," Declan snapped. "Shut your mouth about 'If we hadn't'. We did. That's all there is to it." He caught Isaac's arm hard by the wrist before Isaac would have reached down to loosen the blanket. "*Don't.* Don't scare her."

Isaac huffed. "You're an expert on neonates, now?"

Declan didn't let him go. He tightened his grip. "No, but I'm damn well willing to bet I know more than you." He shook his head at Isaac's dubious look, and let go of his wrist by pushing it away. "Don't ask me about it. Some things, you don't get to know."

Some things about him, no one knew.

"Just… Be quiet," Declan said. He laid a hand atop the blanket to try to soothe the infant. "Just hush. It'll be all right."

The baby didn't believe him. Well and truly angry now, she raised her voice in a high, thin wail and beat at the air with tiny clawed fists. Miserable, and letting the world know about it.

"Shh," he said, and again, blurring them humming white noise. "Hush now, hush."

From his place behind Declan, Isaac made an odd noise and moved to circle around the hawthorn bush. *What is he…?*

Never mind. Declan couldn't be bothered to ask why. What did it matter?

He did know better than to take her out of the cardboard box. He did.

Thing was—he couldn't seem to make himself listen to his better judgment. Startled by movement, the newborn's eyes popped open and her cries dropped to zero when Declan lifted and cradled her to his chest. "Better, huh?"

It could hardly have been worse. Whoever had left the infant beneath that bush had tried to wrap her up against the cold, but they'd done a piss-poor job. The blanket had been hand-knitted. Probably a pretty bit of crafts at one point in time, but age had worn holes through the yarn, and it hadn't been washed since God only knew when. Scratchy, too. Not fit for swaddling brand new skin.

Did she have a diaper on beneath? Declan checked, despite being sure what he'd find, and no. Nor was there any bandaging on the raw end of her umbilical cord stump. Looked like someone had used a rubber band for their clamp, and sawed it through with dull scissors.

She was a girl, though. Possibly mixed race. Hard to tell when they were only hours old.

Funny how it all came back to him. He'd done his pediatric rotations same as any intern and resident, but it wasn't the same. Not even slightly the same.

His foster sister Naomi had been just this size, he remembered. Maybe a day or two older, the first time he'd held her. Her skin had been darker, her eyes opened wider, and Nan Rose had given her a bath with the work-worn hands that were as quick to soothe as they were to instruct.

He hadn't seen either of them since…

"Declan." Isaac shook his shoulder. He'd come back—when?—and shook him again, insisting, "Declan. Are you with me?"

Isaac kept one hand on Declan's shoulder, though whether that was more for Declan's sake or his own, he couldn't have said. *The look of him, God.* Declan seemed to have aged ten years in the thirty seconds it'd taken him to part the hawthorn branches and sink to his knees. He held the infant as if he knew how. No, that wasn't quite right. It didn't take years of training to know *how* to hold a baby.

It did take something else completely to cradle a baby the way Declan did.

Isaac shook his head hard to push the questions aside. Time for those later. He couldn't be sure if Declan had noticed—and he thought Declan might not have—but besides being barely hours old, their foundling wasn't as round with baby fat as a newborn should have been, and her skin looked dry beneath the flaking patches of vernix. Probably hadn't been fed, and definitely didn't need to linger out in the cold.

"Declan," he said, careful not to raise his voice over a murmur he hoped was more soothing than severe. "We need to get her inside. All right?"

Declan frowned, as if he'd heard Isaac but didn't speak the same language. "What?"

Shock, Isaac determined. He didn't know why, or how to fix it, but the job wouldn't wait in any case. Not that he was exempt, either. Every time he turned his back to the bushes, he had the oddest sensation of being watched. Was the baby's mother still out there? Could be, he decided, and it was maybe even likely, but if so they were too good at hiding. He didn't see so much as a twig move, nor hear a stray breath.

He'd deal with that later. Better tend to Declan first. Isaac kneaded Declan's shoulder slowly, carefully, until Declan met his gaze. Perplexed still, and pissed as all hell, but nearer to the real world than he had been before. Good enough. "We need to get her inside," he explained, careful of the pronoun since apparently it mattered to Declan. "It's too cold out for adults to stay long if they're not actively keeping their temperature up by moving. That blanket isn't enough. She needs rehydration, too."

"Right." Declan blinked once, twice, three times. He pressed his lips together in a thin line. Isaac could all but see the thoughts clunking clumsily into gear behind the pale blue of his still-dazed eyes. "My car... No, I left it at the hospital. Meant to circle back around and drive home from there."

"You don't have an infant seat. Nor do I." Isaac fished out his phone and checked for signal. One bar, weak and fluctuating. No luck there. Declan's phone wouldn't be any better off — they used the same service provider, a holdover from the days of residency and subsidized monthly bills for interns.

Declan followed his movements with a frown. "Taxi?" He tucked the infant closer to himself. Automatic movements, Isaac thought. Pure instinct and reflex. "No, they wouldn't have a seat either. One of the neighbors... No." He growled quietly. "I can't think."

"Don't worry about that right now." Isaac clamped an iron band down on the questions. *Not the time.* His mind wasn't operating at a hundred percent either, was it? He pinched a bit of skin on his wrist for the shock of clarity it would bring and wrestled himself back on track. "Your apartment isn't too far away, is it? We can take her back there. Call the hospital and get an ambulance sent out. It's not ideal, but it's the best I can think of right now."

Declan nodded, but not as if he was fully on board, and proved it by asking, "What?"

Isaac shook him again, harder this time. "*Declan*. Whatever's going on in your head right now, I need you to snap out of it. The snow's picking up, and we need to get inside, too. Be a doctor. Can you do that for me? Or do I need to take her from you and do it all myself?"

That did the trick, or at least sank in deep enough to have an effect. Declan's head snapped up, and his glare was as severe as it was relieving. "I'm not in shock," he said. "I'm fine."

"Okay then. Prove it," Isaac said, not letting him look away. "Where's your apartment?" He'd never been there, and Declan had pointedly — to his mind — never made an invitation, but his rough knowledge of residential streets made him think Declan that had subconsciously led him close. "Near? Or too far? More than a mile, and we'd do just as well to walk back to the hospital."

Declan's jaw worked. He'd never admit to leading Isaac that way, even if that had been the intention, but that hardly made a difference. "Less than a block," he said after a pause that went on almost too long. He stood, not asking for help, and not at all willing to take it as far as Isaac could tell, but sounding almost a hundred percent engaged now. Like the doctor Isaac usually saw in action.

"Right," Declan said, picking up speed as he went. "Right. Take your hoodie off — you won't freeze — and cover her. Cut through the backyard of that red brick monster and it's the blue house set cattycorner down the way. Keys are in my pocket. *Go.*"

* * * *

Isaac's hands were almost too cold to manipulate keys and lock, but Declan's brain was back online enough to have given him clear directions. Even so, if any of his neighbors had looked to be at home he would have detoured to knock on their doors. No luck there, though. Lights were out, driveways empty, and yards bare. Snow fell thickly now, covering the winter grass in white and dotting the roads with frost.

To tell the truth, he'd never given much thought to where Declan lived. Declan obviously hadn't wanted him there. The one time they'd...not been rivals...they'd both been miles from home. Isaac had wondered once or twice about teasing Declan into coming over. Maybe for a football game in January. They might root for opposite sides, but they could have done it from the same couch.

Declan's house—it had to be a rental—didn't look like Isaac might have expected. Old, as all the houses in this neighborhood were, but with a new roof and a fresh coat of paint. A five-by-seven square of bare earth, tiller marks frozen into ridges, showed where a vegetable garden must live during the growing season. No yard art, and nothing decorative. Plain navy curtains at every window. A narrow entry with a pile of boots and sneakers mounded by the front door.

"Careful," Declan warned when Isaac stumbled over a hiking boot.

Isaac kicked the boot out of his way and stood back. "Get inside, before you let all the warm air out."

"I turned off the heat before I left last night. Cheaper."

"Still better than the outdoors." Isaac nudged Declan past him, praying muscle memory would take over before he made an ass out of himself groping for light switches.

It did. Declan clicked on a lamp just around the corner from the entry, casting sixty-watt light over a living room outstanding in its plain utilitarianism. Navy-blue couch that still smelled strongly of *new*, a remote control in its plastic factory wrapping on a glass-topped coffee table, and a bowl with a spoon left inside on the breakfast bar ten feet away. No pictures on any of the walls. Almost nothing of personal comfort, and even less of personality. He'd seen hotel rooms with more charisma.

Declan blinked owlishly at the setup as if he'd never seen it before. He shook that off quickly enough, as far as Isaac could tell, but his burst of adrenaline would likely ebb away with equal speed. He'd have a few sharp words to say about it later, but so be it. Looked like Isaac was in charge now.

Isaac shook his head in quiet wonder. Who'd have thought?

"Sit down," he told Declan. "On the couch. No, keep the hoodie. I'll turn on the heat and find some more blankets. Do you have any?"

"Mmm," Declan said as he sank half awkwardly, half gracefully, onto the sofa, the baby cradled carefully in his arms as if she'd been sculpted from frost-thin glass. It might have been a *yes*. Isaac hoped so, anyway.

No linen closet, or at least not one that Isaac could find. Not a problem. He doubted that Declan would mind sacrificing his bedding for the cause, and the third door he opened was— *Aha. Jackpot.*

While Declan's living room might have been bare of all but the essentials, he'd spared no expense on his sleeping arrangements. A California King nearly filled the room. He'd broken his navy streak with a rose and beige Navajo quilt that looked both old as the hills and as comfortable as a cloud, and demanded to be touched.

Isaac's face burned hot, but despite his hurry, the sight of that bed made him miss a step. Soft. Warm. Obviously a long-time favorite, and just as obviously private. Like everything else, come to that, wasn't it?

No pictures on the walls in there either, made conspicuous by their absence. No personal photos. No trinkets. No odd bits of this and that scattered about. The only other personal object was a twisted bit of driftwood mounted over the head of the bed. Looked like lightning arcing through the sky, rendered down in salt-polished cherry.

A flicker of motion outside the window, behind the trimmed-back holly hedges, caught his attention. Isaac leaned toward the pane. *What was that, a bird?*

It might have been, he thought, but dubiously. It didn't come again.

He'd check the bath for towels instead, he decided. Those might work better.

Isaac found the thermostat and switched it to high, and with that he knew he should have been finished with the room. Only he couldn't quite make himself walk away, and not just because of the bed. He had enough of the puzzle pieces to rough out a shape, a guess at the truth, and it was knowledge he never would have imagined, and hadn't asked to receive now. He—

"In the box at the end of the bed," Declan said behind him. Almost close enough to touch. If he wanted.

Isaac couldn't tell what Declan might want. He'd have imagined that Declan would be angry, coming upon him gawking at his personal space like a damned tourist. His face burned hotter, but for all that he could tell Declan wasn't pissed. Wasn't anything but tired. "I'm sorry," he said, just the same. "I didn't mean to, but that's no excuse."

Declan cut him off by waving one hand sideways through the air. The other, he used to support the newborn against his chest with. She'd quieted, which could have been a positive sign or very much the opposite. Hard to tell. "Box at the end of the bed," he repeated. He straightened his shoulders. "Blankets. Towels. Whatever you need, I've got it. The heat's on, I think. Takes it a minute. When the radiator starts to clank, don't stand next to the grate."

"Got it. Did you call for an ambulance, or should I?"

The corner of Declan's mouth lifted in what wasn't quite a smile, but wasn't a grimace or a glower either. "Still no bars on either of our phones. The tower must be down. I used the landline, while your back was turned."

Figured he'd phrase it that way. Isaac gave him another once-over. He couldn't turn off the trained physician inside him, no more than he could stop caring about—about—people. Declan looked better, but nowhere near *good*. "Fine. Go sit back down before you fall down."

Declan's chin came up sharply. "I won't drop her."

"I didn't say that." Isaac rubbed at his forehead. "I don't think that. But you know as well as I do that the human body doesn't always do everything the brain tells it to. You're cold, and you're still—rattled." As good a word as any. "Sit down so you can be sure you don't drop her. Okay?" He kept his hands to himself. "Declan. Okay?"

Declan had heard him. He just didn't have an answer that would satisfy either of them, so he let the question drop like a snowflake, one left to fall unregarded in a crowd of thousands.

Cradled next to his chest with her ear carefully angled against his heart, where she could hear and be soothed by its beating, the newborn squinted at Declan through eyes so new they barely opened. Her head was still misshapen from birth, and there was no definition to her features to set her apart from any other newborn. She looked wrinkled, and miserable, and possibly premature.

All five of her fingers together weren't large enough to fully curl around one of his. He let her try anyway, but when she butted her small head against his chest and began to root, he had to stop that. "ETA was seven minutes," he said. "Because of the snow. I'm not sure how long ago that was."

"Should be any second, then," Isaac said. For once in his life, he'd managed a decent poker face. Declan couldn't tell what he was thinking. It would have to be now, wouldn't it? "Declan. Sit."

He shook his head and turned back to the infant, giving her the tip of his finger to suck on. It wouldn't satisfy her for long before she'd start to cry again. "Don't think I don't know how much I owe you for this," he said, sounding abrupt and harsh even to himself. He must have been snapping out of it, he thought. The shock. "And don't think I don't know you're never going to let me live this down."

He'd hoped the teasing would make Isaac smile, and it did, but he'd also wanted to lessen the man's intense study of him, and that it didn't.

But he'd forgotten that Isaac usually knew what to say. Even though it was a lie, he said after a moment, "Yeah."

"You know what I don't understand?" Declan asked before he could change his mind. "There's a safe haven less than two miles from where they left her. The hospital. St. Hawk's. They didn't have to…"

Isaac sighed. "Go sit down, Declan, or I'll make you sit, and you won't like that." He touched Declan's arm. Rested his palm on the soft skin of his elbow, and left it there. "We've got a job to do. See it through, and then…"

"And then?" Declan asked, with a flash of his customary heat.

"And then we'll see what we'll see," Isaac said. He gave Declan a light push. "And we'll take care of what needs taking care of. All of it."

Declan could tell he meant that, too.

Chapter Three

"And that's what happened?"

Declan had crossed his arms against the chill of the snow. Instead of warming, the temperature had only gotten colder. Normally he loved winter weather. Today it seemed to go straight to his bones, as if they were made of metal and freezing him from the inside out. "Everything I know, you know too," he said to the EMT. He'd worked with the guy before. Lucas. Not a bad choice. Not overly experienced with pediatric emergencies, but capable enough.

He tried to look over Lucas' shoulder to the inside of the ambulance. Strobing red and blue lights and the glare they cast on the snow made it hard to focus, and Lucas had shoulders like the broad side of a barn. He barely caught a glimpse of a slip of a dark-haired woman whom he didn't recognize, but who wore the pastel print scrubs of an NICU nurse.

"Ride along?" he asked, gesturing at the nurse.

Lucas should have been a cop. He didn't blink or look backward. "Katie was just clocking in. She volunteered to come along, and I figured I'd need the help."

"Where's your usual partner?"

"Out sick," Lucas said. He tapped the screen of the tablet computer he carried, entering notes and checking boxes. "You're sure that's all? You didn't see anyone in the area, coming or going? It'd be easy to spot footprints in the snow."

Something in his tone made Declan's neck prickle with indignation. He stood straighter. "My priority was getting her somewhere safe and warm. I wasn't alone. You could ask Isaac, you know."

"Already did. He says he didn't see anything, either." Lucas sighed and shut the cover on his tablet, blocking away anything Declan might have hoped to get a peek at. "Don't give me grief, Declan. You know I've got to ask."

"Not as if you think I did it," Declan said. "Or as if you think I'm lying."

"I wasn't." Now Lucas reacted, giving him an odd look. "Look, things like this get everyone worked into a state. It's a fucked-up world we live in, and sometimes that's just a little too clear for comfort."

Declan scoffed quietly and rubbed at his forehead, trying to stave off an incipient throbbing ache. "God. Tell me about it."

"I would, but I'm not God." Lucas's grin was quick, but surprisingly boyish. He shifted his weight from the right to the left, his gaze fixed on Declan now. Declan wouldn't have said no to Lucas if he'd gotten that sort of once-over in a club, but he didn't care for it in the snow outside his home. "Might not be a bad idea if you got yourself checked out, too."

"There's nothing wrong with me."

"Ah." Lucas made a clicking noise with his tongue against his cheek. "If you say so. You know you're going to have to answer more questions. Someone from the police station, and probably a social worker."

It only stood to reason. Declan lifted one shoulder in a shrug of acquiescence and resignation. "When?"

"Sooner rather than later, would be my guess. Keep your phone with you and turned on. Sure you don't want to come get checked out?"

Declan could feel his face tighten, falling into deliberately blank lines. "I said I'm fine."

"Okay, sure," Lucas agreed. Too easily. "Mind if I have another word with Isaac?"

"I'm not his keeper. Knock yourself out."

Rather than taking offense, Lucas thumped his shoulder in passing. "Give me five, and we'll be on our way. Isaac?"

Declan might have tried to listen in to what Lucas had to say to Isaac, but with the burly EMT out of the way he could finally see. He stood on his toes and stretched his calves for a better look inside the ambulance, at the nurse, and at the safety transport equipment securely lashed to a stretcher. No sounds came from their foundling. He couldn't tell what Katie thought. She didn't look upset, or pleased. Only calm.

Good trait for an NICU nurse to have, he supposed, but it was hell on anyone else who wanted a clue.

"He says he's fine. You believe that?"

Isaac shook his head slowly. He kept one eye on Lucas, and one on Declan. He didn't like Declan's color, too pale for less than ten minutes' exposure to the cold. Neither was he pleased by the man's white-knuckled fists, or the quick respiration that made his chest rise and fall too quickly. "Not even a little."

"Good. If he's got a doctor on site, that means I don't have to worry about sweet-talking him into taking a ride with us," Lucas said. He eyed Declan as well, visibly taking a mental inventory. "Shock, you think?"

"At the least."

Lucas made a small noise of agreement. "You know him better than I do—"

Isaac wouldn't have said that anyone really knew Declan, but he knew what Lucas meant, and what Lucas was truly asking. "He had nothing to do with this," he said in the voice that usually made patients pay attention. "He came straight from work, and we left St. Hawk's together to go for a run. He was as surprised as me when we found her."

Lucas arched an eyebrow. "You usually run out this way?"

"Just luck. Chance. Call it what you want."

He didn't think that Lucas believed him, but the man let it go. Small blessings.

The NICU nurse—Isaac hadn't caught her name—closed the rear doors of the ambulance. Lucas' ears pricked up. "Keep an eye out on him," he said, stuffing his tablet computer in a pocket of his dark blue windbreaker. The same blue that was the only color in Declan's home. "If you need to call us—about anything—then you call us. Got it?"

Isaac knew, logically, Lucas was only doing his job. He'd played cards with the guy before. Shared a beer on a Friday night off. He would've asked the same things of a stranger.

But he couldn't deny that they made his hackles rise now, especially in the face of the sheer blankness that'd fallen over Declan when the ambulance doors closed.

"As soon as I know anything, you'll know it too," he said, watching Declan do an about-face and head for the house. Even odds as to whether he'd lock the door behind him and close Isaac out in the cold, but he'd have to get a move on if he wanted to better his chances. "If you'll excuse me?"

Isaac turned the front doorknob and found it unlocked. Probably only because Declan hadn't thought to throw the deadbolt. Moving on autopilot would be Isaac's guess. Maybe more than that, but he wouldn't know if he couldn't get Declan to settle and talk to him.

And good luck with that.

Walking away crossed his mind. Only for a second. Isaac shrugged off the impulse along with the snow he kicked off his sneakers as he toed them off to join the rest of the pile by the door. "Declan?" he called.

No answer. Not that he'd expected one. He heard movement, though, and in a house this small Isaac didn't have to range far afield to track Declan down.

He'd already neatened the cushions on the couch, Isaac noted in passing. Straightened them as if they were on display in a showroom. The towels they'd wrapped their foundling in for less than five minutes were crumpled into the bathroom hamper.

Declan himself stood in the kitchen, his back to Isaac and his shoulders ramrod straight, piano wire tight. Water clanked full speed ahead through the kitchen sink tap, almost drowning out the clatter of scrub brush wielded against stuck-on cereal in the bowl he scrubbed as if his life depended on it. He swore in an undertone as he picked at a bit on the side — but when he noticed Isaac watching him, the bowl slipped in his hands and nearly hit the bottom of the sink.

"Declan," Isaac said, inclining his head once. He didn't come any closer. "Everything okay?"

"Fine. Why shouldn't it be?" Declan replied without blinking.

"You tell me. Not exactly the usual thing that happens when we're out for a run."

Declan scoffed. A hint of emotion, indefinable, glanced over his mouth. "Maybe not, but it's done with now. Life goes on. If you need to call a taxi to get you back to St. Hawk's or wherever it is you live, feel free to use the landline. It's still up and running for now, but I wouldn't bet on it working for much longer if the snow keeps up."

True enough, but Isaac had been around the block enough times to know when someone was trying to pull a fast one over him. "Declan," he said again. "Turn the water off and look at me."

"No need." Declan attacked the bowl again, scrubbing with a ferocity that would scrape the design off. He did drop it this time, the crash of ceramic and the splash of water it sent up making him swear out loud and shut the tap off in self-defense. "*Fuck*," he said under his breath, holding onto the edges of the sink—and it was that, more than anything, that made up Isaac's mind for him.

Enough was enough.

"Don't," Isaac said.

Declan had nearly composed himself by the time he turned around, drying his hands on his hips. He'd summoned up a hint of his professional shield, blank and impenetrable as virgin porcelain. "Don't what?"

"Just—don't." Isaac rubbed at his face. So things were changing. Up until now they'd both enjoyed the adrenaline, and it'd been fun playing with fire. But whatever they were or might be to one another, under the surface they were friends—and more, Isaac thought, determined not to lie to himself. He wouldn't go for a run through a snowstorm with just anyone.

He was almost sure that Declan knew it, too. He just wouldn't admit to it if he were threatened with hot wires and coals.

Not yet.

Soon, Isaac decided. As soon as he could manage it. Might as well start here and now.

He knew what sort of medicine Declan needed.

Getting him to swallow the dose, though. That could be tricky.

"I said don't, and I meant don't. You heard me. We're not playing that game anymore," Isaac said, pushing himself out of his careful observational post and forward, toward Declan, into Declan's personal space, and even past that. He didn't stop until barely three inches separated them, and he could smell the sharp lemon scent of dishwashing liquid mingling strangely with dried sweat from their run. "You know me, Declan. Now look at me."

"What are you—?" Declan started.

He didn't get the chance to finish. Isaac pressed two fingers to his mouth and held them there. "No. You had your chance to talk, and you missed out. It's my turn now."

He knew exactly what Isaac had in mind, then. It didn't take a trained physician to see the signs. Declan backed away, took a hard left, and pointed himself toward the den. "You're out of your mind."

But Isaac must have anticipated that he'd do that. He was on the move as quickly as Declan, dodging in front of him to block his path and walk him backward. "Ah-ah-ah," he said. "That's not how it works. You think I don't know you, and you're right, but I know you better than most. I think I know what's going on in that head of yours right now."

"Stop," Declan warned him. He tried to put the brakes on.

Isaac ignored him, and kept coming. "Not until I'm finished."

"You're finished now. It's over. We go back to life as usual."

"Not quite." Isaac gave Declan a light push that sent him two steps back, into the edge of the couch. If anyone else had tried that Declan would have given as good as he'd gotten. Maybe even knocked them off their feet.

But this was Isaac, and Declan's knees weren't doing the best job in the world of holding him up. He lost his balance — or told himself that was what had happened — and fell awkwardly onto the cushions, knocking them askew again.

Isaac didn't miss a beat. No sooner had Declan's ass hit the couch than Isaac followed after, one knee braced by his thigh and one foot flat on the floor. "Are you listening to me now?" he asked from just far enough away for Declan to see his face without the features blurring.

What choice did he have? Declan didn't have to like it, and didn't *want* to, but he nodded.

"Good." Isaac's posture gentled. Less warden, more matron.

Declan wanted to look away. To not see the concern molding Isaac's pretty lips, or the line drawn between his eyebrows. To be able to pretend that Isaac didn't now know the last of the secrets he kept close to his chest, the ones he didn't want anyone to know. "What do you want?" he asked.

"To help you," Isaac said. "That's all. I won't tell you what I think I've guessed, because I don't see what it would help."

"Good," Declan shot back. His heart skipped in an odd, sick rhythm. "Is that all you wanted?"

"Far from it," Isaac said, not budging. He laid his hand on Declan's shoulder. Not gripping, or pushing. Just resting it there. Too close, and Declan's body couldn't help but take notice. He breathed in, tasting the scent of cold air and warm skin. Of hospital soap and sterile packaging.

"I'd take you to the hospital if I thought there was a prayer you'd go, but I do know better than that. So here's how it's going to be. I'm going to tell you what to do, and you're going to do it, because I think you need that."

Declan tried to scoff.

Isaac ignored him. He brushed a strand of hair away from Declan's face, the way he had once upon a time. Such a long-ago time, that seemed. Declan's eyes fluttered closed despite his better intentions, and his ears burned hot when he felt Isaac notice.

"There," Isaac said when Declan's eyes stayed shut. "All you have to do is let me help you, and the devil can take care of the rest. Okay?"

He'd gone hard. Declan didn't know when, or why. Only that when Isaac moved his hand from shoulder to groin, he had something to grip, and the touch of his fingers made Declan grit his teeth and tilt his head back in an arc.

Isaac stroked him once, slowly, the pressure of his hand a startling reminder of the single time they'd given in before. Swear to God, he'd never planned to have it again. Too good. Too easy to get hooked, and once he let Isaac in all the way that'd be the end for him, and he *needed* to keep his life in order. He had…reasons…

"I asked you if it was okay," Isaac said again, still stroking him with long, slow pulls. "Can I take care of you, Declan? Yes or no."

Declan opened his eyes to see Isaac looking up at him. He started to shake his head, but his neck wouldn't cooperate, and his face— He didn't know what expression he made, or what hints he might have given away. Whatever they were, he saw Isaac recognize them, and the exact moment when Isaac must have decided that there was no turning back.

"All right," Isaac said. Declan kept his eyes shut as Isaac slipped away—not far, only to his knees. He threw one arm over his eyes, and Isaac let him, too busy first with undoing the drawstring on his sweatpants, and second with drawing his cock out.

Then Isaac's mouth was *on* his cock, and Declan couldn't think of anything else at all.

Damned insightful—

Not exactly the approved treatment for shock, Isaac knew. He'd get a stern talking-to at least and a host of knowing leers at best if word ever got out, but why should it? Declan would never say a word, and Isaac could keep his mouth shut with the best of them when he wanted to.

He took it as gently as he could, one knee braced and one on the floor, as if proposing more than stress relief and emotional vent, and maybe he was. He couldn't tell for sure. God, but he'd missed this, the taste of Declan in his mouth. Even if he'd only had it once before, he knew the signs of addiction.

Call him weak, but he wanted this as much as he wanted to give it, and had for months.

Interesting how quickly Declan had given in, though. Isaac would have bet on it taking much, much longer, and he'd been revved up for the fight. That wasn't necessarily a bad thing. He could draw on that reserve of adrenaline to help make this good for Declan.

Isaac drew off to lick his lips and loose a long, shining strand of spit onto Declan's cock. *Get him good and messy. The nastier, the better. The more he'll feel it.* He slicked the saliva down Declan's shaft, a trickle of it on his balls, and blew cool air over where warm skin had been.

Declan groaned. His hips rocked, not quite thrusting into Isaac's mouth, but in need. He kept his head back and one arm over his eyes, but his other hand had come down to rest by Isaac's shoulder, fingers twitching with tiny jerks, barely brushing the tips of his hair. *None of that.* Isaac took Declan's hand and guided it closer. Made sure that Declan knew what he wanted, and didn't stop until Declan's fist had knotted in his hair.

The prickling sting made him gasp around Declan's cock. Though he hadn't intended to, he found himself shoving a hand down the front of his sweatpants too, taking himself in a rough, clumsy fist. Declan inhaled sharply when he noticed.

"You like that?" Isaac pressed his tongue to Declan's heavy, plum-dark balls between wet, noisy sucks at his cock. He sat back only long enough to give Declan a good look at his hand under the sweats, moving gracelessly and obscenely, pleased beyond words when Declan's lips parted in a better sort of shock. His cock jumped in Isaac's mouth, heavier and stiffer on his tongue.

I guess you do like it.

'Like' wasn't the right word, though. Not strong enough. Declan's breathing altered, clumsy jerks hitching in his chest. Isaac could taste pre-cum, slippery and salty, trickling from the corners of his mouth. He laid his palms on Declan's knees to keep him steady and bowed his head to take Declan deeper, as far as he could go, working his throat in constant swallows. Kneading his thighs, urging him without a word.

Declan jerked forward, tightly curled in over himself, when he came, a steady stream of swearing escaping his lips as his cum drooled over Isaac's chin. Isaac swallowed what he could—not enough—and hitched forward. His hips shuddered as he found the spot he needed and let go, spunk dripping down his fingers.

There. It'd do for a start. Isaac dropped his head heavily against Declan's knee and knuckled him in the shin. He licked his lips and wondered, still foggy, about how Declan had given in once he'd been ordered what to do.

Maybe that was the key. Could be. Isaac put a pin in that thought and tacked it to a corkboard in his memory.

Above him, Declan released a rough bark of a laugh.

Isaac licked his lips again. "What?"

"Just thinking how fucked-up this was," Declan answered, to Isaac's surprise. His lips moved in something less than a smile, but more than a sideways twist. "But if I'm fucked up, at least I'm not the only one."

Startled laughter burst out of Isaac. "Now you sound like yourself." He sat back on his knees and looked up at Declan, not ashamed of himself, not wondering what would come next.

From the looks of it, he wasn't the only one.

Chapter Four

"Snow still coming down out there?"

Declan slowed his pace as he approached the pediatric nurse's station of St. Hawk's Medical. He'd almost worked up the nerve to ask for a look at their foundling's chart. Just to see how she was doing. Now, he and the single nurse who'd done the ambulance ride along eyed the young man who'd spoken to him, a small-framed guy whose caramel complexion spoke of warmer places, and whose crisp diction warned him that he had made a life rule of taking no nonsense from anyone. The kind of guy Declan admired the hell out of under normal circumstances. Not now, when his nerves were as raw as sandpaper scraped over muscle and bone. Especially not considering that the guy wore a lanyard with a Department of Child Services badge dangling on the end.

"I don't know," Declan said, still careful in his observation. "Wasn't looking when I walked past the windows." He'd followed the ambulance with their foundling to St. Hawk's, and when he'd opted to stay for the sake of finding out what he could, Isaac had nodded as if to say he understood. That'd been hours ago. He had no idea where Isaac had wandered off to, or why, but when Declan had gotten the chance to steal a shower and change into warm, dry clothes in the staff facilities he'd jumped at it.

Not one of his better ideas. Stripping down had a psychological aspect. Nakedness and warm water, those had a power all their own. The touch of his own hands on his skin? Deadly. He still tingled from the sense memory of Isaac on his knees. Good Christ, who'd have thought he'd had it in him? Probably the worst thing anyone could have done for shock… If it hadn't worked.

Declan shoved his hands into the pockets of his scratchy jersey. The warmth from the water had almost but not quite faded, making him wish he'd brought a sweater or rummaged through the lost and found to see if he could borrow one. "You've been watching me since I got here?" he asked the guy.

He didn't so much as blink as the shot sailed across his bows, but tapped the side of a book-sized tablet against one palm. "And talking to people. I'm Connor —"

"You're a social worker," Declan said.

"That too," Connor replied. "The nurses tell me you were the one to find Baby Girl Doe. If you have a minute, I'd like to ask you some questions."

Right. Declan knew what that meant when run through normal everyday translation. *I'm going to ask you some questions, and if you know what's good for you, you'll speak when spoken to.*

Without meaning to, Declan glanced about for any sign of Isaac. Nothing. "What do you want to know?"

"Just a few things," Connor deferred. Perfectly pleasant. On the surface.

Not fooling Declan, though. He could see the way Connor's eyes narrowed as he took Declan in. Wondering if he had something to hide, or a reason for recalcitrance with official agencies. Maybe he did it, hmm? Wouldn't be the first time a guilty party was the one to report a crime in the hopes of taking the heat off themselves.

"Including, is that baby mine?" he asked, flat as still water over rocks. "No. I've never seen her before. I haven't had sex with a woman since I was in high school. I'm just a doctor, so what do I know? But as far as I'm aware a fourteen-year pregnancy isn't the norm."

Connor didn't much care for that, though Declan couldn't tell if the rudeness or the over-sharing bothered him more. "Watch it, Dr. Day. You're not helping anyone with the attitude. You say she's not yours and you don't know who her family is. I'm going to ask you again — are you sure about that?"

Declan ground his molars together. "You want me to take a DNA test? We're in the right place for it."

Tap, tap, tap went the tablet. "Do you have issues with social workers, Dr. Day?"

A warm hand landed on Declan's shoulder before he could reply with something he would have regretted. The scent of familiar aftershave tickled Declan's nose. He twisted to look around, but the new arrival spoke before he got a good look, and Declan wasn't sure whether he wanted to throw his hands in the air and shout or just close his eyes in relief.

"Is there a problem here?" Isaac asked.

Funny how an unexpected arrival could change the dynamics of any group situation. Isaac tried not to take advantage of it too often — ruined the effectiveness — but desperate times called for no holds barred on the action. Declan clamped his mouth shut, the social worker who'd been quizzing him frowned, and behind the nurses' station, Katie raised her eyes to the heavens and mouthed a silent thank you.

Situation normal, then. Isaac didn't suffer from any doubts that Declan wouldn't thank him for interfering, but so be it. Antagonizing a social worker wouldn't help either. "Go and get some air. Cool down," he said by Declan's ear, tightening his hand into something more than a comforting squeeze and somewhat less than a warning pinch. He flexed his fingers once to make sure that Declan knew he meant business. "Doctor's orders. Be smart about this, would you?"

Declan shot him an unimpressed glower, but it barely had any heart to it, and he tossed Isaac a tired, careless one-handed wave as he turned.

Connor raised his hackles. "Sorry, did I say we were finished?"

And on to putting out fire number two. Isaac raised his shoulders. "No, you didn't. Is he obligated to answer your questions?"

The social worker pressed his lips together. "It'd be better for everyone involved if he did. Look, I'm just doing my job."

"I know. With all due respect, so am I. Give him a break. I was with him, and I promise you he had no idea she was under there before we heard her crying. My observational judgment is that he's still in shock." Isaac tried to gentle the dismissal. "I'll write a full report, and I'll see to it that he does the same. *After* he's back to normal."

"Meanwhile, Baby Girl Doe gets to pay the consequences." Connor gave a frustrated sigh. "Fine. I'm getting a cup of coffee. You're going to be hearing from me again. Got that?"

"Loud and clear."

Isaac winced internally as Connor turned his back. Pissing off the authorities, rarely a good idea. Couldn't see any way around it, though. "Think I'm going to regret that?"

"Possibly," Katie said. She'd changed into a new set of scrubs, pale pastel blue with fluffy ducklings in doctor's coats and kittens in nurse's caps. She grimaced good-naturedly when he raised a teasing eyebrow at the design. "Shush. Kids love it. That's what matters. I, um… If you want, I'll see what I can do later if Connor comes back around. I know him. We go to the same church. He's a nice guy under normal circumstances, but he takes his job really seriously."

The offer of help was tempting, but… Isaac shook his head. "Don't get yourself in trouble on my behalf. I dug the hole, I'll dig a way out."

"I'm more worried about Dr. Day's blood pressure."

"You and me both." Isaac felt that odd tingling at the back of his neck again, as if someone lurked nearby keeping an eye on him. Probably just paranoia. There weren't any windows around. Then again, it could be alarmingly easy to sneak into a hospital. All anyone had to do was claim they'd come to visit a patient, or gotten lost between their exam room and the john.

He shrugged the tingling off. Most likely it was just his imagination.

Maybe.

Katie chuckled quietly. "You're probably a pretty cute couple when you're not stressed. How long have you been together?"

Isaac blinked in momentary surprise. He opened his mouth to answer...

And partway between intent and action, changed his mind. It was *almost* true. Even more so after the blow job at Declan's house. "Not too long. Feels like half of forever. Long enough to know when he's running on fumes and nerves."

"Mmm." Katie had turned her gaze to the hallway that Declan had disappeared down. "How long was he in the system, do you know?"

"Excuse me?"

"We tend to recognize each other," she said, still frowning after Declan. "I was in foster care for a couple of years after my mother died, while my dad was having trouble coping."

Oh. Isaac's mouth had gone dry. That would make sense, wouldn't it? Would explain a hell of a lot, actually. "I don't know," he fibbed to cover himself. "He's never said. I figure probably a while. Longer than he wanted."

"He has the look." Katie sighed and dropped into a rolling task chair at what Isaac guessed would be an angle to watch the hallway from. "And I'm guessing he hates the thought of anyone, especially a baby he feels responsible for, getting dragged in there."

* * * *

Isaac found Declan in the cafeteria, where no one in the know ventured after ten p.m. without a good reason, two Styrofoam cups cooling on the table before him, a tablet computer in hand, and a death glare into the middle distance on his face. Talk about 'knowing the look'. Isaac had that one down by heart. Wise men would not dare to interrupt Declan in that kind of mood.

But Isaac had never claimed to be wiser than average.

He stopped in front of Declan and nudged the eye-searingly bright orange chair facing him with one shoe. Declan barely flinched, but his gaze cut upward and quickly away. Acknowledgment of a sort. "Is this seat taken?"

"Yep," Declan said, still not looking at him. "Saved for my arresting officer. It'd just be bad manners if I let you have it."

"You're not going to be arrested. At least, I don't think you are." Isaac used his foot to hook the seat out, far back enough for him to drop into it. "Thirsty tonight, or did you buy the hypothetical officer something to warm up with?"

Declan huffed as he lifted one of the cups to his mouth. "You don't give up, do you?"

"Not as a habit, no. But you already know that."

"Don't I just." Declan tasted the murky liquid inside his cup and grimaced. "What the *hell*, Isaac? This stuff is bad enough when it's hot. Let it go cold, and I can't even tell if it's coffee or tea or pick-and-mix."

Isaac tried the second cup and winced. All he tasted was *bitter*, and it left a nearly oily coat on his tongue. Must have been on the burner for hours. Next project up on his recommendation list? Update the cafeteria. "God, that's awful."

Declan shuddered in reply.

Another sip went down clotted-thick and nearly evil. Isaac replaced the cap on the Styrofoam cup and pushed it aside. He could save it for paint stripper, but he wasn't sure how that might affect the environment. "So I talked to a couple of the nurses after you took off. Found out what I could. Seems as if people are a hell of a lot more likely to talk to me than they are to you. Wonder why?"

Declan's ears almost visibly pricked up, though he pretended cool indifference. "And?"

"And I expect it's pretty much the way you think," Isaac said, keeping as careful a watch over Declan's reactions as he would any patient's. "They have to ask us both if we're responsible. I know it's not fair, but it's their job. They'll be asking again until you answer, and they find proof otherwise."

Declan said nothing. Just glowered.

Isaac took a deep breath. "They're keeping the baby in the hospital nursery for right now," he said, more gently than before. "She seems healthy, and her weight puts her at close to full term, but she did get pretty cold and she was dehydrated."

Declan nodded. "And after that?"

"You know the answer," Isaac said, though his chest twinged with sympathy. "Foster services. They'll find a place for her. I'm not sure if there's anything St. Hawk's can do to help make sure it's a good one, but—"

"Some good ones exist," Declan said, shuttered. Not quite shuttered enough to hide a flash of pain. "Mostly they don't. Even the good ones can go sour."

Isaac didn't know what to say to that. He probably wasn't wrong.

Declan fell into silence without further prompting from Isaac, which—fine, he could suit himself. Gave Isaac a chance to study him. Update his parameters. Same old face, but Declan looked a good ten years older at the inside minimum, the lines at the corners of his eyes starker and deeper than they usually seemed. Still shocky.

"How old are you?" Isaac asked.

Declan frowned, as if the question threw him. "Thirty-three."

"A year younger than me. Wasn't expecting that."

"Isaac..." Declan pressed his knuckles to his forehead. He sat back. "What do you want? Or do you just get a kick out of pestering me every time I get something to drink? Should I start watching my back every time I pass a water fountain?"

Isaac let the sarcasm ride over him in a bristling, but mostly harmless, wave of prickles. He tucked his hands, fingers curled together, beneath his chin and propped his elbows on the table. "That new nurse, Katie. She thought we were together."

"Wouldn't be the first," Declan said. "Won't be the last."

"She said we made an interesting couple."

"Interesting times make for interesting couples. I take it you didn't correct her?"

"No," Isaac said. He could tell when someone was trying to make him back down. He wasn't ashamed. "It isn't untrue. It's just not quite what they think, is all."

"Which makes it...untrue?"

"Stop that. You know what I mean."

Declan shook his head in darkening silence. He switched off his tablet and raised one hip to stuff it in his right front pocket. "Splitting hairs awfully thin there, Isaac."

"As long as they'll bear the weight, I'm fine with that."

"God!" Declan growled. "And you just... Why do you even care?" He turned his hands palms up and held them wide apart. "I mean it. I swear I don't understand. You want sex? You already had a drink from that well. What's in this for you, Isaac?"

Isaac held his breath for a beat. This was important. How he answered mattered like no other question before. "Nothing," he finally said. "Believe me or don't, but I'm not doing it for a reward. And why do I care? Fuck, Declan. I've told you before. Because I can see there's so much under the surface, and I want to know what that is. I like what I've found so far. Now, this is the way it's going to be."

Declan sent both eyebrows arching up. "This ought to be good," he said, but sounded gut-punched. "The way what's going to be?"

"Tonight," Isaac said, warning Declan with a look that he wasn't in the mood to give any quarter. "This coffee-tea hybrid isn't fit for consumption. You and I can walk to the Whistle Stop for something to eat, or to the Palomino if you want a harder kind of drink, or we can run circuits around St. Hawk's all night long. Up to you. But we're doing *something*, you and me, that isn't just sitting here and stewing. And that's the what and why. So there you have it." He sat back with a clatter of industrial chair legs on linoleum. "Any questions?"

Shit. Shit, fuck, shit. Declan could tell that Isaac meant what he said, and it'd take a steamroller to sway his course. And then…

Declan's stomach tied itself into a knot around the mouthfuls of inky caffeine he'd swallowed down. He tried, just once more, to stall. "Why would I agree to that?"

Didn't faze Isaac. "Because I know you," he said. "I know what you need. It's just common sense."

Declan scoffed. "You really don't know me as well as you think you do."

Isaac only raised one shoulder in response to that. "I know you were in foster care for a while," he said, as calm as if they were conferring over the likelihood of more snow, while his words doubled up both fists and punched Declan in the gut. "I know it wasn't a good time for you. I know I'll do what I can to help, whether or not you let me, because that's who I am, Declan. You know *me* well enough to be sure of that."

Fucking hell. Declan tilted his head back to stare up at the ceiling, counting the speckles on the drop tile until he had enough breath back in him to speak. "You know facts. Inferential guesses. You don't know *me*."

"Maybe not," Isaac said, implacable. "It's still a place to start."

He would see it that way, wouldn't he?

"You want to help me?" Declan asked, moving focus from tiles to colleague, and holding him there. He felt his knuckles go white. "Then shut up and listen while I tell *you* how it's going to be. I'll tell you what you want to know, to stop you from fucking *asking*—" He could live with that, he'd have to, and at least it could be on his own terms— "And after that we don't mention it again. One-time offer, so you'd better take me up on it before I change my mind. And it's conditional. Follow?"

Isaac's eyes had gone wide, like a boy's, but he didn't break or back down. He leaned forward in his chair and folded his hands. "Let's hear it."

He just wouldn't quit, would he? Declan stood. His chair slid away from him with an almighty rattling screech, but so be it. "You want to help me? Fine. I want to forget. Come home with me and make that happen."

At last, he had the satisfaction of seeing Isaac taken off guard. "I don't know if that's a good idea."

Or so he said, but Isaac wasn't the only one who could observe signs and symptoms. As Declan scanned him, he saw the telltale giveaways. A shift of the legs, a contracting of the stomach, a pinkening of the skin. Lips parted briefly. Eyes hooded. Only for a second, but *he* knew Isaac better than Isaac was aware, and he'd use that to his advantage, by damn.

"Thought so," Declan said after the first beat had passed, when Isaac would have had to acknowledge it to himself. "You can tell me you don't want me, but I won't believe you. So. That's your choice. Are you in? Or are you out?"

Chapter Five

Whoever had chosen the clock that hung on the St. Hawk's cafeteria wall must have liked being reminded of the time. Every second of it, unless its mechanics had worn even less well than its heavy burnt-orange casing. Each jerk of the second hand made the glass reverberate, time tromping by in thick-soled army boots.

Declan's knees didn't want to hold him up. Took all the strength he could muster to plant his feet and keep his hands loose. Looking down at Isaac. Willing him to make the connection. *Come on, man, just get it. Use that big brain of yours. You're plenty insightful at the worst of times.*

Action. He needed action, not more questions. Let Isaac ask another, and Declan knew he'd break and run. He could barely think like this — wound up as tightly, finely stretched as a garrote wire — much less talk. Part of him burned with shame over what he'd reduced himself to, but he'd come too far to back down now.

He needed — He *needed* —

He saw the moment when Isaac understood. Comprehension widened his eyes and parted his lips—then consideration brought him forward to lean on his elbows and narrow those eyes at Declan for far too long.

Tick. Tick. Tick.

Declan refused to count how many seconds slipped by, but the world almost ceased to register with him as they did. The cafeteria in all its outdated glory, the uncomfortable non-fit of the jersey with its scratchy seams on his shoulders, and the sourness of his stomach twisting around a mouthful of bad coffee.

Finally—finally—Isaac made a small *huh* sound and nodded. He stood in a long, fluid stretch, his arms long enough to reach across the table as if it wasn't in his way at all. He rested one palm against Declan's cheek and angled Declan's face up.

Declan drew his tongue across his lower lip.

"All right," Isaac said after another warm-rubber stretch of time. "We're not officially on duty. We can leave. If you really want what I think you want, then follow me."

Declan didn't ask where they were going. He shut his eyes and shuddered with relief on the inside. Isaac had his finger on the pulse. He *got* it. Knew what Declan needed, even if Declan couldn't ask for it with words, and was willing to give it to him.

To take charge.

Good. They could go now.

* * * *

This would be the tricky part. Isaac thought it might have been better if they'd gone back to Declan's place, but he knew better than to ask. The man's façade had cracked, but it wasn't open yet. Push him too hard in the wrong direction and he'd slam down the security gates. Besides, if he wanted Isaac to take control, then he could start by following his lead.

It'd be a decent test, if nothing else.

The snow had let up temporarily, though going by the thickness of the steel cloud cover that made the early afternoon almost as dark as night, that wouldn't last long. They'd walked most of the way, not quite side by side but not so far apart as to lose track of each other. A silent agreement, but effective.

Isaac slid his house key into the lock and opened the front door to his apartment, then stood back to indicate that Declan should go in front of him. Declan gave him a slight frown, but rallied like a champ, squared his shoulders, and stalked inside with a hint of his usual stubborn pride in place. *Good*. Fire worked better for purging. He hadn't left the heat on while he was out, but he doubted they'd be hurting for warmth any time soon.

He waited until Declan had all but disappeared into the darkness — the flat he rented was on the back of a Georgian-style home divided into apartments, with neighbors above and behind, and not many windows of his own — to reach for a lamp and press the switch. Buttery yellow light filtered through the paper shade to illuminate Declan from behind.

Stubborn. Angry on the inside. Asking for help, even silently, turning to look at Isaac with wide, uncertain eyes.

Isaac toed off his snow-covered boots and gestured for Declan to do the same. Again, he waited, and again, he pointed to show Declan where he wanted them to go. Not far. The advantages of an apartment carved into an old house weren't exactly legion when it came to modern conveniences, but it was abundant with angles and nooks for this kind of business. He put a hand on Declan's shoulder to guide him into the best light, his back to the wall.

Fine shivers ran beneath Declan's skin, but he held his head high. "What are you doing?"

Isaac could have answered him in words, but he preferred to show the man instead—and he'd been saving this up. He lifted Declan's chin as he had done in the cafeteria, where he'd held himself in check, and pressed two fingertips against the hard line of fragile bone. Declan's pulse fluttered against the side of his hand, almost stutter-stumbling when Declan caught his breath, then let it unfurl in a long sigh when Isaac pressed his mouth to Declan's.

There. Isaac didn't press his luck with the slight parting of Declan's lips, not yet. He angled his head to one side and lingered there. Almost sweet, almost chaste, but for Declan bringing a hand up to rest on Isaac's chest.

Better. Covering Declan's hand with his own, Isaac traced the tip of his tongue across Declan's mouth. A mouth like a kiss waiting to happen, he'd said? It delivered on its advertising. As he coaxed Declan's lips into slow, uncertain responses, it occurred to him that they'd never kissed before now.

Somehow, it seemed to suit them.

He didn't laugh. Would have ruined the mood, and Declan had gotten with the program now. Though he let Isaac do the pursuing, he allowed himself to be caught. Curled his tongue where Isaac stroked it, sliding together, replacing the flavors of coffee and uncertainty with his own taste. Declan moaned into his mouth as he put an arm, hand fisted, around Isaac.

Isaac let him. However he needed to hang on, that was fine.

Though he wouldn't let that go on forever. Especially not now. Hate to end it though he did, Isaac withdrew before Declan could wrestle too much closer. He nudged the man's chin with his nose, and bit lightly at Declan's cheekbone, dark-burn pleased with the startled swearing he won with that venture.

"You asked what I was doing," he said, tapping one fingertip against Declan's neck in time with his pulse. "Do you want to hear the answer now?"

Uncertainty and wariness chased each other over Declan's face, but he nodded.

"Good." Isaac took Declan's hand and led it down, down, down to cup his cock through his jeans and show him how to knead. This would be the trickiest part of all, but if he wanted to cede control he'd do it right or not at all. "Unfinished business," he said. "And fair is fair, Declan. It's your turn."

Now. Would he bite?

Normally, Declan would tell anyone trying to get him on his knees without a serious discussion where to step off, and if they didn't listen, then he was in the best place possible to make his point — with teeth, if necessary. But these weren't normal times, not at all, and his knees would have given way with relief if he hadn't allowed them to buckle and drop him.

Isaac did understand.

Declan butted his forehead against Isaac's thigh, not surprised by the hard runner's muscle, but pleased not to find it too soft a pillow. *Soft* wouldn't do, not just then.

He looked up before Isaac could break the role to ask if he'd hurt himself, warning him with a sharp glance to keep his questions to himself. Though he might have expected a laugh from Isaac any other time, Isaac only watched him now with hooded eyes and a quirk to one side of his mouth. He reached down to trace the shape of Declan's lips, and stopped with the pad of his thumb pressed to the very center.

Do it.

Declan breathed out, knowing it would feel warm, almost hot on the bare strip of skin between Isaac's rucked-up blue thermal and the sturdy leather belt threaded through his jeans. The muscles there jerked gratifyingly, but that was only the beginning. He pressed his nose to the hard line of cock behind Isaac's zipper and breathed *in*.

"Declan," Isaac warned, one hand coming to rest on the top of his head.

He hadn't needed to. Declan licked his lips as he slid the belt free of its loops and drew Isaac's zipper down with a faint *click-click-click* that reminded him of the sound the second hand had made on the cafeteria clock. Kinder, though. Less merciless. Building toward, not counting away. He eased denim, still new enough to be stiff, down Isaac's hips. Not far. Only past the firm rounds of his ass. Enough room to work with.

Isaac kept his hand on Declan's head as Declan drew his cock out, careful of the zipper, and groaned behind his teeth. Declan blew another unsteady puff of air over the length. He'd seen it before — barely, with his memories clouded by champagne and summertime hurry — but he remembered the feel of it in his hand, thick and long, salty and heated.

When he slid the tip into his mouth, he had to take hold of Isaac's knees. Isaac allowed it, and *allow* was the right word. He'd shifted to hold Declan by the back of the head, almost too hard, just as Declan wanted. His hips jerked, the man eager—Declan could tell—to hold him tight and fuck his mouth.

Declan swallowed away a mouthful of saliva that rose at the thought. *Do it*, he said by kneading Isaac's thigh and sinking down, taking more of Isaac into his mouth. *Do it hard.* He made a grunting noise and pushed Isaac's hips against the wall. *Do it.*

And Isaac did. With a hiss barely caught behind his teeth, he tightened the joints in his hand until there would be no fighting back against them. *Good!* Declan let the man fill his mouth, hard and fast over his tongue—not too far, but saliva ran down his chin now, wetting Isaac's cock until it almost glowed in the dim light of the lamp. Would have been better if he'd let Isaac stay up against the wall, but he could make this work.

His own cock demanded attention, but he barely had the presence of mind to pay it any heed. Just a hand down the front of his jeans, a tight circle of his fingers, and let friction do the rest. Jerking forward as Isaac pushed into him, a continuous circle that made Declan first dizzy, then sore, then let him slip away into the white space.

God damn, it'd been a long, long time, but Isaac knew how to—

Isaac tugged at Declan's hair in warning. Nice of him, but not necessary. Declan dug in with his short-clipped nails that wouldn't cut but might leave scratches to remember him by—and did—and breathed in through his nose. He urged Isaac's hips forward, wanting more of him even as he came over his own hand, slick-wet heat ruining his jeans. With his tongue underneath and a scrape of teeth on top, he demanded his share.

"Oh, *fuck*," Isaac groaned as he came. Too much to swallow. He only got half, if that, and let the rest drip down between them. Instead of a thank you, Isaac gave his hair a sharp pull, and a light clap of the hand against the back of his skull.

Declan dropped his head again. That was — better.

He didn't have to say anything, either. That was almost the best part.

Or — didn't have to say anything *yet*, that was.

He swallowed, and chased the flavor of Isaac on his lips. Building himself back up for keeping the promise that he'd made.

* * * *

"Here. Brought you this." Isaac tapped Declan's shoulder with one hand, and offered him a damp facecloth with the other. He'd lingered at his bathroom sink long enough for the water to heat up for Declan, but had taken care of his personal business with a shock of cold. Under the harsher white light above the mirror, he'd looked almost strange to himself. Nearly as shocky as Declan, and for the first time he admitted to himself that maybe the events of the day had had their effect on him too.

Physician, heal thyself.

Declan didn't seem to want to move even so far as taking the damp cloth from Isaac, but Isaac had been prepared for that. He held it over Declan's head and squeezed the terry in his hand. One drop of water fell fat and heavy to splash on Declan's nose. "That means 'take it'," he said as Declan spluttered.

Declan shot him a dour look, but tweaked the cloth out of Isaac's hand and ran it over his face. "Thanks," he muttered.

"Not exactly what I had in mind, but it's a start."

"Unless you feel like a rinse cycle and a tumble dry, it's as good as it'll get," Declan said, wiping his hands.

Isaac raised one shoulder. "Is there a reason I shouldn't offer that? Because I was going to. There's two people in this room, and the hardass isn't me."

"You would put it that way," Declan muttered. He balled up the cloth and tossed it back to Isaac.

"You didn't finish," Isaac remarked mildly. He'd expected as much, and had come mentally prepared. Declan would always be a challenge. Luckily for both of them, a man who never knew when to take no for an answer thrived on challenges. He dropped to a crouch, then to a kneel behind Declan, putting one arm around his chest and one around his waist, and tucked his chin over Declan's shoulder. "As I recall, we made a deal. It's your turn to pay up."

Declan huffed a small laugh and said nothing.

Isaac didn't react. He could be patient enough to let Declan find the words in his own time. He closed his eyes and listened to the man's breathing, and the small, subtle ways it changed as he struggled with himself. Pride went toe to toe with need, and shame with stubbornness and a sense of honor. All the things that made Declan a damned good doctor, and a hot mess of emotions.

He waited. Not for long.

"Answer me one thing," Declan said. "Why do you care? I can't get my head around it. Why even like me?"

Isaac took the question seriously. Idly, he stroked the skin-warm cloth of Declan's jersey, smoothing it down, then rumpling it back up again over Declan's stomach. "Because you're worth it," he said. "Hard work, but with a decent reward. Like a truffle wrapped in barbed wire."

"Jesus." Declan sighed. "Fine. But only if you admit you're a truffle balanced on the end of a blunt instrument."

Isaac snorted. "Yeah, I suppose that's accurate." He nudged Declan in the side. "I would tell you that I could guess almost everything you don't want to say, you know. But that wouldn't be the point to all this. You're the one who needs to say it more than I'm the one who needs to be told. Do you understand what I mean?"

"I'm probably the only one on the western seaboard who *would*." Declan plucked lightly at Isaac's hand, though not as if to move it away. More like a guitar player might run a pick over strings, or a religious man would grasp a rosary, grounding himself. "Do you promise you won't ask me about any of this stuff again?"

"Hell no."

"Figures," Declan said. "Hell with it. Fine. Okay. I grew up in foster care. That's the first thing you need to know, even if you already did, because that's the backbone. I have no idea who my real parents are. I haven't gone looking, because I don't want to know them. Fuck them for missing out. I didn't even want to look when I was younger."

Isaac held himself as still as could be, wanting to listen but encourage too. Light stroking over Declan's chest and a noncommittal murmur had worked so far to keep the man soothed. He carried on and kept his ears open. "Go on."

"I did find out the circumstances of my surrender," he said, turning his head to give Isaac a dark look. "Any guesses?"

Isaac didn't give him the satisfaction of reaction. "Underneath a bush, or in a safe haven?"

"An open dumpster behind a shitty diner," Declan said. He stared straight forward, fixated on the floor, as his mouth moved and words came out. "In July. No cloud cover. Hotter than hell. Covered in the kind of germs most people can't imagine. I shouldn't have survived, you know?"

"Stubborn even then." An idea had been filtering through Isaac's head. He stood to lose a hell of a lot if it didn't work, but if it did... Carefully, lightly, he touched his lips to the spot where Declan's neck met his shoulder in a small, open-mouthed kiss. "Always stubborn. A survivor."

Declan groaned, but tilted his head—willfully or subconsciously, either would work. He popped Isaac's knuckles for him as he worked their hands together and made Isaac wince with appreciation.

But he'd gone quiet. Isaac used a light prickle of teeth as he said, "Keep going."

Declan bent forward, almost straining against him. "Fuck! Okay. I was in foster care. You know that. You know it's a shitty system. Mostly bad. Some not so bad. I had a good one, for a while. Don't remember how old I was. Ten? Eight? I thought she was an old, old lady, but she would have been in her late forties. Just looked older. I called her Nan Rose—I think it was Helen Rose, but I can't be sure. She'd had a hard life, but she had these hands, these work-worn hands that were so kind, and she liked to sing, and..." He stopped, swallowing with a painful sound. "She had diabetes. I remember that. She did her best, but she couldn't keep up with us—me or the little girl she had. Naomi. I tried. Swear to God, I *tried*."

Jesus. "You were eight years old," Isaac said.

"You think I don't know that? Fucking *hell*." Declan ground one hand against his face and let out a long, shaking breath. "After that, I got stupid. Did some things I regret."

"Juvenile record?"

"Sealed. And I'm not going to tell you anything except that there is one." Declan moved his elbow back and into Isaac's ribs—not hard, but firmly enough to warn. "Let that sleeping dog lie. I got over myself. Mostly. Grew up, and tried to do the right thing. I did look for her, but I never found a trace before I went to medical school, and then when I graduated I couldn't stand to think about what I'd find. And then I met you. And now you know it all."

All? He barely knew anything, Isaac thought, but it was—like he'd said before—a place to start.

"Okay," he said, smoothing his hand beneath Declan's thermal, up and over warm skin. "All right. Thank you for that."

Declan turned his head as far as he could, likely searching for signs of sarcasm.

Isaac made sure there were none for him to find. Instead, he pressed his lips beneath Declan's ear, then took the lobe between his teeth and squeezed.

Declan turned his head. "Pavlov? Really? The dog barks, so you give him a treat?"

"So you recognize it," Isaac said. "Doesn't make it any less useful or worthwhile."

"Isaac..."

"Declan..." Isaac echoed his tone. He loosened his hold just enough to let Declan look at him without straining his neck past the point of cramping, and nudged stray spikes of hair away from his forehead, away from the Arctic eyes that only looked tired now. "What do you want me to say? You needed to get that out. I'm not sorry I made you. This is why you matter to me. Even if you can be prickly and difficult sometimes, and you like to pretend otherwise, you *care*. You care so much that it takes me out at the knees, you know that?"

Declan shook his head.

Isaac found the button of Declan's jeans and flicked it open. Let there be quiet for a moment, let Declan adjust. Gave him a chance to say *no* or *stop* or *back off*, and when he didn't, Isaac kept on going. He drew down Declan's zipper and slipped his hand inside.

"Messy," Declan said, though he arched into Isaac's touch.

"I'm a doctor. Mess doesn't bother me too much." Isaac nipped lightly at Declan's nape. "So that was what you didn't want me to know. Why, though? I'm not degrading it, but it wasn't the end of the world. Look around you. We're still going."

"Spoken like someone who's never been in a position to judge."

Fair enough. "Okay. You're right about that. I'm sorry." He hesitated. "Have you ever thought about becoming a foster parent yourself? You'd be a good one."

Declan made a noise that said, more clearly than words, that he wasn't any too sure about that. "Until you've been there, you wouldn't believe how people look at you differently. When they know."

Isaac could easily accept that as a truth. He splayed his palm wide over Declan's lower stomach, and let him adjust once more before saying, in his ear, "Then think seriously about joining that committee Dr. Gabriel wants you on. Just for a start. So you do care about what I think of you? I wondered."

He expected the backward swing of Declan's elbow, and dodged in time — then took Declan's cock in hand and found him not quite hard yet, but willing to go there. "Don't flatter yourself. No one at St. Hawk's knows," Declan said, with a reluctant smile tugging at his lips. "That doesn't make you special."

"Liar." Isaac moved his hand downward.

Declan let a smaller moan escape. "Isaac. You think this'll fix anything?"

Isaac didn't have to think about his answer. He took a better grasp on Declan's slowly growing erection and made him pay attention. "No, I don't. But I think I'll be there tomorrow to know that. And the day after, and the day after, until the problems *are* solved. I think you know that, too. Else we wouldn't be here in the first place."

Chapter Six

Have I thought about becoming a foster parent, he asks? Only every day or so. More than that, lately.

With a paper cup of sinfully dark Italian roast in hand—black, two sugars—showered, dressed, and rested, Declan stood off and to the left of the viewing window in St. Hawk's nursery, deliberately minding his own business. Or that had been the idea.

Funny how life tended to change the best-laid plans.

A week after her arrival, their foundling's bassinet did not take center stage. Understandable, he supposed. As he understood it—via second-hand information—she'd needed a few hours with a bilirubin lamp, and they'd run as many tests as her little body would tolerate. Hard to do that while keeping her on display, and for who?

Declan tilted his head as he watched her. Someone had wrapped her in a pink and purple blanket that looked as soft as a kiss and was the size of a spiderweb, and planted a knitted hat the size of a teacup on her head. God. That was full term? She'd barely had any weight to her, when he'd held her.

And to have all that hair, a lock of it stubbornly sliding out from beneath the brim of that hat. As far as he could tell she'd fallen asleep while chewing her fist.

They'd told him he could hold her. He wanted to. Thing was, if he let himself do that, he wasn't any too sure he'd be able to let go.

Only a few days ago he'd have kept his distance. Done the smart thing.

The best-laid plans, indeed.

Declan blew out a breath and shook his head, grateful when movement to the right caught his eye. As small as St. Hawk's was with regard to patient capacity, they did have a respectable handful of new parents who swore by the pair of comforting, comfortable middle-aged midwives on staff. Aside from a few athletic mothers to be, Declan didn't get involved much in that end of the business. He didn't recognize any of the new fathers or partners crowded around the glass, but the looks of shell-shocked awe made his mouth change its shape into a small smile.

One thing about being quiet—it made people-watching all kinds of interesting, when they forgot you were there.

Two men took front and center. Must have been a bumper crop last night, Declan thought as he nursed his coffee. One of them looked almost too young to be a father, but there was no mistaking that particular expression on a man's face. One part awed, one part terrified, one part 'just got slapped in the face with a mackerel'. His hair stood out at crazy angles, as if he'd had something sticky on his fingers when he'd run his hands through the tangled mess.

Another, a calmer sort of guy—probably his second or third time around the block—chuckled at the gobsmacked young man. "Your first?"

Odd Hair Day covered his mouth when he laughed. "Is it that obvious?"

Calm and Cool thumped his shoulder companionably. "Little bit. Which one is yours? See right there, straight ahead, that's my newest boy. My wife says she's not building me a baseball team, and if the next one's not a girl she'll buy a pair of hedge clippers from the general store and settle the matter herself."

Declan hid his grin in another sip of coffee. He'd slept in, nearly till ten a.m., and he wasn't accustomed to taking in the world quite this clearly. Seemed like it'd been months since he'd gotten a decent night's sleep.

He'd been missing out.

"That one's mine," the younger man said, gazing at another pink-filled bassinet. The slightly crazed panic in his face slowly faded from wild to delighted. "She looks like her mother. Lucky kid."

Declan studied the foundling, still sucking on her fist. Her tiny legs kicked idly beneath the blanket. *Who do you look like? Who will you be?*

He both was and wasn't surprised when Isaac stepped into place beside him. No idea where he'd come from—the man could move as quietly as a mouse when it suited him—but he carried with him that same sense of assurance, as if wherever he went, that was where he belonged. "How's she doing?"

"Healthy," Declan said. "Surprisingly so. She's a tough cookie."

"She's beautiful," Isaac said, tapping one finger lightly against the glass. He looked fascinated. "I didn't realize they lost that wrinkled look so fast."

Declan swatted his hand away. He wasn't wrong. She might not have been in the spotlight, but their foundling was as pretty as a doll. "Stop that. You'll wake them all up, and besides, they're not fish in an aquarium."

A warm roll of low laughter made him look up. Odd Hair had wandered off, but Calm Guy had lingered on. "You two are cute, man," he said, giving them a thumbs up. "She's a lucky little lady to have the both of you for her daddies."

Isaac and Declan weren't so much as touching elbows, but Isaac would have sworn he could *feel* Declan tensing up. He shook his head minutely and said to the new father, "Thank you."

Declan shot him a narrow-eyed look, but didn't make a fuss until the man had exited stage left. "Why did you do that?" he asked in an undertone. "She isn't ours."

"One, he didn't know any better. Two, he meant well. Three, we're not on duty. Neither of us have our doctor coats on. She isn't officially our patient."

"But—" Declan bristled over the idea that he lacked reason or right to keep watch over their foundling.

Which, in Isaac's opinion, was worlds better than refusing to even ask a nurse about her. "I know. We're invested. But do you really want to explain to strangers why we're hanging out at the nursery?"

Declan's expression shifted subtly from annoyed to resigned. "I know what you're doing. You're trying to get me to stake a claim."

"Good. There's hope for you yet." Isaac grinned at him. "Have you had lunch yet?"

Okay, sometimes it might be too easy, but Isaac hadn't stopped enjoying a good pull to Declan's pigtails. So to speak. Declan held his paper cup up with an inquisitive shake that sent coffee sloshing against its sides. "This is breakfast."

"It's nearly one o'clock," Isaac said. His stomach rumbled in secondary agreement. "You've been standing here for almost an hour. If you haven't eaten yet, you're going to."

Declan started to argue—but he stopped when Isaac put a hand on his shoulder, deliberately atop a spot he knew he'd left a mark on the night before, and squeezed. *Then* his mouth shut with a snap and his cheeks bloomed pink.

Unexpected, with everything it entailed, but Isaac wasn't above taking advantage. "There's a new food truck down on the street. Asian fusion. If you've never had it, you'll love it, and I'm buying. Follow me."

The one thing Isaac didn't love about buying from a food truck was, often, a lack of definite seating. Still, the low wall that lined the sidewalk on Hawk Drive would do. Plenty wide enough for the pair of them, and out of the way of foot traffic to boot. With most of the snow melted and surfaces dried, the cold wasn't so bad that he couldn't enjoy being out of doors.

What he *did* love about street food was everything else.

Isaac cradled a wax-paper basket in one hand, filled to the brim with spicy peanut rice that seared his nose when he took a test sniff. Chunks of chopped nuts, bright green scallions and sesame seeds made it as good to look at as it tasted. Declan had ordered lemongrass chicken and smoked tea noodles gamely enough, though he kept prodding the noodles suspiciously.

"Plenty of room," Isaac said, gesturing to the wall beside him. "Feel free to help yourself."

Declan didn't take him up on the offer right away. "You're sure? I'm not much good for company right now."

"Somehow, I like you anyway. You already know that. Unless we're pretending last night didn't happen? I wouldn't mind convincing you again that we're actually almost friends now. Especially the final act." He waggled his eyebrows and his chopsticks at Declan.

"Oh God," Declan said with a wince and a badly hidden light of humor flashing briefly over his face. "If I sit, will you stop that?"

"Maybe. Come and find out."

Declan shook his head, but he dusted off a section of wall and took a careful seat. "You're trouble, aren't you?"

"You have no idea."

"I think I have *some*." Declan sighed as he slid his chopsticks free of their paper wrapper. "Pretending last night didn't happen? No. I'm not that good, or that bad, depending on your point of view. But what are we now? That's what I can't figure the answer for."

Fair enough. "What are we?" Isaac tried a morsel of peanut. *Mmm*. Salty, sweet, spicy. "Honestly?" he asked after chewing and swallowing. "Aside from 'probably are actually friends' instead of 'possibly could be', I have no idea."

Declan made a huffing noise. "At least you're honest, I'll give you credit for that."

"Even so." Isaac tried a second bite of rice and crunched down on a hidden pepper. He yelped and fanned his mouth, while Declan rolled his eyes and offered him the bottled water he'd bought to go with his meal. Isaac took a hearty gulp and said, with the clarity that pain sometimes brought, "So maybe neither of us are what we are now. But do you think we could agree to be just this while we're figuring it out?"

"Depends," Declan said. The corner of his mouth lifted. "What's 'this'?"

"Shut up and eat your food before it gets cold, wiseass."

"Aha. *This*," Declan said. He dug his chopsticks into his noodles. "And that. Before I commit myself, what's the likelihood again that it'll kill me?"

"Low probability of stealth peppers."

"Comforting," Declan said, drier than old bones.

Isaac laughed quietly to himself as he sat and, with a contented noise, dug in. He wasn't sure he'd like canoodling and crooning with anyone else half so much as he loved trading jabs with Declan. With a contented noise, he dug in to his lunch.

"Son of a—"

He looked up, and laughed, at Declan. Apparently the man couldn't work a pair of chopsticks to save his life. "Hold them from the..." Isaac motioned in mid-air. "Or use a fork. There's no shame in it."

"Says you. It's personal now." Declan glowered at the utilitarian balsa wood disposables.

"Then keep on trying. But like this, not that." Isaac showed him again, leading by example, and moaned at the explosion of taste and flavor when it hit his tongue.

Declan tapped his chopsticks together like castanets or a ruler against a blackboard. "See, now. If you keep making sex noises at your food, I'll start to feel unnecessary."

Isaac very nearly snorted rice up his nose. Laced with liquid napalm as this was, he devoutly thanked his lucky stars that hadn't happened. "Food doesn't give blow jobs. You're safe. And by the way, does your definition of 'this' and 'that' include your coming to my place again tonight? If it doesn't, see above re — willingness to convince you."

Declan's face was dark pink, but pleased, as he bent his attention to his food. "It might," he said. "If you play your cards right. Or you could come to mine instead."

Nice.

Isaac waited for him to successfully wrangle a bite of noodles before he spoke up again. "One thing I always wondered about you. Why sports medicine?"

"Huh?" Declan nearly lost the noodles balanced on his chopsticks, and made a small, triumphant noise when they stayed put. "Nice try, Isaac. Come again?"

"Uh-huh. Funny guy." Isaac flicked a spicy peanut missile at him, which Declan batted away with his free hand. *Nicely done.* "Why sports medicine?" he asked. "I'm not asking with any kind of agenda. I'm just curious. Always have been."

Declan frowned, as if this was one of the odder questions Isaac had ever tossed his way. "You have met me, right? Occasionally we cross paths in the mornings, that kind of thing." He shrugged. "I love to run."

"That's it?"

"Should there be more?" Declan successfully transferred noodles to mouth, then clacked his chopsticks together. "Running makes me happy." He sobered as he spoke, taking the question seriously, and Isaac liked him all the better for it. "There was a good long while there when nothing else did. I wanted to do something with my life that I knew I would enjoy. It isn't hard."

No... It wasn't, was it?

"I think I envy you that," Isaac said. "No, really. I do. Although I admit I'm kind of at a loss here. I was expecting some backstory about tearing a tendon when you were fifteen or something."

Declan snorted. "Again—you have seen me run, right?"

"Fair enough." That'd gone well. Better than Isaac had expected. Why not push his luck? "One more question for you."

Declan shot him a sideways look that was equal parts resignation and wariness. "And that is?"

Isaac would have held his breath, if he hadn't needed it to speak with. "I mentioned foster parenting last night. Have you given that any more thought today?"

Yep. Pretty much what he'd expected Isaac to come out with. Declan sighed as he wedged his chopsticks into the noodles and set them aside.

At his side, Isaac looked as much like the earnest Boy Scout he was at heart as he ever had. An intense kind of guy, wasn't he? "I'm not asking out of curiosity," he said. "I do have an agenda this time."

"Again, with the honesty," Declan commented. He folded his arms. To him, Isaac had the look of a man who wasn't going to stop before he'd gotten through the entirety of his prepared speech. He'd seen that look a few times in his life. For once, he found himself curious about what a lecturer had to say. "I'm listening."

Good thing, too. Isaac blinked, as if surprised that Declan had given in, but was quick to pounce on his advantage. "I know it isn't tactful, given what you shared with me. But I'm asking because I want to know how you feel about it. No jokes. Just the truth."

Hmm. "Why?" Declan asked, deliberately not giving anything away.

"Because..." Isaac floundered momentarily. He lifted his chin when he recovered. "If I'd had a camera, I would've taken a picture of you standing at the nursery window, watching her. Because of the way you held her in your apartment, waiting for the ambulance to come. Because I know you remember what I said about the way you care. And because that guy who spoke to us wasn't wrong. Any kid would be lucky to have you as a father."

"Foster father."

"Caretaker," Isaac countered. "Guardian. I think you have a lot to offer, Declan. Maybe more than you're willing to admit, and not everyone is going to go after you with a nutcracker and a pair of tongs the way I do."

"Nice choice of imagery."

"You know what I mean." If Isaac had worn glasses, he'd have pushed them up his nose with one finger in his eagerness to make his point. Declan just knew it. He'd have trouble reconciling this version of Isaac with the one who'd taken control so ably the night before if it didn't all dovetail just *so* with the rest of the man's passions. "Just think about it. And come to my place tonight, because I don't know about you but I missed my workout run this morning, and I have a hell of a lot of adrenaline to work off now. Wonder why."

Declan couldn't help it. He tipped his head back and laughed out loud.

Isaac laughed too. He knocked shoulders with Declan. "That's a good look for you. Do it again sometime."

"I make no promises."

"Then I'll make it happen," Isaac threatened-slash-promised.

He probably would, too. Declan's chest warmed in time with the tips of his ears. If he wasn't careful, he could fall for a guy like Isaac all too easily.

Assuming, of course, that he hadn't already.

He checked to see if Isaac had noticed, but he'd already moved on, attention distracted by the sight of Dr. Gabriel returning from lunch out. "Or you could start small. Start from a place you're mostly familiar with. Dr. Gabriel's been trying to get you to participate in that family medicine committee for how long, now? Next thing we know he's going to start passing notes."

"Will you work with me? Check yes or no," Declan said. He could see where this was going now, and it ought to be good.

Isaac waved to Dr. Gabriel. The older man tossed Isaac a wave in return, but didn't break his stride or let his focus swerve overly much from the tablet in one hand and mobile phone in the other.

Mr. Multitasking at work, ladies and gentlemen, Declan mused, amazed. He cupped his hands around his mouth and shouted, "Hey! What time's the core meeting today, again?"

"Three thirty, I think," Dr. Gabriel called back. Without his taking off the sunglasses he wore, no one would technically be able to tell if he'd blinked or not, but he gave a good impression of not batting an eyelash over the question.

Isaac's jaw dropped.

Declan tapped it with his forefinger. "Close it up before you catch flies. Nan Rose used to tell me that all the time," he said in an undertone – then, to Dr. Gabriel, called, "Save me a seat if I'm late."

"Bring me a coffee and I'll think about it," Dr. Gabriel called back, tossing a thumbs up to him.

Declan pretended great innocence in the face of Isaac's questioning glower. "So I might have forgotten to tell you about that."

Isaac's punch to the arm landed almost exactly where and when Declan had thought it might. "And how long were you planning on keeping that secret?"

"Truthfully? Always. But families do sports too, let me remind you."

"Son of a gun." That sounded almost admiring. When Declan checked sideways, he saw that it had been. "You sneaky dog."

And Declan almost – basked. He allowed himself a broad, quiet grin instead, then dug into his pocket and brought out his secret weapon. "Here. It's a good way to work off extra energy mid-day. Ever played?"

Isaac wrinkled his nose at the crocheted beanbag. Declan would allow him that. Its grubbiness confirmed the frequency of its use. "Hacky sack? Seriously?"

"I have layers." Declan pushed off the wall, and tossed the ball from hand to hand. "Layers like an onion."

"Ahh. So that's why you tend to make people cry. Now it's all making sense," Isaac said as he followed Declan, his curiosity visibly leading him by the nose. "You carry that around with you all the time?"

"Most of the time. Otherwise I leave it in my locker. And I take it that's a *no, I haven't played*. I'll teach you."

Isaac frowned down at his brogans. "How much damage does it do?"

"Not enough to cry about. Come on. You can't work at this hospital and not play hacky sack." Declan feinted the ball at him, feeling his sideways, crooked smile growing wider than usual. "Unless you don't think you can keep up with me."

Isaac's head came up like a shot. "Oh, now it's *on*."

* * * *

Hot and sweaty, but not bothered by it, Isaac waited for Declan to disappear back inside St. Hawk's before he took one last look around the now quiet sidewalk backed by evergreen bushes. He'd hoped that their silent observer would slip up and let him get a good look. No such luck. A time or two he could have sworn he'd felt someone watching, but nothing more.

Which didn't give him license to give up. Isaac felt in his pocket for the folded square of paper he'd scribbled on before going to find Declan. Its edges had rounded from being carried, but it would still be readable. He slid it between two cracks in the wall, where it waved like a quiet white flag.

There wasn't much in there. A name, a contact number. If all they wanted was to know their baby was well and being cared for, at least he could provide them that much. If he could ask them why they'd done it—just so he could understand—then all the better.

And if they never said anything to him at all, then at least he'd tried. But he couldn't not try. It wasn't who he was.

Declan would understand that. Surely.

* * * *

Declan stood alone at the nursery window. All exhausted new parents had succumbed to the temptations of an afternoon nap, he supposed, and just when the babies were waking up. Though as he understood it, that would be pretty much par for the course for the next year or so of their lives.

Their foundling waved her fists above her, utterly fascinated by the mittens someone had dressed her in.

Declan resisted the urge to tap on the glass. Isaac and his power to influence people, hell. "You think I could do it?" he asked her, wondering if she would recognize his voice if he did hold her after all. "What if I tried? You think I should?"

She didn't answer. She was less than a week old. He hadn't expected it.

But in a way, that was his answer. Someone that new needed someone who'd been around the block a few times to take them under his protection. She could do worse. So could he.

Maybe he could name her Naomi.

Isaac would never let him hear the end of it if and when he found out, but... Declan thought he'd be able to live with that.

"Okay," he said out loud. "All right. But only for you."

Here we go.

* * * *

That night, instead of turning left out of St. Hawk's Drive, Declan turned right.

And took himself to Isaac's house.

The stubborn—very dear—punk had left a light burning for him, after all.

Chapter Seven

"Give me your hands."

Declan let Isaac take them both. He lowered his head to rest on his elbow, the bend slick with sweat and almost fever-warm. His lips parted with the effort to draw in enough air, his shoulders rose and fell, and his cock hung heavy between his thighs. He watched with one eye half open as Isaac lifted his hands and arranged them on the headboard of his bed. They'd both turned so that they faced the wall, the back view of them observable, as if putting on a show for an invisible audience. It almost embarrassed Declan, but at the same time it lit a fire in him. Made him harder, hotter, more willing.

This was the fourth time he'd spent the night at Isaac's home. Fifth, if he counted the first night of snow, and he preferred to. Almost three weeks had gone by since then. He'd done his best to keep it in check, not to push the boundaries more than either of them could manage—and arranging a booty call wasn't the easiest with a doctor's schedule—but when he needed this, truly needed it, Isaac never made a big to-do about his just—showing up.

Nor had he put up a fight about not being invited back to Declan's home yet. Sometimes Declan thought Isaac understood more than was good for either of them. Sometimes, though, he just wanted to mutter a *thank you*.

Isaac tested his grip with a gentle tug on each wrist. "Think you can hold on?"

"Going to make me wish I could let go?"

"I'll do my best. God, you're gorgeous," Isaac said behind him. He thrust up with three fingers, curling them inside Declan.

"Says the man—*oh*—about to get laid."

"Damn right."

Isaac slid his fingers out, and slapped Declan's hip. Declan might have had something to say about that if he hadn't heard the unmistakable crinkling sound of a condom wrapper as a follow-up. He bowed his head with relief and canted his hips up. "About time, too."

"Greedy, greedy bottom." Isaac delivered a love tap to his ass. "Sexy bottom. Sweet as peaches."

"Shut *up* and fuck me."

Isaac laughed. *Smug so-and-so.* He loved tweaking Declan's chains until Declan forgot himself and growled at the man, and Declan...

Well. Declan wasn't about to say no.

But what exactly do you think he'd say if you told him you were in love with him?

Declan groaned and thumped his head forward.

Isaac caught him before he did any damage. "Hands where I can see them," he said in chiding, readjusting Declan's grip. "Focus on me. Just me. Tell me if you're ready."

Declan rolled his shoulders, doing the best he could to let go of the tautness he'd carried around. At least he had good reason. Later that day, he had an appointment scheduled to discuss becoming a foster parent and his possible fitness—or lack thereof—for the job. *No pressure, right?* The way Declan saw it, that'd put any man on edge.

It was fitting, somehow, to come to Isaac for the medicine he needed.

He hissed as Isaac pressed his cockhead between the cheeks of his ass. Slick enough, open enough, he knew that the man could slide home without any teasing— but tease he did, nudging himself an inch in, and back out. He made shushing noises and stroked Declan's sides, then pressed his mouth to Declan's shoulders and bit at the skin below his nape.

Declan groaned in protest. "Do it right, or not at all."

"Is that you saying 'please'?"

"It's saying 'do it before I flip you over and fuck *you*', is what it's saying. I'm saying. Damn it, Isaac—"

He'd never laughed while being fucked, before Isaac. He'd had no idea what it was like for laughter to be choked off into a moan that came core-deep out of him, or how *different* it was to feel the same rippling through Isaac and to him. They stopped when he'd seated himself, his chest snugged up skin to skin with Declan's back.

Declan's fingers creaked from holding on to the headboard, but he turned to lift his chin at Isaac as best as he could. "Is that—all you've got?" he asked, knowing a fierce grin had stretched his lips wide. "You can do better."

Isaac showed teeth in *his* grin. "I know I can." He thrust deep, jolting Declan forward with a gratified moan. "Hold on tight, Declan. See if you can keep up."

Declan rolled his neck. *I love him*, he thought. *Love him, love him…*

But what do I do about it?

* * * *

Isaac lifted his face to the sky above them. The last of the most recent snowfall had nearly melted, and if the sun kept beating back the clouds, they might get away with a winter-green weekend for once. "Don't laugh at me," he said without looking at Declan. "I can feel you holding the snark back."

"I wasn't saying a word."

"Uh-huh." Isaac nudged him gently in the side. His friend, no 'almost' about it anymore, and his — his —

Well. Right there was where his brain seemed to stall these days.

He sighed and opened his eyes reluctantly. "Feels good, is all," he said. "We both need the Vitamin D, since we've been missing out on a good half of morning runs."

"And whose fault is that?" Declan asked, cocking his head.

"No idea." Isaac checked his watch. "What time's your meeting with the Department of Child Services, again?"

Declan visibly winced. "Four." He lifted his head. "I'm ready."

Was he? Possibly. He'd been doing better about it since the crash and burn when he'd first gotten an email from the department asking for a conference, but Isaac had to remind himself that 'better' was something of a sliding scale for Declan. It had a tendency to veer toward 'worse' when he remembered that he'd managed to insult the initial social worker on the case.

But if he managed this... It'd change their lives, wouldn't it? His too. He couldn't imagine Declan would shut him out. He'd need help more than ever, and Isaac meant to be the one there to give it to him. Anything he needed. Or even anything he wanted. He'd let Declan poke fun at his lack of baby-wrangling skills with no complaints, and encourage Declan to teach him. And when he needed to wind down, Isaac could do that for him too.

He'd spent most of his adult life being useful to those who asked for his help. One doctor among many. Funny how good it felt to, for once, be *necessary* to someone who needed what he, and only he, could give.

It could become an addiction, and fast.

"Four," he said with a nod. "Okay. Call me after it's over, no matter what happens."

Declan wrinkled his nose. "Could be they just want me to fill out some more paperwork," he said, making a poor job of faux diffidence. "It's probably nothing."

Isaac raised one shoulder. He nodded at Dr. Gabriel as their colleague passed them on the opposite crosswalk, and—thank God—waited for Declan to look away before he shot Isaac a double thumbs up. How domesticated they must look, the pair of them.

And that wasn't a bad thing, was it?

Who would have thought I'd fall in love with him? Not me. And yet, here we are.

I wonder if he could ever fall in love with me?

Hard to tell, and Isaac wasn't in any hurry to push that particular button. Too much at stake to rush in where angels feared to tread.

On the other hand...

Declan had hunched his shoulders as he walked, glaring down at the pavement. Worried. Isaac could interpret the various shades of Declan's moods now, and knew the signs of a deep and intense brood coming on.

"Hey. Listen to me." Isaac took hold of the back of Declan's head, both holding his attention and cradling his skull. He bent forward to brush his lips against Declan's, and chuckled at how adorably dumbstruck Declan looked afterward. "Don't worry so much. All right? It'll be okay. I promise."

Declan licked his lips once, as if chasing after Isaac's kiss. The side of his mouth lifted. "The way you say that, you know... I almost want to believe you."

"Good." Isaac kissed him once more, for luck. "Do."

He checked the wall bordering the sidewalk as Declan stiff-upper-lipped his way toward St. Hawk's to put in half a day's shift. They likely wouldn't meet again before the evening, but that was all right.

The notes he left there for his silent observer kept disappearing.

Including the one from last night, asking them to meet with *him* today. Time for answers, Isaac thought. With luck, he might finally get some.

* * * *

Four o'clock came. Four o'clock went. At fifteen minutes till the hour, the social worker — Connor, of course it was — blew past with his arms loaded full of files and opened his office doors to Declan. The kid looked more exhausted than some women who'd just been through labor and delivery, which a philosophical man might say was more or less the definition of the job on a daily basis.

Connor gestured at the office. "Well?"

Great start, Declan thought as he followed the social worker.

It'll be okay, Isaac had said. And Declan had listened to him.

But he had a sinking feeling that it wouldn't be okay at all.

Seated in a straight-backed desk chair too small for him, with one rickety leg, Declan stared at Connor. Who stared back at him. He looked painfully young and hip with his odd cat's-eye glasses, but his cluttered office showed the signs of someone doing a man's job. Every surface was jammed with folders and files, crayon drawings and finger-paintings, schedules and dossiers and overflowing in-trays. The walls boasted a clock almost as bad as the one in the St. Hawk's cafeteria.

Tick. Tock. Tick. Tock.

Connor had a singular gift for not blinking.

Declan gave first. "I'm not good at apologizing," he said.

Connor didn't bat an eyelash. "Is this you trying to do that? Because if so you get full points for intention, but your follow-through is a little lacking."

Declan rubbed at his face and sighed. Thing was, in a different life he'd have adored this kid. Tough and clever were his favorites. He could just hear Isaac now — *the power of sass is strong with this one. You do realize you have a type, Declan?*

"This is me trying to try," he said. "Does that count in my favor or against it?"

Connor folded his hands beneath his chin. "Mmm... I'd say it sets you back to neutral. Neither good nor bad. Can you live with that?"

Which was better than the alternative, Declan supposed. He tried shifting his weight in the chair and grabbed at its pointy arm when it gave an alarming creak. A slight soreness, the reminder of how he'd spent his morning trying to overcome his nerves, made him wince.

Connor noticed. Of course he did. One neatly shaped eyebrow went up, and the other side of his mouth lifted.

Kill me now. "You got my application," Declan said. "I mean, did you get my application?"

"You're not here to discuss the stock market," Connor said.

And nothing else.

Declan wanted to tap his foot. He restrained the urge. Partly because he felt fairly certain it wouldn't count in his favor. Partly because he had no idea when the chair would give way, but odds were it'd be sooner than later. "And?"

Connor exhaled heavily and sat back in his chair. "And I wanted to know if you were serious."

A pulse of hope tickled in the pit of Declan's stomach. "Very."

"Okay," Connor said, not giving anything away. "Why?"

What? "Why, what?" Declan asked, the hope dying away as quickly as it'd come. He knew that tone of voice. The slow no. The kind denial. Still, he pushed the line he'd drawn in the sand. "I don't understand the question."

"Tell me why you want to be a foster parent," Connor returned with a shrug that didn't fool Declan. There was nothing casual at all about his narrow-eyed focus. "Do you want to do this in general, or just for this one little girl? Do you feel a sense of responsibility, or of guilt?"

Declan tightened his hold on the rickety arms of the chair. "She's not mine by blood. I don't know how many times I have to say that. But I could be a family for her. I want to be. She deserves a chance. That's your 'why'."

He wasn't sure how he could tell, but he had the strongest sense that hadn't been the right answer. He was certain of it when Connor picked up a manila folder to tap against his desk. "You were pretty forthcoming when you made your application, especially the personal essay you included. I appreciate the effort. I'm less thrilled with your suggestion that all foster homes are the armpits of society. No, don't interrupt. Do you know how hard it is to do this job, especially when you care?"

Maybe not, but he had an idea. Declan leaned more heavily into the chair, his shoulders slumping — but he didn't apologize. "People are people," he said. "I know there's good out there along with the bad, but in my life experience there's more bad than good. I'd rather she didn't have to go through what I did. I want to keep her safe."

A flash of a smile passed over Connor's lips. Had that been the *right* answer? Declan growled internally. Swear to God, he'd never understand guys like him, not even the ones he liked or could have liked.

"Okay," Connor said, dropping the folder flat on top of a pile of battered envelopes. "Honesty is always the best policy. So I'll ask you to keep that in mind when I tell you that at this time, I don't think we can approve your application or allow you to take that baby home with you."

He'd expected it. He had. It still hit like a baseball bat to the gut.

"And it has nothing to do with us getting off on the wrong foot."

Declan couldn't quite see how it wouldn't, but...

"Did you know almost everything you're thinking is right there on your face?" Connor asked. "Not obviously, but once you learn the tells it's like having a master key code. Look, Doc. If you want the straight-up truth, here it is. I think you'd make a hell of a foster parent — *someday*."

"But not this day," Declan said. His fingertips were numb, as were his lips. Strange that he hadn't realized how much hope he'd built up before it went *pop*. "What am I doing wrong now?"

"Right now? Nothing. Except for keeping a house like a monastic cell. It's not a home. It's a prison cell, and I wonder if you realize that."

Declan kept his mouth shut.

Connor didn't let that stop him. "But there are things you could do, and should do. Take some classes in parenting. Fix up your house and make sure the yard is child-friendly. Adopt a dog from a shelter. Trust me, I know it's not the same but it's good to know just how much you can cope with. Look into all the furniture and accouterments a baby needs, and start a budget. Regulate your schedule. Volunteer with a boys' and girls' group. Get some *experience*."

Declan's temper burned with the indignity. "People with zero experience do this every day."

"Some do. Some of those end up here, because it's so much more of a commitment than the uninitiated think before it happens to them. You're a doctor, for crying out loud! You should know this. It changes your life. Full stop." Connor shook his head. "I'm not saying 'never'. I'm saying 'not now'. If you really mean it, then help me to help you, because as it stands all you've got is a pocketful of good intentions and a sixty hour work week average. At *minimum*. That's not the best thing for her right now. Am I getting through to you?"

The damnable thing of it was that—yes. Connor was. Yet even so, Declan had to swallow down a hard, spiky knot in his throat, and had to make an effort to unclench his hands.

Connor didn't back down from whatever look Declan must have given him.

Slowly, unwillingly, Declan made himself nod.

"Good," Connor said decisively, sitting forward. "Then that's a place where we can make a new start. Are you in?"

He understood where Connor was coming from. If it'd been anyone else, he'd have backed the guy's play.

But it wasn't anyone else. It was him, and a little girl he'd broken his own rules for.

Knowing that Connor was right didn't stop the understanding that he'd *lost* from tearing his heart down the middle, wide open and raw. A wound not even Isaac might be able to fix—and it was Isaac's fault for sowing the seeds in the first place.

* * * *

Six o'clock.

Isaac tapped the face of his watch then shook it gently next to his ear. Ticking away just fine. Silly to do that, though. The sun had just finished setting, and though a fresh batch of storm clouds covered the moon with silver billows, anyone with half a brain could make a reasonable guess that Declan's appointment was likely over and done with.

They said no news was good news. Isaac, stubborn in all things, refused to give up hope. Who knew? Maybe the paperwork was taking forever. Paperwork usually did. He should have done more research into the steps involved in becoming a foster parent. A twinge of guilt niggled at him. He really should have made more of an effort — there had to be something he could have done to help. He'd thought that letting Declan handle it all would serve as a sign of trust, but... *Hell.* Wouldn't be a surprise if Declan thought he wasn't all that concerned.

He should call. Wouldn't hurt anything, would it? Declan would have his phone turned off while in the meeting. If he didn't get an answer, that'd be something to build on.

But he left his phone in his pocket. The storm clouds had brought a strengthening wind with them, one that made him shiver and wrap his arms more tightly around his chest. It'd be sanity and reason to go inside, away from this, if he hadn't wanted to give his lurker just one more chance to show themselves —

He felt them before he saw them. A presence at his back.

"Declan?" he asked, just to be sure.

"No." The voice had a hoarseness to it that made it sound both young and indeterminate of gender. "Don't turn around. *Please* don't turn around."

Isaac's nerves tingled with uneasiness and the desire to disobey immediately. He gritted his teeth and made himself stay put. Just because he hadn't felt the tip of a knife tickle him yet didn't mean someone who sounded so desperate wouldn't go there. "All right," he said carefully, staring straight ahead. "I won't. I promise."

"I didn't want to," the person said. "I swear I didn't want to. She said if I didn't, she would. They'd have seen me at the hospital and they would know who she was because I'm always with her. I tried to leave her by the doctor's house, but I got it wrong. I'm not smart. I didn't mean to mess up—"

"It's okay." Isaac tried raising his hands, palms out, to show he meant no harm. "It's all right. We found her just the same, and she's going to be fine. She's going to have a good home. We'll take care of her. I promise."

"No. I mean, yes. Okay. That's good." The more they spoke, the more they sounded male. Young and male and terrified. Either damaged or developmentally delayed, but plenty sharp enough to understand consequences. "Is she like me?"

"I don't know what you're like," Isaac lied. "But she's healthy. I promise. She's had every test she can be given, and I saw her myself. She's going to grow up normal and happy and she'll be loved. Please believe me."

A long pause, then, "Okay," the boy said.

God, how old was he? No more than fifteen or Isaac would eat his hat. He'd buy a hat *then* eat it.

"Okay, that's—that's good. Don't turn around. *Don't* look at me. Stay there until I'm gone." The laugh he gave was bitter as dry almonds. "You'll know."

Isaac's pulse kicked up. "Let me try to help you," he said. "If you just give me a chance, I'll do what I can and you won't get in trouble."

The hesitation he'd hoped for didn't come. "I said *don't*," the boy barked, and shoved Isaac with surprising strength, knocking him forward. Startled,

Isaac hit the pavement, breaking his fall with his palms at the last second. Before he could so much as get to his feet, he heard the rustling clamor of awkward footsteps over grass, diving into the bushes that ringed St. Hawk's.

"Damn it!" Isaac swore. His knee twisted when he tried to put weight on it, and he barked out another obscenity. Messed that up good, hadn't he?

He'd...

He blinked, oddly dizzy.

He didn't see the blood until it fell in crimson drops in front of him.

Messed up, indeed, he thought. *Damn.*

Chapter Eight

"What the hell happened to you?" Declan stopped before he'd fully walked through his own front door, leaving his keys forgotten in the lock. He'd given Isaac a spare key to keep on hand, but they always ended up at Isaac's place instead of here. Finding him there now, without warning, was a surprise.

Isaac stood over his sink with the water running full blast over his hands. He grimaced at Declan's question. "I'm an idiot."

"No kidding. Is that blood?" Declan jerked his keys free of the lock, tossed them aside, and shut the door behind him with a shove of one foot. Instinct, whether good or bad, could be a bitch of a thing. He reacted as he would to any patient, the doctor half of his brain propelling him forward to take Isaac's hands by the wrists and examine them.

Isaac sighed and tried to withdraw his hands. "It's not that big a deal. I think they're just scraped halfway to hell and back."

"For starters, maybe." Declan wasn't going to let him get away that easily. He turned Isaac's hands gently over for a close inspection on both sides of each. The backs weren't bad. The palms, though... Scuffs, scrapes and one cut that looked like it might need a stitch or two. Declan frowned. "Did you fall?"

Isaac's hesitation at the question set warning bells clamoring in the back of Declan's head. "Yes."

What wasn't he saying? Declan narrowed his eyes at Isaac. "Did you fall onto broken glass?"

Isaac all but chewed his lip. And he said Declan had a poor poker face! "I might have, yes. Only one piece of a bottle. It could have been worse."

"Could have been..." Declan mentally counted to ten. "You *are* an idiot. Stand there. Keep your hands under the water, and don't move."

"Where are you going?"

"First aid kit. Where did you think?" He hadn't *stopped* spoiling for a fight. Hell, he'd walked for nearly an hour trying to cool his head, and that hadn't done the job. Nor had the dark edge of anger at Isaac and his smooth tongue abated. If he hadn't listened, he wouldn't have gotten his hopes up. And if he hadn't started to hope, it wouldn't have mattered so much when the whole thing had gone up in smoke.

Maybe it wasn't all Isaac's fault, but there was enough lying at his doorstep to make Declan itch to shout at him.

Instead, he found his first aid kit, brought it back to the kitchen, and slammed it onto the counter.

Isaac, for once in his life, wisely had no comment. He'd done as he was told and only watched Declan with wide, uncertain eyes.

Declan groaned in frustration and rubbed his face too roughly for self-comfort.

"Declan..." Isaac started.

"Don't." Declan took Isaac's left hand, the one worst damaged, and turned it palm up. Stitches wouldn't hold well on a palm, and neither would a butterfly bandage. "Any allergies I should know about? Any problems with surgical glue?"

Isaac raised one eyebrow as quick as a gunshot. "What are you doing with surgical glue, Mr. Sports Medicine?"

"Kinky shit. What do you think? It's an emergency preparedness kit, so I'll take that as a 'No, no allergies' unless you correct me."

Isaac's lips twitched, though the rest of his expression remained both haunted and worried. "No allergies that I'm aware of."

"Good." Declan dried Isaac's hand, then began his work. It wouldn't take too long, but he used caution and worked slowly all the same. And as he did, asked, "Why are you here?"

"Ah… Long story."

"We've got time." Declan pressed the open edges of skin together on Isaac's palm and held them, waiting for the glue to seal. Inaction and silence wasn't Isaac's way. He was counting on that to work in his favor.

And it did. "It's established that I'm an idiot, right?"

Declan glanced up sharply. A sinking feeling formed in his stomach, a sensation that seemed oddly almost heavier than gravity. "What did you do?"

"I, um… Oh, fuck it," Isaac said, shoulders going loose with release of restraint. "You might as well know now instead of later. It's not something I should have kept from you in the first place. I had a run-in with the baby's father."

Isaac had expected that Declan wouldn't take it well. He hadn't expected that Declan would take it quite this badly. He dropped Isaac's hand like a hot potato wrapped in burning coals and took two steps back. The color had faded from his face, leaving his expression a wax mask.

"Let me explain." Isaac used his elbow to shut the spigot off. He didn't want to shout this over the racket of running water. "Because it might not be like you're thinking."

Declan gave a dry bark of a humorless laugh. "How can it not be exactly what I'm thinking?"

"Okay, fair point." Isaac started to run a hand through his hair, grimaced, and stopped. He hadn't meant to come to Declan's house. He had a first aid kit of his own stashed in *his* bathroom, and he was fully capable of cleaning up scrapes and scratches. To be honest, he hadn't fully comprehended his decision to go to Declan's instead of his own home before he was at the door.

Shock? Probably. A bad turn could do strange things to people.

Or possibly it was that he'd automatically gone somewhere *he* felt safe. Animals and people retreated to their dens when they were hurt.

In which case, Isaac decided his psyche had some definite issues.

He exhaled. "I've noticed someone watching me for a while now. They never approached, and I never got a look at their face, but they kept after me like a sniffer dog. I figured they wanted something they were afraid to ask for. It only started after we found the baby. It wasn't hard to put my finger on why."

Which was all true, but it didn't take a trained physician to be sure that Declan wasn't in love with this situation. His lips pressed together into a tight line, and a muscle in his jaw jerked.

Isaac hurried on before the storm he knew was coming could touch off. "I know, okay? I know. But what were my options? I thought maybe it was the mother! What was I supposed to do, tell the cops? The social workers?" Damn it, he'd almost forgotten about Declan's meeting. *It might still have gone all right*, he lied to himself. "I thought if I talked to them and promised them she was all right, that she'd be fine, it'd ease their minds. Give them some closure."

Declan's eyes had gone narrow. "Okay," he said. "And?"

"And? And nothing."

"Bullshit." Declan snapped the catches on the first aid kit closed with sharp precision, the plastic on plastic loud as firecrackers going off in his small kitchen. "See, I know you, you stubborn ass. So tell me, and *what* or I swear to God — "

"I wanted to know why they did it! Okay?" An accidental twitch pulled sharply on the glue in Isaac's palm. He hissed with the sting of pain and cradled his hand. God, he'd been a moron. Obsessed. He could see that clearly *now*. "I wanted to ask them what they were thinking. Why they didn't take her to a real safe haven. What makes a person act that way."

Anger glowed in the black depths of Declan's irises. "You could have gotten yourself killed."

"I know."

"And it's none — I mean, *none* — of your fucking business, Isaac. You know that."

He did. He could get his license revoked for less, and he knew it. He'd just gotten in too deep to remember it.

"What the hell were you thinking?"

"I wasn't," Isaac said, frustrated. "I was trying to help you."

There. The last bit that he had to offer.

The truth didn't set either of them free this time.

Declan shook his head. He took two more steps away from Isaac, widening the distance between them in more aspects than the physical. Isaac could feel his withdrawal, and almost hear the walls going back up. "Yeah. Maybe that's what you told yourself, but I know you. Remember? What you wanted was to figure out what made me tick. To figure out why my mother dropped me in a dumpster, and I told you that's not something I ever want to know. *Ever.*"

Isaac's heart sank at that, because he wasn't wrong, even if it'd taken him far too long to understand as much. "Okay," he said, hoping that surprise would give him an advantage. He'd take anything to stave off the 'get out' he could see shaping itself on Declan's lips. "For what it's worth, I'm sorry. Like you said, you know me. Did you think I would do any less when it came to helping you? I told you I would do anything, and I meant it."

"Yeah," Declan said, looking away. "Anything, no matter what. Thing is, Isaac, I don't know if I can live like that. You take too much."

"I give as much as I take," Isaac said. "Declan, please —"

He wasn't sure what he would have said next. He never had the chance to find out.

Declan's phone, tucked in his hip pocket, pealed out like a string of bells. There wasn't a question of not answering, Isaac knew. Not for doctors on semi-permanent call status, when they had patients whose lives depended on them. "I am so done, Isaac. Swear to God, I am a thousand percent done with — almost everything except this. We're not done here," Declan warned as he lifted the phone to his ear. "Dr. Day speaking. This had better be good."

Then he fell silent, listening to whoever had called him, and going paler than porcelain as they spoke.

"Declan?" Isaac asked, alarmed by the man's utter silence, and by the shock of pain that glanced over him. He wanted to shove his body up next to Declan's and give him something to lean on, only he was ninety-nine percent certain that Declan had meant 'finished with you' when he'd said 'I am so done' — fuck, that hurt — and on top of that would take his head off if he tried.

He almost did it anyway.

"What happened?" Isaac asked instead, giving Declan's shoulder a shake. "Talk to me. What's going on?"

* * * *

Isaac hunched into the deep, warm folds of his coat in the parking lot of St. Hawk's and thought to himself that he wasn't sure he could remember the last time he'd hoped so hard not to be right. For a doctor, that wasn't just whistling in the wind. He prayed for tests to be negative and suspicions unconfirmed on a weekly basis.

Never quite like this, though. Because this was Declan, and the worst possible thing.

I should have asked him how the meeting went. Or, no. I shouldn't have lied to myself. The second I saw him, I knew.

I didn't want to know. So I told myself I didn't.

How many other ways had he fooled himself — was still fooling himself?

Maybe Declan had the right idea to call them 'done'.

So help him God, the notion didn't sit right with Isaac. At all. Could be stubbornness. Might be a drop of sense for once in his life.

But he couldn't say anything then. Life worked that way sometimes.

Declan stood next to him, unmoving and unspeaking. The social worker—Connor, wasn't it?— bundled up to his nose, stood maybe four feet away and two across. He held a sheaf of paperwork in one arm, and a tablet in the other. Nurse Katie stood next to him, holding their foundling. Who would be leaving the hospital that night to go to her new foster family.

Not to Declan.

"I didn't tell you earlier because I didn't know earlier," Connor said. He looked tired, but resolute as he nudged his glasses back in place. "A place opened up for her this afternoon. I found out after you'd gone. It's a couple I've worked with before. They're good people, not just in it for the money, and they have a history of doing well with infants. They'll look after her like she was their own."

"And when she's not an infant anymore?" Declan asked. He might as well have been a statue.

Only Isaac saw the bunch and curl of Declan's fists, even tucked away as they were in his coat pockets. He crossed his fingers, whispered a half-formed prayer, and stepped sideways, closer to Declan. Close enough for their shoulders to touch. Whether Declan liked it or not, Isaac was and always would be there for him.

"When she's not an infant, then maybe she'll have someone to adopt her," Connor said. He gave Declan a speaking look that Isaac wasn't sure Declan noticed. "Just give that some thought, okay?"

Declan's jaw worked, as if he were biting down on iron. He said nothing.

Connor sighed. "We need to go. It isn't good for her to be out in the cold. If you want to say goodbye, then this is your chance."

And there it was. The reason he'd called, the reason that Declan had taken on the look of a man who'd been shot but hadn't fallen yet, and the reason that Isaac had rushed over to St. Hawk's with him.

Partly so he could watch Declan's back. Only partly.

The rest was so he could do *this*.

Carefully but firmly, he placed a hand at the small of Declan's waist and nudged him forward. "Go on," he said when Declan glared at him. He knew the dark looks for what they were now. A plea for help. "If you don't, you're going to regret it for the rest of your life."

Declan's throat jerked as he swallowed. "If I hold her now, I don't know if I can make myself let go," he said, low and raw.

Isaac didn't let himself budge. "Then I'll help you."

"Fuck," Declan said under his breath. He scrubbed at his eyes. "Okay. Let me have her, just for a minute."

Connor mouthed a silent *thank you* to Isaac as Katie eased the baby into Declan's arms. Isaac nodded back, saying nothing out loud.

Let Declan have his moment.

Isaac's heart ached at the sight. Unless caught up in a competition, Declan wasn't and never would be a man for overblown displays. A person had to know him to speak his language. Isaac could read volumes in the careful positioning of his arms, the twitch of his lips, and the focus of his stare at the infant's face. She blinked up at him, curious and content as so new a human could be, and waved one mittened hand outside her swaddling blanket. Katie exchanged a glance with the social worker and stepped away, giving them some privacy.

Isaac promised himself he'd buy her flowers for that later.

Declan let the tiny mittened hand smack against his palm. "Be good," he said, so quietly that Isaac almost didn't hear. "Be a good girl, Naomi. Live a good life. Be happy. Okay?"

The baby—*Naomi*, and even if it wasn't on her birth certificate it *was* her name now—made a quiet babbling noise and produced something almost like a smile.

Not even Isaac could interpret Declan's reaction to that.

"I hate my job just about as much as I love it," Connor said quietly to Isaac. "He'd be a good father if he was ready for such a big step. He just needs to come into his own."

"I know," Isaac said. "And I'll help him get there."

"Oh yeah?" Connor eyed him. "I thought so. You two are something to each other, aren't you?"

Isaac nodded. "We're—something, all right."

"Okay." As if that cinched some decision for him, Connor folded his glasses and hooked the earpiece over his collar, then held out the sheaf of paperwork. "That's why I'm going to give you these, and not him. It's all the information prospective adopters need. Don't let him quit. Understand?"

Isaac took the paperwork, and tucked it under his arm. "Never have before," he said. "And never will."

Which answered that question. He and Declan weren't done with each other yet.

As long as Declan would let that happen, that was.

When the social worker's van pulled away, Naomi strapped into a snug car seat, there was a moment's silence in the parking lot of St. Hawk's that seemed to Isaac somehow redolent of Bethlehem. Of tired shepherds slouching down dirt roads with their hands in their pockets and the collars of their jackets turned up to keep their ears warm.

"I'm sorry," he said. Blurted. Not smooth, so not smooth, but once begun he had no reason not to get it done. Not even if Declan *had* pinned him with a dark and warning glower. "I am. I know I messed up, and I know this looks hopeless, but there are things we can do. I'm still in it. If you want me to be. I want to be with you." He bit the inside of his cheek, a sharp stab that grounded him. "I love you."

Declan stared at him. He said nothing.

For a long damn minute, he said nothing.

Then, and still without a word, he turned his back on Isaac and walked away, walls like Jericho shooting up tall and standing starkly behind him.

Chapter Nine

Isaac would follow him. Declan knew he didn't have long. *Think fast, Doctor. Where are you going? What do you want?*

And so he didn't go far. Only to the edge of his block, not such a rough walk now that most of the last storm had melted and another had yet to truly sink its teeth in.

To the bushes. Springtime was *just* around the corner, but so far no signs of new growth or healing showed on the bush they'd disturbed to get at its strange fruit. Rumpled evergreen, a couple of cracked branches. Beneath that, a hollow just big enough for their foundling's box to fit.

Declan dropped to one knee and laid his palm flat on the bare earth, untouched by snow or melt. He'd be lying if he said he hadn't wanted to know, too. Apparently, Isaac was ballsy and brash enough to go there. Who would have thought he'd actually do it? Jesus.

And he did it for me. At least in part.

He'd be lying, again, if he didn't admit to himself that it was likely the larger part. Curiosity drove, but the heart compelled, that great big giant hero's heart that confused him but not as much as it awed him. Was there any challenge Isaac wouldn't stand up to?

Probably not. *He said he loves me.* Declan made a small noise of disbelief.

And I believe him.

Which means...

Well. *Think fast.*

You going to give up now? a warm, molasses voice demanded in his mind's ear. *Boy, I might not have raised you for long, but I raised you better than that. You are not a quitter and you never have been.*

Declan clenched his fists until the knuckles ached.

I don't think so, Nan Rose's voice scolded. *Don't you tell me this is the end of anything, baby. It's a new beginning. Now you get out there, and hit the ground running. Understand me?*

Slowly, finger by finger, his fists loosened. He took deep breaths of the crisply cold air that hit his lungs with the bracing ferocity of snow and wintergreen. His lips tingled, as if he'd just bitten into a leaf of spearmint.

He heard Isaac behind him, the only foot traffic on this road late at night.

Okay then.

Isaac knew how things stood — or thought he knew — when he laid eyes on Declan. He couldn't have said why. The set of his shoulders, or the lift of his head even though he didn't look back. Something about him. Ready to fight a different battle. One that put them squarely on the same side. Odds were he could trust his intuition. He'd known where to find Declan, after all.

But he had to be sure.

"Declan?" he called, as quietly as he'd coax a stray cat to his hand.

Declan made a noncommittal noise, but Isaac thought that he understood the man's meaning.

He crunched softly over the winter-dry grass and small weeds in the lawn to stand by Declan's side. Strange how small the hollow beneath the bush looked. Too little to contain a life, and too insignificant to hold as much meaning as it did.

"For what it's worth," Isaac said, "the baby's father told me he put her here so you would find her. He knew you were someone he could trust."

Which opened the door to so many questions. How did they know Declan? Did Declan know them? He must. Otherwise they would — could — have chosen any other doctor for the job, and they weren't exactly short on those in Blue Creek.

"He must have thought you were a good man," Isaac said thoughtfully. He tucked one hand in his pocket, and laid the other on Declan's shoulder. When Declan didn't shrug him off, he tried a light squeeze to Declan's arm. "So do I."

"Mmm," Declan said, gaze fixed on the hollow beneath the bush. "I love you too. Just so you know."

Once upon a long ago time, Isaac had tried to teach his nephews T-ball. One of them had belted him in the stomach with a giant Nerf bat and knocked the wind clean out of him. Didn't hurt, but dear God.

Declan's shoulders moved slightly with his nearly silent chuckle. "So I guess you didn't know."

"Not as such," Isaac said with a wheeze. "What—You—" He shook his head hard to clear it. "You mean that?"

"I do." Declan looked sideways, at him. All that focus just for Isaac. "I'm going to adopt her."

Hope licked at Isaac's heart. "I thought I'd have to talk you around to that."

"You're not the only one who can put up a fight," Declan said. He shivered once, but seemed stronger after it'd passed through him. "But I'm only good at fighting. Not so much at what comes next. I won't quit. But I need you to help me to not fail. Can you do that?"

Isaac exhaled with relief—and something more. "What do you think?" He took Declan's hand—and Declan let him. Twined his fingers with Isaac's. Isaac pressed his palm to Declan's and let his eyes close for a beat. When he opened them, Declan watched him at a tilted-head angle, a faint smile curving his mouth.

"All right?" Declan asked, tentative but willing, the start of a flame kindling brighter and hotter in his eyes, and a dark, appreciative edge to his gaze as he ran it over Isaac. "I'm in. Tell me you are, too. That's all I need."

A mouth like a kiss waiting to happen. Isaac made it happen. "All in," he said, knowing his words would be warm on Declan's cheek. "Look out, world. Let's see what we can make happen when we're officially on the same team."

* * * *

And so here we are.

Declan clicked the switch on his bedside lamp, finding it through sense memory and by touch. His eyes were closed, and his mouth occupied with kissing Isaac. Though Isaac had wanted to take Declan to his home, they'd been there a good half-dozen times since this whole affair started, and Declan wanted to see how Isaac looked in his bed.

Isaac hadn't even bothered to put up a fight.

I can live with that, Declan decided as Isaac opened his mouth for him, letting Declan slide his tongue inside. Warm, sweet lips—arms around his neck—his breathing short and shallow through his nose. Hard runner's legs and harder cock nudging up against Declan's stomach, next to his own. He took both shafts into one hand, and though he couldn't quite wrap his fist all the way around them alone, Isaac joined him and completed the circle.

Declan hissed with pleasure through lips that tingled from kissing. "Get naked, would you?"

"Oh, I see how it is now. The romance is gone."

"As long as it gets you naked faster."

Isaac swatted him, then pushed him lightly with one hand on his chest. "Get naked yourself, big man, and lie down. It's not a party of one we're talking about here. And the sooner there's no clothes in the way, the sooner you can fuck me."

When he put it that way…

Declan managed to get his sweater off and cast aside. He managed to kick his shoes off before he had to stop lest he lose his balance. With a growl, he thumped down on the bed, putting his back against the headboard and his legs on the mattress before him. *Finally!* A decent spot from which he could enjoy the show.

Good Christ, he loved the way Isaac stripped out of his clothing as casually, as carelessly, as if nudity had never bothered him a day in his life. Though leaner and narrower at shoulders and hips than Declan, his sensitive face set in serious thought, he would have knocked Declan's socks off if they hadn't already gone.

Also, that ass. Mmm. Declan whistled softly.

Isaac gave him an arch look. "Like what you see?"

"You know I do." Declan opened his jeans, but before he could do more than raise his hips, Isaac caught the cuffs at his ankles and pulled. "Helping me now?"

"It's a bad habit I seem to have developed." Isaac guided the jeans and boxers down Declan's hips and legs, all the way off, and tossed the lot behind him. He made a satisfied sound and dropped to his hands and knees on the mattress to crawl up to Declan and over him. He stopped when he'd braced himself four-square over Declan and grinned at him. "Hello."

"Hello, yourself," Declan said. He licked his lips. "Going to do something, or are you just hanging out?"

"Give me time," Isaac replied, studying him in that way of his. "I'm glad to be here. You scared me, earlier."

"I scared me," Declan admitted, tucking one hand beneath his cheek. "How do you know how to do that?"

"Do what?"

Declan felt himself go pink with embarrassment, warm and red as a rising sun, but he cleared his throat to speak and he didn't back down. "Find me. Follow me, and bring me back. Who taught you how to do that?"

"Nobody." Isaac touched Declan's cheek. "You're a good runner, but so am I. When you try to make a break for it, I give chase. That's who I am, which makes us both lucky. No arguments, and now pay attention. It's your turn to have me. Want to?"

"Oh yes. God, yes."

"Good." Isaac reached out a hand to rummage through the half-open bedside drawer. "Because I'm all yours."

Instead of handing Declan the tube of slick, almost full, that impatient son of a gun knelt over him, straddling his hips, and reached between his own legs.

Declan thumped his head hard against the bed when he realized what Isaac meant to do. "Fuck," he said shakily, reaching up to rest a hand on Isaac's stomach. "Fuck."

"Hmm," Isaac sighed. He tilted his head back and made another pleased sound, better than the first. "That's the idea. You like watching, too. This is for you."

"I don't know whether I want to thank you or wrestle you for that," Declan admitted. "Or turn you over my knee the next chance I get."

Isaac only laughed. "All of the above. You can't fool me anymore, Declan. You like me."

"I do, actually." Declan dragged a thumbnail over Isaac's nipple. God, the sight he made, working himself open with his own fingers. Imagining was almost better than doing it himself, especially when he had a front row view of the warm red flush spreading from cheeks to collarbone to navel, of the drops of sweat rising on Isaac's skin, of the way his cock jerked when he uncurled his fingers. "I really do."

"Good," Isaac said. He bowed forward as he took his hands away and wiped sticky lube on the sheets. Declan didn't care about that. He took Isaac's hips in his hands and held on, knowing what Isaac would want before Isaac had to ask.

And he'd guessed right. Slow, slow, but never stopping, Isaac sank down and took Declan inside him.

"God," Declan said, breathless still, when Isaac's hips were nestled against his groin. "What kind of crazy person…?" He stopped to laugh, a quick bark. "Look at you. Still on top."

"So I am, and you like it that way."

He did. He truly did.

When Isaac moved again—too soon, and not soon enough—he moved slowly still, and rode Declan as if they had all night. Declan found Isaac's hands and locked them together with his, each giving the other something to lean and push against, to brace and to battle at the same time. He couldn't raise his hips and fuck deep as much as he wanted, but Isaac knew how to ride a man. Gentle rocking, deep squeezing, and never a hand on himself. His mouth hung open, and his eyes fell nearly shut as he worked Declan's cock. Slow waves, long rushes, and coming with a groan that tumbled out of his lips.

He bent forward to kiss Declan when Declan swore, stuttered, and nearly stopped. Thrust his tongue between Declan's lips, filling him from both ends and taking as much as he gave, giving as much as he took.

"God," Declan said when Isaac lifted his head. His head swam, dizzyingly drunk on touch and sensation. "Are you trying to kill me?"

"Yes," Isaac said. "And no. You'd better stick around. I have plans."

"I bet you do."

"Mm-hmm." Isaac held still to let Declan slip out. He rolled his shoulders and sighed, then dropped down again to lie on Declan's chest, fully heedless of sweat and mess. There for the long haul. Declan liked that. Isaac brushed his fingertips through Declan's hair, one slow and lazy swish at a time with a noise like rustling silk. "Much better. Wouldn't you say?"

Declan wet his lips with the tip of his tongue. His eyelids were heavy as sailcloth, but he could feel his skin humming in satisfaction. "Much," he said.

"Good." Isaac tipped his chin up and brushed one last kiss over his lips. "Because we have a lot of work to do, you and me. And we'll start as soon as you're ready."

Epilogue

Six months later

Isaac's key still shone a new bronze, with only three tiny scuffs, and it slid easily into the lock. Nothing remarkable except for what it meant. He could have picked it out of the others on his ring with a blindfold on in the dark. He turned the knob, then bumped the door open with his hip. "Declan?"

No answer. Isaac shrugged as he stepped inside and bumped the door shut again.

And nearly tripped over the cord to the vacuum cleaner.

"Well, at least I know he's here," Isaac said to himself as he stepped free of the entanglement. "Declan! The vacuum cleaner just tried to eat me."

Still no answer. Isaac grinned. Understandable, all things considered, and he didn't mind chasing after Declan even now.

He eased the two grocery sacks full of odds and ends onto the kitchen counter—their kitchen counter now, as crowded with his juicer as with the coffee maker Declan guarded with the zeal of a true aficionado. Mismatched dishes sat in the drying rack, and soap that smelled of pink grapefruits still faintly scented the air.

Home. Once just Declan's, and only a house.

They'd changed that, the two of them. Carpet, thick and plush, had gone down over the scarred wood floors. Isaac loved kicking off his shoes to wiggle his toes against the velvety surface, and liked even better the occasional wrestling match that put them both on the ground, naked and eager. Of course, that would have to stop, but they'd broken the place in good and proper. Curtains hung at the windows, bright and clean-smelling and crisp. They even had pictures on the walls now. Framed photos, most of them. Diplomas. A candid shot Dr. Gabriel had caught of them playing hacky sack at a St. Hawk's employee picnic.

Isaac would have to admit that one was his favorite.

He worked out the pleasant stretch in his arms, earned from carrying heavy bags, as he meandered down the short hallways and poked his head into each room by turns. Nope, nothing, and nada. No Declan to be found, though the vacuum cleaner had been parked at the door of the bedroom.

Which only left... Aha. When Isaac opened the back door of the house, the one that led to the new deck they'd built together, he found Declan biting at his nails and staring into the middle distance as if he'd like to set it on fire.

Frustrated then, with a side order of anxious. He glanced sideways at Isaac and made a rueful grimace. "Should have known you'd find me."

"Did you expect anything else? And hey, stop that," Isaac chided, tapping the back of Declan's hand. "Don't start a new bad habit at this stage of the game."

Declan grinned. "I will if I want to. Try to stop me."

"Bite me, big man." Isaac kissed him. "Don't ever change too much, okay?"

"Not likely when I have you around to pull my pigtails. Are they late?" He craned his neck. He would, Isaac felt sure, have stood on his tiptoes if dignity hadn't disallowed it.

"They're not late. I am early. Calm down."

Declan ran a hand through his hair. "You're not nervous at all? Really? Because I don't buy it."

"Nervous as hell," Isaac said candidly. "But I'm not worried about me. It's your big day. You're the dad."

"Good God, I must be crazy," Declan replied. He blew out a breath, and shook his head. Isaac felt the empathy straight down to his core. Six months ago, some would have said that Declan was only chasing a pipe dream. That no matter what an encouraging social worker had to say, no one could make quite so many changes—that it couldn't be done—but by damn, Declan had done it. He hadn't gotten the dog that Connor had suggested—allergies—but he'd managed everything else, including a new kitchen sink.

So in Isaac's opinion, if anyone could tackle fatherhood without looking back, it'd be that guy.

"Like you're any saner, signing up to do this with me," Declan said. He took Isaac's hand and squeezed. "If you leave me now, I'll gut you."

"Always the poet." Isaac snorted. "Leave you? As if. I don't think you need to lose sleep worrying over that."

Declan's lips moved into the shape of a smile. "I know," he said, turning to Isaac as if meaning to kiss him, and—

Then they did hear the sound of a car in the drive.

Declan closed his eyes and muttered something like a prayer, but opened them again and grinned at Isaac straightaway. "Connor, you think?"

"I think." Isaac swatted Declan's hip. "Go on. Be the first one to say hello to Naomi. I'll be right behind you."

"Better be," Declan said. He stole a kiss that Isaac willingly gave, and cupped his cheek for one moment. "Don't wait too long."

"I won't." Only long enough to let Declan be the first one to welcome their foundling to her new home. As it should be, with Isaac coming up behind, giving chase.

He sighed, content under the early July sun, and inhaled the scent of rich green growth. When they'd built the deck, they'd transplanted the hawthorn bush to pride of place beside it. Summer had treated the bush well, and it seemed to like the new spot where it grew. Isaac plucked one leaf and flicked it into the air, followed it until he lost the flash of green to the sun, and nodded once, satisfied.

Then he went to the front yard to find Declan. Fair was fair, and he wanted a turn at holding their daughter, too.

About the Author

Willa Okati can most often be found muttering to herself over a keyboard, plugged into her iPod and breaking between paragraphs to play air drums. In her spare time (the odd ten minutes or so per day she's not writing) she's teaching herself to play the pennywhistle.

Willa has forty-plus separate tattoos and yearns for a full body suit of ink. She walks around in a haze of story ideas, dreaming of tales yet to be told. She drinks an alarming amount of coffee for someone generally perceived to be mellow.

Willa Okati loves to hear from readers. You can find her contact information, website details and author profile page at http://www.totallybound.com.

Totally Bound Publishing

Home of Erotic Romance